Bricks and Mortar

Bricks and Mortar

A Novel

Volume 1

Ten J. Howard

To inquire about author interviews or speaking engagements, send inquiries to: info@tenjhoward.com

ISBN: 1514119536
ISBN 13: 9781514119532
Library of Congress Control Number: 2015908564
CreateSpace Independent Publishing Platform
North Charleston, South Carolina

Bricks and Mortar

A Novel

Volume 1

TEN J. HOWARD

To inquire about author interviews or speaking engagements, send inquiries to: info@tenjhoward.com

ISBN: 1514119536
ISBN 13: 9781514119532
Library of Congress Control Number: 2015908564
CreateSpace Independent Publishing Platform
North Charleston, South Carolina

Dedication

To those who have the courage to reinvent themselves
and live the life they imagined.

Acknowledgements

To Tyler and Brooke Lyn, you complete me. Thank you
for your love and support to help me realize a dream.
You inspire me every day.
I am blessed and honored to be your mom.

Thank you to my editor K. Salikof for helping me to connect
with my fears and vulnerabilities and stretch my limits to create
a beautiful work of art.
I couldn't have done it without you.

To my soul sister P. Young, thank you for reading every word
and offering your professional and cultural critique. I am deeply
appreciative of our friendship.

To those whom I loved and lost, our journey together taught
me valuable life lessons and insights that I continue
to glean from and grow from.

To my family and friends who love me no matter what.
My life is so much fuller with you in it.
I thank Almighty God for his love and undeserved kindness.
I am sincerely grateful.

One

December 11, 2008

New York City! The real-estate mecca of the world. Everyone wants a piece of it. It's the topic of dinner parties, newspapers, TV shows, magazines, and blogs: "How's the market? What's happening in the market?" People are fascinated with it. It's an alluring seduction, and they can't get enough of it. Thousands of deals are made in New York City every year. And for a real-estate professional, there's nothing more gratifying than bringing two parties together and closing a deal. Especially knowing that the only reason it's happening is because it's a direct result of *you* consummating it. It's the art of making the deal, and there's one real-estate aficionado—namely me, Omega Bouvier—who has no shame in her game.

Dressed in a signature Prada suit, I felt it was just the right statement of strength and femininity that I wanted to express on this particular Monday morning. All my work over the last eight months was about to pay off. Royally. The view of the city from the penthouse office in the Chrysler Building was boastfully spectacular, and it complemented the scene happening inside. Rotating from side to side on the leather swivel chair, I scanned the room full of men wearing expensive suits and crisp monogrammed shirts, exchanging dialogue, with a Chinese interpreter translating. Documents were traded across the mahogany boardroom table from one set of attorneys to the other, then to the buyer and to the seller. This was the moment I had envisioned for months, and I was taking it all in. A harmonious symphonic orchestration was playing out right in front of me.

The closing concluded successfully, and congratulatory handshakes between the men were exchanged. I stood and made a slight bow to the very distinguished Chinese businessman who was now the stately owner of some of the city's most revered properties—an off-market sale of eight buildings acquired by Mr. Zhang for nearly a billion dollars. I couldn't contain the smile on my face as I was handed the commission check for my services. It was one of the single largest New York City real-estate transactions of the year, and it was compensation well earned.

"Congratulations, Ms. Bouvier!" Drew James announced. "It's time for a celebration!" Bottles of Pernod Ricard Perrier-Joüet champagne were popped, and bubbly was poured into crystal flutes. A celebration indeed. Closing this all-cash deal was nothing short of miraculous.

The best years in the history of New York City real-estate sales were 2007 through the first two quarters of 2008. Properties were trading at the highest numbers ever. And then everything came crashing down. Wall Street collapsed. The housing market bubble had burst all over the country, and now New York City was no exception. Barack Obama, the first African-American US president, would inherit the worst economic disaster in our history since the Great Depression. The excitement that came with establishing my own firm a few years ago quickly dwindled in light of the financial crisis. It felt like the end of everything I had dreamed of and there were so many times when I almost gave in to the pressure of it.

Everyone at my firm was grateful that most of our deals closed successfully, although we had our share of disappointments. Each of us had to hustle and grind through the toughest year of our careers in order to stay in the black. Our tenacity and skill were tested, and it was an emotional roller coaster to say the least. Many in the real-estate industry couldn't survive. A fortunate few who were able to guide their clients through the crisis would remember it as their best year and would spend the rest of their professional lives trying to re-create it.

Manhattan was still a playground for the privileged and super wealthy. As 1-percenters, they're recession proof. Now the upper echelon was looking to my firm *The Omega Group Real Estate* to provide them with opulent residences for their diverse portfolios. Half the young CEOs stationed between 59th and 77th Street could dig up the deeds to their lavish penthouses or West Village brownstones and find paperwork prepared by Drew, my trusted legal counsel.

Drew James's belly had grown over the last few months from all the late-night Chinese, which had led to huge stacks of empty white takeout boxes crowding his office. However, every contract that came out of that office was clean, crisp, and airtight. He sat at the opposite end of the table from me and ordered two dozen oysters to go with his whiskey neat. Though he ordered them for the table, he would wolf down all of them himself, probably even dribbling cocktail sauce on his Brooks Brothers suit. The young waitress flirted with him blatantly as he handed her our corporate black AmEx card. Drew liked to expose the card at the beginning of dining to ensure better service. I laughed a little to myself, knowing that while the waitress assumed he was the head honcho in charge, in reality the man behind this empire was a woman.

Our group was overly happy, drinking quickly, and toasting to our well-deserved success. I was their fearless leader, although through every obstacle we faced, I'd been terrified. I wouldn't have let them see it, of course. It felt wrong boasting any sole claim to our success, because it was due to the efforts of everyone in our well-oiled machine of a company and many long hours from everyone at the table. It wasn't just those in charge, namely me.

I suppose it was finally time to pat myself on the back, but as usual I was reluctant to do so. I had started the firm with a stack of résumés. They were all young, eager, and green, but they were my top candidates. With a little carrot and a little stick, we became one of the most prestigious luxury boutique real-estate agencies in the city. With three offices in Manhattan and Brooklyn, I had to keep reminding myself that forty was still a young age to be heading a multimillion dollar company.

Forbes credited us with being the country's leading African-American owned firm, with an extensive client list of A-list black millionaires living in the Northeast. I was honored to be such a strong representative of the community, but it was telling how we were given such a specifically racial title. I had made a point to take this given title graciously while still emphasizing that we had no intention of catering to any one type of client in particular.

We were built on a foundation that was different from the other companies I had worked at in the past; I'd made sure of that. Some of these firms were more polished than most and others more tech driven. But they all operated in a similar way, treating their agents like employees instead of dignifying them as the entrepreneurs they were. The diversity of my firm represented the melting pot of cultures that make New York City the greatest city in the world. Our firm's success came as a direct result of trusted relationships with our clients and concrete knowledge of our business. Our work was based upon honest, top-notch service, and our results were indisputable. The op-eds and industry kings and queens could say whatever they wanted about us now, as we'd just blown them out of the water in the last few weeks. I would keep my mouth shut about it and pretend it was no big deal. However, I secretly hoped the presence of my company made them shake with fear in their custom-made shoes.

I was certainly proud of the type of company we had become. My core team was such a dynamic, fun group of people to work with, which was starting to show more now as the second round of drinks was delivered.

Tonya and Deborah, the only two other female agents on my team, were sitting next to each other, engaged in an intense conversation. They likely were discussing something to do with their thriving social lives. They were in their late twenties, so there was quite a lot of drama to visit. Strong, vigilant women, they had teamed up to supervise the office, keeping the rest of my staff in line during office hours and after hours. They even tried to clean up after Drew and possibly teach him basic manners, which wasn't an easy task. They brought a necessary personal touch to the office as well as adaptability to the team, all without sacrificing their ambition or success.

They both were impeccably dressed. Tonya's semi sheer lilac blouse was paired with a deep-green skirt that hugged her copious curves and complemented her even caramel skin tone and natural kinky, curly hair. Deborah, who, as the more conservative of the two, often donned cream and black, wore her thick straight hair in a bun and always wore a set of pearls. They represented two ends of the spectrum of professional women—reserved versus brazen—but they worked amazingly well together and had become best friends shortly after I'd hired them.

My outfit for this celebratory occasion mirrored my powerful mind-set. My black suit pants and satin black tank top felt sleek, as if I just wouldn't be shaken. The bright-red blazer I'd picked up from Bergdorf's earlier that week spoke of attention and more. I didn't normally lean toward such a bold statement piece, but it felt necessary for that day. I was marketing myself as the sophisticated, eloquent woman I finally felt I had become. I finished off the look with simple, black, red-bottomed stilettos, because every powerful woman in New York City needs a pair of Christian Louboutins, and they looked damn good on me. Classic Deborah and chic Tonya complemented me well.

We sat there flanked by our four male cohorts, strong men in perfectly tailored suits who were constantly adjusting their expensive ties and cuff links. I'm not one to judge someone based on his or her attire, but this industry was one where image was connected to sales. My team knew their business; we knew how to execute and close; and we knew how to dress and portray the most professional images possible for ourselves. I emphasized these factors with Tonya and Deborah when they first started out with me, and they both took to the suggestions superbly. The images they portrayed for the company were perfect, and I wanted their appearances to inspire their personal confidence as well. I tried to look out for them, hoping they would look up to me in some capacity. I tried to guide them correctly in their professional lives and otherwise.

At one point during the year, Deborah's work was suffering for an unexplained reason. It was very frustrating, and Drew thought the best route was to let her go. I asked her into my office and told her to give it to me straight. She admitted to being caught up with the wrong type of man. It was forgivable, although I didn't give her much room for sympathy. I made it clear that work was her top priority and that she obviously wasn't at the top of this man's list; if she were, he would treat her accordingly. It was basic advice, and Deborah took it well, turning herself around shortly thereafter. While my demeanor and delivery may have been tough, my heart went out to her. She had so much faith in an obviously doomed relationship. I missed the feeling of falling in love and being blissfully ignorant as I listened to her relay the past few weeks of her life that had led up to her heartbreak.

Yes, forty was still a young age for someone to grace the cover of *Forbes Magazine*. However, it wasn't an age to be foolish with love and men. The women I employed were ahead of the game and some of the smartest in the business, but occasionally I had to remind myself that they were still young and tender on the inside. I wanted to save them and keep them from making the mistakes I'd made along the way, but they were bound to make them anyway. Deborah and Tonya were women of New York City now, which could be dangerous for the weak of heart—not that the men in the firm were any less soft and inexperienced in their hearts, and I supported them as well. We had become a very productive close-knit family within the company, demonstrating that iron does in fact sharpen iron.

The oysters arrived, along with beef Wellington and Maryland crab cakes. Tonight we were going to be as luxurious as we liked, expense account be damned. I ordered a reserve Bordeaux, which was only sold by the bottle at $800. I knew I wouldn't finish the wine, and I normally wouldn't order in such an ostentatious way, but tonight I wanted to taste the finest French grapes and remind myself why I put in seventy-hour workweeks.

"I'm working with developers interested in buying more in Red Hook. The prices there have been rising significantly, and the industrial sector in that area is moving out," Damien said confidently. He was born and raised in Brooklyn and had been a significant figure in our last few deals in the ever-growing and desirable borough. He also was stunningly handsome and sharp. Sometimes, however, he was too hard-shelled, and getting him to trust the rest of the staff was difficult because his upbringing had taught him the skills of defensiveness above all.

"There's no subway access. A neighborhood without the presence of the great MTA is a dead zone. Red Hook is just riding on the coattails of Dumbo and Brooklyn Heights. There's no future in residential development there. Plus who wants to live near that stinking Gowanus Canal?" This was offered by Jay, who sat next to Damien and was unafraid of the long, drawn-out argument that would certainly follow. Disputes were always amicable or at least they were for now. The beginning for us had many varied battles.

After the appetizers were cleared, the steaks were brought out. It was a much larger cut than I ever would have been able to eat, but the swish of Bordeaux and the juicy prime fillet launched me into a heavenly state. Everyone at the table had ordered steak at market price. We had a statement to make. Our table of brokers may have been a bit out of place in the iconic Midtown establishment, where there was a faint, lingering smell of cigars, even though smoking hadn't been allowed in restaurants for years now. The selection of Scotch and bourbon was just as extensive as the wine. In fact I could have bet that the cellar below was filled with a small fortune in wine, champagne, and liquor.

I looked around at the diners, an older elite crowd enjoying the tradition and prestige of the establishment. Some of them were our competition, but some of the patrons were our clientele. Our table wasn't the only group of brokers, but my team was a little livelier. We also were notably younger and browner. The *Forbes* write-up moved to the front of my thoughts again, and I made a silent toast to myself. I also made a small note that this dinner should become a tradition in the firm, and even as we grew, we could come back and remember this original core group.

"Omega, does this mean you're finally going to take a vacation?" Deborah had finished rehashing all her drama to Tonya and was reaching out to me across the table. This garnered everyone's attention.

I couldn't help but laugh and say, "I guess I should. A coconut mojito on the beach sounds fantastic."

My assistant, Ty, added his two cents to the conversation. "Sun and seafood. I'm headed to the Caribbean as soon as I can. Well, as soon as you let me, Omega."

"Try the Turks and Caicos, Ty. It's a bit far, but well worth it," I said.

"Have you been there?" Tonya asked over the rim of her cosmopolitan.

"I have, yes. I've been to most of the Caribbean, including Cuba, which is a beautiful country," I answered.

"What were you doing in Cuba?" Ty asked, bewildered.

"Oh, if I told you that, I would have to kill you," I said kiddingly.

"Did you have to go through Canada? Or South America?" Ty continued.

"I believe we flew directly in from Switzerland, although it depends on which time I went," I said.

"When was this?" Ty was certainly curious about this whole matter.

"Probably around nineteen ninety-eight," I said.

"Ah, yes. The Clinton years! You could get away with just about anything during that time." Drew jumped in with a mouthful of steak and swung his fork around wildly for effect.

"I don't know about Cuba. I was just thinking somewhere far away from e-mails and sales negotiations and last-minute client demands," Ty said, settling back into his seat.

"Well, you'll have to go to Antarctica to get away from cell signals and Wi-Fi. Otherwise Omega will find you," Damien said, winking at me.

"Oh, I'm sure they have Wi-Fi in Antarctica," I said jokingly, and the table agreed that unless I was on vacation they would never truly be able to escape me. I knew they meant it in jest, because while I knew I could be a tyrant, I tried to be a benevolent one.

They definitely wouldn't be complaining about their commission checks over the next few months.

The wine was settling more inside my head and making me fuzzy. As the night went on, the team was only laughing louder. It was a perfect evening.

Excusing myself from my crowd, I got up from my leather wing-back chair to head to the ladies' room. There was a new strut to my walk now, which was probably from the wine, but it also could have been from how well the night was going or, really, how well the day was going.

It's funny to think now that the biggest deal to save us that year wasn't on the golden isle of Manhattan but instead in good ol' blue-collar Brooklyn, which was becoming a preferred residential area to an established middle class. The borough was growing with wealth and development, and the neighborhoods were being gentrified, which I had mixed emotions about. Brooklyn was where I'd started my career in real estate and where I ultimately opened my first office. The culture, diversity, and architectural landscape of the neighborhoods set Brooklyn apart from the other boroughs. There's no other place on earth like it, and a growing number of people were moving there to discover it for themselves.

Restaurants, stores, hotels, and theaters had popped up and taken hold in areas like Williamsburg, downtown Brooklyn, Bed-Stuy, Crown Heights, and the neighborhood where we closed our billion dollar deal, Dumbo. It was being called the "new Manhattan." However, Barbra Streisand, Spike Lee, Anne Hathaway, Chris Rock, and Jay-Z, to name a few, called Brooklyn home long before its panache and popularity. I was fortunate to notice this trend happen early, and with my skilled and sought-after agents, we swooped in and snagged our very own chunk of Brooklyn's new development market.

We were progressive strategists who understood the market trends of real estate, and we aligned ourselves with the most prolific developers who were creating a new Brooklyn. We provided our services to liaison with community groups, local politicians, and businesses to strike a balance. We avoided the fiscal disease by focusing on what mattered: ingenuity, adaptability, service, and hope for future growth. We had dodged a bullet.

I had suffered through many ups and downs in my career, and as I walked through the swanky Manhattan restaurant, I was grateful to feel high off this current upswing, because I truly had earned it.

When I passed the bar on the way from the restroom, I stopped in my tracks. I tunneled my attention to the TV screens above the shelves of spirits and couldn't look away.

I wasn't the only one. Everyone sitting at the bar was watching as well, not a word between them. Even the staff had stopped to notice.

CNN was on every screen, showing the biggest headline of the day, which was probably the biggest headline in years. It was December 11, 2008. Madoff Securities was being indicted for fraudulent investment claims and accounting. Bernard Madoff, the prominent Wall Street financier, was being escorted out of his office by police officers. Mr. Madoff was in a suit and tie as well as a black topcoat to keep out the cold December air. For a moment I wondered if they'd let him keep his coat in prison. I knew of the man through some of my clients, who believed he was a financial genius, but I'd never met him. There had been such a bad taste in everyone's mouth lately for those who worked on Wall Street. This story certainly wasn't going to help.

Madoff's company was worth billions, and now CNN was saying that decades of his books had been falsified. The reporter enumerated the long list of high-profile investors and international banks that were involved. Many were family, trusted friends, and icons of the religious and cultural community. This was followed by a string of questions. How much damage was there? Who would be affected most? How would this hurt the already bruised market? Was anyone honest still working on Wall Street?

It was obvious that Bernie was a very greedy man. Although, when I watched the clip that was being looped of him leaving his office, arrested and flanked by members of law enforcement, he looked somber. His face was calm and controlled despite the flashes from cameras and the crowds of reporters. The police were stoic and moved quickly. Bernie looked down but didn't appear hurried or flustered. It seemed as if there might have been a glimmer of remorse on his face, or maybe it was just shock. I continued to watch out of curiosity.

Then the reporter described the modus operandi of the firm. She mentioned that it was set up as an elaborate Ponzi scheme.

Something turned in my stomach. It was a feeling I'd long forgotten—a feeling I'd thought I had buried and left behind. I was hit with a flood of memories. Pounding and intoxicating salsa music, bodies synchronized to the rhythms. Late nights wrapped up in big, strong arms. A passion that was so intense it blocked out everything around it, even the most sinister of things. A feeling of love that had been seared into me, and even after so long, I still felt it. I was becoming lost for a moment in the memories of it, just as I'd been completely lost in it back then.

A hand on my shoulder brought me back to the present. There, in the dimly lit steakhouse, in the middle of Manhattan, Damien was standing next to me.

"Ms. Bouvier, you've been gone awhile."

I turned to him and pulled together a smile. It was strange to have him so close to me with all the thoughts that had just been coursing through my mind.

"Oh, I'm fine. I was just watching all of this," I said, motioning to the TV.

"Yeah, we just found out about it. It's insane," he said, keeping his hand on me but turning to look at the screens. "It's not real money anyway." Damien sighed deeply.

"What do you mean? It was a multibillion dollar company," I said. I knew his touch was meant in comfort and affection with no other intentions, but I was still very aware it was there. I tried to pull myself back into the moment and forget my thoughts from before. It didn't matter anymore.

"Yes, but those billions of dollars were built on investments from already wealthy people—people with money to spare," he said, removing his hand and shrugging. To a certain extent, he was right.

"It can still ruin some people's lives. It's still dishonesty," I said defensively and perhaps with a bit too much mothering.

He nodded and smiled then turned to walk back to the table. "Are you headed back?"

"Yes. I will in just a minute."

I kept watching the news. It was the same clip of Madoff leaving the office over and over, with the same sound bites about the whole ordeal, but I kept listening to them. I couldn't turn away—it was as though I were hypnotized.

Then the coverage switched to a live news report. There on the screen was an older blond woman wearing a black coat, sunglasses, and pearls. She looked distraught but pulled together. The video captured her as she was getting out of a black sedan. She put her hand up to try to shield the glare from the ambush of camera flashes. It was Mrs. Ruth Madoff, dodging a barrage of questions from reporters about her husband as she tried to enter their Upper East Side apartment building.

Her husband the charlatan, liar, cheat, manipulator, swindler. Mrs. Madoff was still there, wedding ring on, her face and tone calm. Her reputation was ruined. Her friends likely would mistrust her and eventually abandon her. She wouldn't be able to see her husband while he was put on trial and sentenced to prison. She would be left behind to pick up the pieces.

Yet there she was. She adjusted her coat a little as she tried to push her way through the sea of reporters. Mrs. Madoff was keeping it together. *Good for her*, I thought.

She was in a terrifying, disheartening position. It would quickly become one of the hardest times in her life. I knew this because I'd been there myself. I was once the woman who had to learn to keep it together, in lieu of losing all my dignity and grace. It had made me stronger and a better woman, but I wouldn't have wished it on anyone.

The bartender was wiping down the bar as she spoke to a man in a gray suit who sat in front of her.

"She knew. She had to know," he said. "There's no way her husband could've been stealing all that money without her knowing."

She may not have, I said to myself. There may have been signs in front of her everywhere, basically clobbering her over the head, but the heart can make you do crazy things when it wants to. I felt queasiness in my gut, and my heart began to palpitate.

I looked down at my diamond and gold Omega watch and released a long sigh. Instead of heading back to the table, I stepped outside onto the sidewalk for some fresh air. It was late, but the streets were still busy. It was close to Christmas, so the streets were lit and decorated. There was no snow to be seen, but the air was bitingly cold.

My body may have been outside in the chill of northeastern winter, but my mind was transported to a tropical heat. The kind of sweltering heat that makes your body drip with sweat and a cool breeze feels like heaven up your dress. I was transported back to memories I'd long suppressed. I remembered the sound of ocean waves in the middle of the night.

Two

Some of us search our entire adult lives, looking for the one thing we didn't have as children. It's a haunting feeling. The first time I got my period was also the first time I learned the truth about the events surrounding my birth.

I'll never forget the moment. I was in the family room, lying on the sofa, staring for some reason at the red bricks that made up the fireplace. I had come home from school and wasn't feeling well. My lower back was hurting, and I had a strange pain in my abdomen. I was watching an afternoon special on TV and suddenly had the urge to go to the kitchen, maybe for a drink of cold water. But once I was there, I felt frozen in place. As I stared out the kitchen window at the cornstalks in the open field, I felt weird. And then it came—an unusual wetness from between my legs.

Having been prepared for this moment by my sisters, I rushed upstairs to the bathroom to examine myself. Then I called for Mom. She came in a rush and asked me what was the matter. I showed her the blood.

She took a look at my soiled panties and said, "Don't worry. It's going to be all right."

Then she turned away and left me alone in the bathroom.

It was a familiar feeling. I'd felt this so many times before in the presence of my mother. In fact my very first memory of her, dating back to when I was around three years old, is of me going over to give her a hug and her pushing me away, turning her back, and walking out of the room. I cried out to her, but she kept walking, never looking back.

Imagine what that will do to you, having your first memory of your mother being one of rejection. I craved the attention of my mother but often felt it denied. It was something I struggled with throughout my childhood and, to tell the truth, one that has plagued me well into adulthood.

As I sat on the edge of the tub and waited for her to return, I thought about that moment and so many others. And they all added up to the same thing: my mother didn't love me.

I was the youngest of ten siblings; I had seven brothers and two sisters. I knew other families that had many children, and it was always the same thing. The youngest, the baby of the family, was doted on by one and all, given extra love. Yet that wasn't the case with me. In fact the opposite was true. My mother didn't have the usual portion of love for me, let alone extra love.

When I asked my older brothers and sisters about it, they demurred and said Mom had been the same way with them. But as they said this, their eyes would slide to the left or right and not meet mine, which I took as a sign that they weren't quite telling me the truth.

In bits and pieces, one of them or another would fill me in on our family history, what I had missed out on by being too young to comprehend anything important.

For one thing it took me a long time to realize we were only one of three black families in our neighborhood. We lived in a middle-class, rural community in western Maryland, and it seemed exempt from the prejudice against people of color that was prevalent in other parts of the South below the Mason-Dixon line. Or at least, in my youth, that was my perception of it while I grew up there.

I guess in that way my parents were pioneers, but their frontier was moving into the great white unknown of this rural county neighborhood. My father was a college-educated man who possessed a good business sense. Even though the asking price of the home they bought in 1952 had been increased by 25 percent because the owners didn't want to sell to anyone black and the realtor tried to steer them away from homes in historically white neighborhoods, they bought the house anyway. As hardworking law abiding citizens, my parents weren't inclined to allow anyone to dictate where they had a right to live. They knew they might not be popular with some of their neighbors, which became painfully evident when someone painted "Niggers get out!" on our garage door. My parents knew exactly what they were up against and who they were dealing with.

My mom and dad also were pioneers when it came to our education, particularly my mother. Everything was segregated back then. She grew tired of having her two oldest children, six and seven at the time, bused twenty miles away to the nearest black school. So after the vindication of *Brown v. Board of Education* in 1954, she was there to help integrate the white elementary school so my two oldest sisters could attend, hence opening the door for all children of color to receive a quality education.

My mother was very proud that she had achieved her goal. In our kitchen, framed on the walnut-paneled wall, was a yellowing newspaper photograph that showed her holding up a protest sign in front of that school. She stood there with that sign in all sorts of weather—on hot summer days and on cold winter days and when it snowed and when it rained and on those blessed days when the weather was fair under a blue sky. She stood there with that sign, along with other protesters, until she broke the back of the segregationist standard for the school district, allowing black boys and girls to attend for the first time in our county's history. And on that day, as my sisters proudly marched into that school, my mother was there on the sidelines to cheer them on. There was a newspaper photograph of that too, and its place was next to the other newspaper clipping on our kitchen's wood paneled wall.

My mother was a strong woman. She had to be in those days, raising all those kids and living during a time of social unrest in the 1950s and 1960s. Never a religious woman in the traditional sense, she had thrown herself into the civil rights movement with a zealousness that almost bordered on religious frenzy. The proof of this was the way she had helped to integrate my sisters' elementary school. There was constant conversation in our house about the assassination of John F. Kennedy, the work of Dr. King, and bus boycotts and lunch counter sit-ins. Each new outrage my mother took personally. After all, she had her children to protect, and she knew how the world perceived them.

She grew apoplectic when that Mississippi sheriff, Bull Connor, turned fire hoses and dogs on innocent black children. And she sorrowed when the bodies of white voting-rights workers from the North were found dead in a shallow grave, also in

Mississippi. She followed these stories the way other housewives in our town followed their favorite soap operas on TV. The major difference was these stories weren't made up of actors fantasizing a script. These were real-life demonstrations of racism and bigotry being projected onto people simply because of the color of their skin. My parents wanted change and were advocates for better lives for themselves and their children.

But the stress of those years began to take a toll on my mother. They seemed to sap her of her strength. She was in her early thirties, with nine children at the time. Raising seven boys, one right after the next, also took its toll. Almost overnight her hair went from dark to gray and she began dyeing it. Her energy level began to sag, and by the time I came around in 1968, she was exhausted all the time and seemed to have little left to take care of her youngest child. Never mind that her youngest was her baby girl.

This was, more or less, the tale I pieced together based on various statements made by my older siblings, who, I realized even later, had been less than forthcoming with me. Often these were conversations I overheard and put together later in my head. I took this received wisdom and understood it in the limited ways a child can. But the words and images and stories stayed with me until, at age twelve, I had a very good sense of where my mother stood in the world.

I sat on the edge of the bathtub for what seemed to be the longest time, waiting for my mom to return. Time seemed to stand still the way it does on a hot Sunday in summer when there's no cool place to be found. But return she did, after a while, with all the accoutrements I would need to be ushered into the society of women.

We were alone in the house. My father was off at work, and my siblings were either no longer living at home, at work, or outside playing, and this was one of the few occasions when I had my mother all to myself and she wasn't busy doing anything else, which was rare in those days.

As we sat in the bathroom, there were questions I wanted to ask my mother. Actually it came down to only one question—one question that was more important than any other. And this seemed as good a time as any to ask it. There was one big problem, though: I couldn't get the words out of my mouth. It was as though each word were a weight too great for my tongue to bear. It felt weighed down, and no matter how hard I tried, the words weren't light enough to lift off my tongue and fly out of my mouth and through the air to my mother.

I recognized that this was my way. I was shy, insecure, always unsettled on the inside, afraid to tell people what I really wanted. I did this all the time—refused to stand up for myself, even after I finally became aware of this shortcoming. And I even knew where this tendency came from: my mother. By turning her back on me, in both the literal and figurative sense, she had undermined my sense of self. It was up to me to change the way I was. And I was determined to do so. It was a journey, I knew, that started by confronting my mother.

"Mom," I said, unable to get any more words out of my mouth.

"Yes, child," she responded.

"Mom?" I asked.

"Yes, child," she repeated, this time with a slight edge in her voice, a sound that was very familiar to me.

"I've been thinking," I said, "and there's something I want to ask you."

"Yes, Omega, what is it?"

I looked into her face and wasn't sure what I saw there. Was it fear? Apprehension?

I had second thoughts about asking her. Maybe putting her on the spot wasn't such a good idea. I quickly rummaged through my mind for a substitute question that I might ask. But I couldn't think of any. And it was a good thing too, because it forced me to return to my original intention and ask the question for which I desperately wanted an answer.

"Mom," I said for the last time, "why are you so cold to me?"

I wanted to look her in the face, to see her reaction to my words. But I couldn't do it. I couldn't lift my eyes to her face, to her eyes. Feeling a stabbing sense of shame, I kept my eyes lowered. The only way to alleviate it, I realized, was to lift my face and see the look on my mother's.

Disappointingly there was no look on her face. That's because it was covered by her hands. I was afraid they were there because my mother was crying and didn't want me to see her with tears streaming down her face. But when she finally lowered them, I saw that her eyes were dry, as dry as the Sahara Desert, which we had seen a filmstrip about in class. I understood that my mother had raised her hands to her face not to cover nonexistent tears but because of the shock she felt at hearing that question come out of my mouth.

Her mouth, visible once more, let out a sigh. It was a long sigh, freighted with all sorts of hidden meanings. And when she was finished with it, she sighed again. This one had a note of resignation in it. And then she said my name, Omega, in a tone of voice I'd never heard before. That's when I knew that she was going to answer my question.

She took a deep breath then said, "All right, Omega, I'm going to tell you the story of how you were born."

And she did this in terms that a twelve-year-old could understand, detailing the events that had led up to my birth. But that, of course, would prove to be a completely expurgated version of the story. The real events were something quite different. I would learn of them much later in life, when I pieced together different accounts my siblings gave me. Most of what I'm about to tell you is true, part of it maybe conjecture. But to the best of my knowledge, this is my mother's story, which I have put in her voice. And this is the version I remember her telling me on the day I got my first period.

"Omega, honey," she said, "I was so tired in those days. Tired because of all of our work fighting for one thing or another. And tired from all the time I spent raising your brothers and sisters. I'd just given birth to my ninth child, and I was suffering from a depression that was so bad that sometimes I had trouble getting out of bed in the morning. I'm ashamed to say that I left it to the older children to feed the younger ones and get them out the door to school."

My mother was describing what we now know as postpartum depression, but in those days it was called the baby blues.

"That's when I found out that I was pregnant again, for the tenth time. At first I said nothing to your father. Kept the news to myself. Didn't dare share it with anyone. Because this time, unlike all those other times, I didn't want to go through another pregnancy. I was exhausted and, even though I didn't know it for what it really was, so darn sad all the time. So frankly, Omega, my dear child, I decided I couldn't go through with another nine months of being pregnant. The road was too long. And at the end of it was yet another child to raise. It was too much for me to contemplate. And that's when I decided to get an abortion."

My eyes began to tear, but I was determined to hold them back.

"Oh, don't look so shocked," she said. "It wasn't something I thought lightly about doing. I thought long and hard about it. I searched my soul, even as I held my own council. I prayed to God for understanding, wisdom, and compassion. And in the end, I decided this was the course I was going to have to take.

"Now this was nineteen sixty-seven, back in the days before *Roe v. Wade* became the law of the land. Abortions were still illegal. I asked around and found out about a clinic that wasn't too far away, where abortions were performed and the doctors wrote them up as an emergency D and C. I made all the arrangements on my own. There was no one to confide in. And made the appointment for a day when I knew your father would be out late. I had an excuse all made up and prepared dinner in advance for your brothers and sisters to eat while I was away.

"I started out in the midmorning. The clinic was located in the next county, about an hour away by car. As I got into the car to leave, gray skies were already gathering overhead. I remember noticing them because I thought that they fit my mood perfectly. But as I drove north, the clouds became darker and darker until they opened up, and rain began to spatter down on the car.

"This rain, child, it got worse and worse until it became a real drenching downpour. It was truly like the heavens had opened up. It was coming down so hard that I barely could see through the windshield. And so loud that it was drowning out the radio, which was playing the Edwin Hawkins Singers doing 'Oh Happy Day.' And the sky was so dark that it seemed like I was driving at night. I turned the headlights on, but there was little for them to illuminate but the rain. I seriously thought about pulling over to the side of the road to wait for the storm to pass over. But I didn't because it didn't look like the rain was ever going to stop and because I didn't want to be late for my appointment. So I just kept on driving.

"Well, it took me longer than an hour to get there, more like an hour and a half. But I still managed to make it to my appointment on time because I'd had the foresight to set out earlier than I had to. So I got there, to the clinic, and checked in with the receptionist behind the counter and went and sat in the waiting room, where I tried to watch TV—I think *The Guiding Light* was on—but couldn't concentrate on it or anything else because all I could think about was what I was about to do. I sat there and prayed that I was making the right decision."

Still holding back my tears, I sniffled as my mother continued to recall the moments of that day.

"I looked through the window of the waiting room and saw that it was still raining outside, still coming down as hard as Judgment Day. I could barely see my car in the parking lot. And now the storm was accompanied by lightning and thunder. And it must have been close, and getting closer all the time, because there was almost no time to count 'one Mississippi, two Mississippi' between the lightning strikes and thunderclaps.

"Finally a nurse came out and took me to a small room where the procedure was to be performed. She told me the doctor would be with me shortly and gave me a white gown to change into. So I changed and pulled myself onto the table and waited for the doctor to arrive. I was getting more and more nervous by the minute, still wondering whether I'd made the right choice for my future.

"He eventually came in, the doctor. He was a white man, with a white head of hair and a white beard, and there was something about him that was biblical and deeply trustful. He gave me a brief examination and asked me a bunch of questions and put me totally at ease.

"Meanwhile I heard the rain drumming hard on the roof of the clinic. And there was more lightning and thunder to punctuate the sound of the rain. The nurse came into the room, and she and the doctor began the procedure. They had me lie back on the table. I watched as the doctor filled a syringe with some sort of liquid and approached me with it. 'Now you might feel a pinch,' he said as he swabbed my hip and prepared to give me an injection there. *This is it*, I told myself. *No turning back from this point.*"

I couldn't hold them back anymore, and finally the tears fell from my eyes. I wiped my face as my mother continued her horrible tale. It was as if she were in a confessional and finally relieving herself from the burden of her concealed sins.

"And then, just as the doctor was about to inject me, something happened. The room was plunged into darkness."

I gasped.

"The lightning had struck a power line somewhere and knocked out all the electricity. We were in the middle of a blackout. The doctor cursed, damning the fact that the clinic was too poor to afford a generator of its own. Once he got himself under control, he turned toward me and said in a calming voice, 'Don't worry. I'm sure the lights will come back on in a few minutes.'

"But I couldn't wait. I knew what I had to do. I jumped down off the table, ripped off my gown, and fumbled around for my clothes, which I began to put on again."

"'Where are you going?' the doctor asked me, in a confused tone.

"'It's a sign. Don't you see?' I said. 'It's a sign from God.'

"And I believed this with all my heart. The lights and the power going off were signs from God. He was telling me I wasn't supposed to have this abortion. I wasn't supposed to go through with this procedure. So, pulling my clothes on, I thanked the doctor then fled the clinic and got back into my car and started back home. Shortly after, the lightning and thunder stopped. And so did the rain. And by the time I got back home, the sun was actually starting to come out a little. I made it back in time to serve dinner to your brothers and sisters.

"And after that, dear child, I never looked back. Never thought again of that day. It was like it never happened. And

I never thought again about having an abortion. Seven months later I gave birth to you. But I was still so tired, so bone-deep tired that I didn't have the strength to care for you the way I knew you needed to be. So it was easier to just turn away from you, let your father, brothers, and sisters assist in the raising of you, as they'd done for each other, but with my supervision. You most certainly are Daddy's little girl.

"Your father and I grew distant over those seven months before you were born. He didn't know what was happening or what to think of me at that time. God bless him. He was patient and remained supportive and did the best he could to prepare himself for yet another mouth to feed. We went back and forth with so many names and still hadn't come up with one by the time you were born. But that night, in the hospital room, after giving birth to you, as I held you and fed you a bottle [I was the only one my mother didn't breastfeed], a name came to me. And I knew it was the right name for you and the most fitting name possible. I named you Omega, after the last letter in the Greek alphabet and because in the Bible it means the end or conclusion of all things. Lord knows I knew you were the last child I was ever going to have."

Listening to my mother's story in the bathroom that day gave me insight into what her life had been like. As painful as it was to hear, especially at such a tender age, I finally understood what she had gone through and why she'd treated me the way she had. But to tell the truth, it didn't change anything. All it did, at a very young age, was make me more determined to prove myself that much more. How dare she even contemplate getting rid of me! I would be extraordinary, too special for my mother ever to ignore. Surely I was meant to be here to fulfill a higher purpose. That's what I told myself anyway.

These were defining moments in my young life that shaped the very foundation of my existence. It seemed as though my mother made herself available to everyone but me. Her emotional and psychological abandonment set the tone for how I approached the world and saw myself in it. I became an overachiever and strived for perfection, which played out academically and in sports. I vowed to leave home as soon as I possibly could and make a life for myself. And I pledged that if I ever were blessed with a child, I never would treat him or her as my mother had treated me.

Although my heart had been broken, I managed to love my mom despite her limitations and choices. Forgiveness is the beginning of healing, and love covers a multitude of sins. I tried not to judge her. I stood in her image, more than I even knew at the time.

Three

I fell in love with the buildings at Dartmouth. They were hundreds of years old, adorned with classic brick facades and stately white pillars and embellished with gargoyles that actually spooked me out a bit. When I arrived it was summer, and the buildings were covered with green vines. The exteriors of the buildings were misleading. Although they were gorgeous and dignified on the outside, the insides were decayed and had been sloppily repainted—at least in the hallways of the freshman dorms, which happened to be the first part of Dartmouth I ever saw.

The guts of the ancient halls and archways teemed with students. They were hauling trunks, crates, boxes, acoustic guitars, and dreams of running the campus. I was surrounded by many people with the same drive and ambition I had. Although 99 percent of the population didn't look like me, we were all searching for the same sense of importance and acknowledgment. We all shared the history of hard work and stressful habits that had transported us to these hallowed halls. We were all clones of the ignorance and thirst for something more.

Despite this, I stood in the shadow of the buildings, my vision full of young bodies, green grass, and red bricks, and never had felt more alone. I recalled the stories as told by my sisters when they had integrated the elementary school, and for the first time in my life, I got a real glimpse as to what that experience was for them. As I recalibrated my bearings, there inscribed on the brick wall in front of me was Dartmouth's Latin motto, "*Vox clamantis in deserto*," which translated into English is "The voice of one crying out in the wilderness." That statement couldn't apply to me more than it did at this moment.

I was late to meet my RA and neighbors for orientation. I'd gotten lost on the way from the bus stop. Although beautiful, the buildings all looked the same, so I was dragging my bag and trunk all over campus. Many of the students pulled their cars right up to the residence halls. They were all shiny, new, and expensive, to match their owners. Even though my own car was just a figment of my imagination, it wasn't nearly as nice as the ones I was trailing my bags between. It also didn't help that I was perspiring through my denim dress. It was my favorite dress, and I thought it looked great on me, but I was starting to regret wearing it in the heat of summer.

Great first impression, Omega, I thought. *Late, carless, and sweating out my freshly pressed hair.*

I might as well have played into the poor black, country-girl role that undoubtedly would be assigned to me and showed up barefoot with a hog on a leash: "Hey, y'all. Is this where them smart people get schoolin'?"

I was homesick for just a moment and I was nervous. I was used to being the only black student in the classroom, I knew what that felt like. However, I'd never experienced white privilege displayed so conspicuously at this level. *Oh, my God!* I quickly collected myself and was reminded of my father's parting words to me: "No one is better than you, Omega!" I hadn't busted my butt for years in school to be defeated by fancy cars and berets. Why were all the girls wearing berets anyway? Did that mean they all spoke French? I had taken Latin in high school, which I thought was good enough. Did I have to learn French now too to get a leg up?

Later I would learn that berets were "just so totally in."

I followed the typed-out directions on my residence letter and found my way to the River Cluster, where I would be spending my days and nights for the next nine months. Alone. Well, technically I had a roommate, but I had yet to meet her. I only knew her name at this point. I essentially was going to be alone in a world without my family and friends around me. A lump in my throat reminded me of this fact, but a part of me also whispered, *Finally.*

I was imagining Dartmouth as a sanctuary for studying, learning, and exploring myself. The students wandering around were some of the most intelligent young people in the country, and they'd be sleeping across the hall from me. We'd have long, insightful conversations. We'd invent and develop brand-new ideas that would shape our generation. The future would be better because of the experiences we would share. At least that was what the admissions packet said would happen.

I finally located my floor and was standing in the common area, when a tall girl with frizzy red hair tapped me on the shoulder.

"Are you Omega Booveer?" She mispronounced my last name with a distinctive Boston accent.

"Ah, yes," I answered.

She looked down at a folder and said, "You're late. You missed the orientation walk-through."

"Oh, sorry. I got lost on the—"

"Yeah, it's fine. Your roommate will tell you about it." She looked back at the folder then wrote something down. She held the folder very close to her face, as if she needed to wear glasses but didn't have them on.

I apparently didn't provide a response quickly enough for her. Before I could think of anything at all, she ushered me toward my new room, 76A.

A paper was taped to the thick wooden door with two names written on it: Omega and Samantha.

I propped open the door and dragged my trunk though. There, sitting on the twin bed next to the window, was my new roommate, Samantha. Being the youngest girl in my family, I was accustomed to sharing a bedroom. I was curious to see if we would get along or at the very least share similar decorating styles. To my pleasant surprise, despite the musty, ancient state of the room, Samantha had managed to make the small space into a haven of frill, floral, and pillows galore. She had passed my style compatibility test. Yay!

"Hi, there!" Samantha said brightly. I recognized the drawl. She was a Southern girl, which meant she'd be friendly, which was good news. It also meant she'd be nosy, which wasn't.

"You must be Omega. I'm your roommate, Samantha. Not Sam, although that's what my Grandpa calls me, but it's a boy's name and I surely hate it." She stood up and hugged me then leaned over and started to help me move my trunk. "I'm from Savannah, Georgia, in case you didn't hear already," she continued. "My grandma got all in a tizzy because she wanted me to go to Stetson, but I wanted to live in the snow. I think it'll be real fun, right? You ever lived somewhere where it snowed?"

"Um, yeah," I said. I had a nervous habit of saying "um" when I was a little unsure of a situation.

"Well, hot damn. Good, then you can help me pick out a ski suit. I want to get one of those ones that are all one piece. Probably a pink one. You ever been skiing?"

"Um, no," I said.

"All right then, Omega. Come winter, you and me will just have to learn on the bunny slopes together. Oh! We should go to Vail. Ain't it funny that we would have to go south to go skiing?" She laughed at her own joke.

I laughed along with her, as I couldn't seem to help it. She kept talking as I unpacked everything I owned and put my life away into the shabby dresser and desk drawers.

Although Samantha was from the South, we didn't share a similar upbringing. Her last name was Watts, which was also the name of one of the biggest mining companies in the Southeast. She had been raised in the city of Savannah on sweet tea and Derby Days. She was a debutante and a socialite in training. Her mother was a constant critic of her etiquette, while her father did nothing but buy her everything she asked for. Still she admitted to being nervous about being in a new place, so I didn't feel as bad about my first day. Her stream-of-conscious way of talking was slightly comforting.

"So did ya meet our angry witch of an RA?" Samantha asked.

"I think so. She told me where my room was and said I missed the orientation."

"Oh, yeah! She got her hair stuck in one of them low-hanging branches. It was real funny, and she didn't get over it for the rest of the tour." Samantha laughed lightly. "It's not right to be poking fun at someone right after first meeting 'em, but she was grumpy before the whole hair-catching incident."

Samantha was charming and beautiful. I found her incredibly intimidating, because clearly she had come from wealth. She was the cliché Southern belle. I wondered if she had any black friends back home in Savannah or if the only people of color she might have known worked as the help. I imagined myself as the opposite of Samantha, and everything I admired about her on the first day I started to see as missing in myself. I was both nervous to be living with her and excited.

Samantha somehow had mastered the art of portraying perfection while not caring about anything having to do with being perfect. I suppose that was the luxury her upbringing afforded her. During all the years I lived with Samantha, I always wondered if she was treating me like a charity case or if it was her kindness that had allowed me to trail her through the first part of college, learning about a world I'd never been exposed to before. I was grateful to her, but at first I resented the ease with which she glided through social situations.

Later on, when Samantha and I reconnected in New York City, both in our thirties, successful and far removed from the insecurities of being young women, she explained how she'd really felt from the first day we'd met.

"I knew you were different than every person I grew up with and everyone else at that school," she said. "I actually liked that about you. I was so nervous I'd have some country-club Connecticut girl with a closetful of cable knits. You walked in our dorm, and I thought, *Thank the Lord!* Although we came from two very different experiences, I learned so much from you that I wouldn't ever have known if I hadn't met you. You're one of the smartest women I know, Omega. I may have introduced you to our friends Prada, Louis Vuitton, and Chanel, but you helped me to be a more socially conscious and responsible human being. My life is so much fuller with you in it."

We were sitting in the Loeb Boathouse in Central Park, fifteen years later, sharing a bottle of wine and nibbling on cucumber salad. We hadn't seen each other in a decade, but we had picked up our friendship right where we'd left off in college. Samantha was just as strikingly put together as I remembered, and even with a hefty career and a toddler, her energy still made my head spin.

"Sam, we did all of those things."

"Yeah! I know. That's what I'm saying." She smiled and laughed at my comment. We toasted to our friendship and re-hashed our lives in between our time apart.

Dartmouth wasn't a cheap school in any sense, and while Samantha had little worries about the price of groceries or her new Betsey Johnson dress, I had much more limited funds for an eighteen-year-old. My parents had converted to the Jehovah's Witnesses faith, which discourages the pursuit of higher education, and decided that since attending college was my decision, I'd have to find a way to pay for it. They made it clear that they wouldn't be giving me any supplementary income. Fortunately Dartmouth had given me a full scholarship based on my grades and my position on the tennis team. However, when it came to anything else, I was on my own. I was pretty resourceful and thrifty from having grown up in a large family, so with a part-time waitressing job on the side, I was able to stay afloat.

It wasn't a bad job either. There was a small diner near downtown that stayed open twenty-four hours, and I worked the overnight shift there a few nights a week. The owner, a small Greek woman who never let me call her anything but Yaya, allowed me to study all night when there were no customers and made sure I ate and had a ride to and from work, since the hours were late. Besides these concessions, however, she wasn't a gentle woman. Her eyebrows were menacing, along with being attached across the top of her nose, and her mustache didn't lighten up her appearance any. She constantly criticized the cooks for being useless and lazy and gave me dirty looks if any of the booths had stray French fries in the seats.

Most of the customers were Hanover locals, getting eggs and coffee at 5:30 a.m. before work or a milkshake after church on a Sunday afternoon. Most people were very friendly and warmed up to my presence quickly. A few were impressed by my background and my attendance at Dartmouth and every week asked me about my courses. They would brag to the other customers about how I was going to be a doctor or engineer, and I would change the world, because that's what kids from Dartmouth did.

A few times students would stumble into the restaurant. When they did they were mostly drunk and incoherent, since the cheapest bars were only a few blocks away. They usually were older students who didn't recognize me, nor did they think to ask if I was a fellow student.

I liked the anonymity of the job. Working on campus would have meant running into my classmates and professors while laboring over food or trash or whatever menial job they gave to freshmen for work study. Spending my nights at the diner meant escaping the world of Dartmouth and the bubble that surrounded its inhabitants. My customers had bills to pay and families. They'd strike up conversations about the local news happenings around town or relay to me their worries about fixing the broken washing machine.

More important, they all saw me as some great anomaly. I was a shy, still-developing black girl from the rural South who had managed to make it to Dartmouth and was doing it on my own. They sat at the counter as I poured coffee, impressed that I was trying to tackle everything they never imagined they could take on. Back on campus I was just another eighteen-year-old trying to figure out how to get around from class to class and how to make ramen noodles in the sink. None of the other students thought of me as anything but one of them—and a poorer, inexperienced version of them at that.

Finally, after my return from Christmas break, I decided to open myself up to the many possibilities that college life offered and see what would happen.

I was standing behind the diner counter, going through my spring semester schedule, trying to clock the hours I would be studying between shifts, when a group of large, hunky college boys rolled through the door of the restaurant.

I didn't recognize their faces, but they were my contemporaries and had just finished a bout of beer pitchers at the bar down the street. There were four of them, and they took up every inch of the vinyl booth closest to the coffee machines. I brought them their sodas and burgers quickly and quietly then returned to safety behind my counter. I heard them echoing through the restaurant, not thinking to cover their conversation.

"I really love a good townie girl. They'll let you do anything to them," said a blond one in a lacrosse jersey. He had the kind of voice that seemed as if he were forcing it down so it would sound deeper and more impressive.

"Yeah, but then there's no challenge. I prefer the poli-sci department girls," replied another blond one, who was shorter than the first but had the same general broadness of stature and deep-toned voice.

"That doesn't make any fucking sense, Mathers."

"Listen. Hear me out. Poli-sci girls are all liberal and outspoken and shit. If you just listen to them blather on about their causes and volunteer hours, they'll definitely let you make it with them. And since they're feminists, they're probably into kinky shit."

"Have you tested this idea out?" a third guy, this one with dark hair, chimed in. His face and voice were notably softer, and the tone of his question was obvious mocking.

"I'm working on it. I'm taking women studies this semester," Mathers replied. The other three laughed at this comment and gave him a round of punches and bumps in his side. "Anyway, Yarb, what would you know about all the chick options? You've only dipped into one kind. The high-school kind." The other guys responded with teasing and taunting noises to the one with dark hair.

"Yeah, yeah. Maybe I'm just not crazy about banging girls I don't know very well."

At this point in the conversation, the guy called Yarb looked right at me. I guessed he was trying to see if I'd been listening in. I'd been so fascinated by their inane conversation that I was, in fact, staring straight at them. He locked eyes with me, and a chill ran through me. He smiled, knowing I had heard the whole thing.

I looked down and away, trying to focus on filling the sugar caddies or anything that wasn't in the direction of the tableful of testosterone.

I'd never been so flustered before, and I was incredibly embarrassed. I was used to being around guys—well, specifically my brothers—and they'd never spared me from conversations about girls. The difference had been they were my brothers, and they were more respectful of women, at least in my presence anyway.

When Yarb looked over at me, it hit me that he could have in that moment been thinking about "banging" me. Granted he had prefaced his statement by saying he would get to know me first, which was noble enough, but there was something about the look on his face that made me feel like the process of learning about me would be very revealing.

I couldn't think of a time when a guy ever had looked at me the way Yarb did that one very cold night at the diner. He looked like he had wanted to eat me alive! It was terrifying, yet I was intrigued by the thought of what it would be like to be devoured.

The group paid the bill then noisily left the diner. Yarb lagged behind for a minute while the rest gathered in the parking lot, exclaiming loudly about the frigidly cold weather. He leaned over the counter and got close enough for me to smell the beer on his breath.

"Hey, you go to school with us, don't you? I feel like I've seen you."

"Um, yes. I'm a freshman," I replied.

"Cool. I am too. What dorm are you in?" He cleared his throat and stood up, which made him wobble a little.

"The River Cluster," I said quietly.

"Oh, cool. I am too!" He looked at me for a minute, saying nothing and making my skin heat up involuntarily. "Well, then I'll definitely see you around..." He looked at my name tag. "Omega."

Yarb glanced up at the foam-tiled ceiling and laughed to himself then said, "Hey! You can just call me Alpha." He smiled wickedly, and I almost couldn't stand it. "Okay, well, see ya." With that he sauntered out to join his friends, and they disappeared beyond the yellow streetlights.

I was shaken up for a few minutes after they left, but I couldn't think of a reason I was so tormented by the feeling. I didn't know them, nor did I think Samantha did. It was likely they wouldn't even remember me because of how much they'd had to drink before they showed up. Yet I had an overwhelming worry that I would run into one of them on campus. Especially Yarb. There was something about the look of him that kept me awake when I finally got home to sleep early the next morning. Even Samantha said I was acting strange, but I denied it.

It was my first real crush and not the innocent kind. This crush was riddled with warm, powerful feelings inside my body that I couldn't seem to stop or control. I thought about my one encounter with the mysterious Yarb for days and days afterward. Every time I thought too long about how he had looked at me from across the booth, I would blush.

I finally got up the courage to ask Samantha about him.

"Yarb? Oh, yeah!" She was doing aerobic leg lifts on the floor between our twin beds, wearing an adorable pink sweatband, even though no one would see her except me. I was drinking hot chocolate and sitting at my desk, telling her about the night I'd met him, but without all the scandalous details.

"His name is George or Charles or something, but his last name is Yarborough. So they all call him Yarb, which I personally think is just plain dumb. Yeah, I know there are a lot of Georges and all, but that's a real terrible nickname."

I nodded. "Well, he said he lives in our dorm."

"Oh, I didn't know that. Probably. It *is* a freshman dorm, you know." She pumped out a few more reps then looked over at me. "What? Do you like him or somethin'?"

"I don't know. I just met him for a second, and he was drunk." I shrugged and took a sip from my cup.

"He's on the rowing team, and all of them are hot—up in the morning doing all those boatin', rowin' things. I know a few of them through Momma. Do you want me to ask around?"

"Oh, no! It's fine." I realized Samantha might already be plotting to introduce us, even though I protested. She had a firm belief that somehow eventually everyone should know and meet everyone. It was the only way the world could continue on working, because if you needed to know something or someone, you should just ask and figure it out. In her own quirky way, Samantha was practicing the principles of social media long before anyone had come up with the idea.

I spent the next few weeks slumping around the halls of our dorm, half hoping I would run into Yarb/George/Jocky/Hunk/He-Man and half hoping he would never set eyes on me again. Then again he knew where I worked, so if he wanted to see me, he could always just show up there.

Finally, on a hurried, hectic morning when I was late for my business principles class at 9:00 a.m., I saw him sitting on a bench along the sidewalk. I had no choice but to pass right by him. I did so, speed walking, trying to seem as if I were late for class, which I was, but my primary concern was avoiding his glance. He spotted me, though. He looked up from a book, dragging his eyes from my Keds all the way up to my eyes, and locked them with his again. The same rush as before blew through me.

He smiled at me and raised his hand as if to stop me, but I continued on and into my lecture.

It was after the second encounter that I became disappointed with myself.

I was back at work that night, rushing through dinner, dropping plates and messing up customer orders. I'd been running that tiny ten-second moment that morning through my head over and over, like a film loop. I felt utterly ridiculous. When the customers left, and everything cooled down, Yaya demanded that I go into the bathroom and "pull it together for good." It was her Greek-accented version of American colloquialisms, which basically meant she was telling me to chill out.

I was frazzled. My hair was sticking out of my ponytail at every angle, eclipsing the extra frilly scrunchie my sister had given me. My face was flushed, and I felt like a crazed psych patient. I had no reason to feel anything at all, as it was just another normal day. This boy, this silly representation of varsity ego, was making me feel like I was lost.

I looked in the mirror for another ten minutes or so before gripping the sink and scowling.

"Stop it, Omega. You're better than this. Yeah, okay, maybe you don't know anything about boys or men or whatever they are, but that doesn't mean you can't figure it out. Mom and Dad might get mad, but you don't live with Mommy and Daddy anymore." I sighed and ran my palms over the sides of my face. "It's time to grow up."

I was talking aloud to myself in my work bathroom, but it didn't matter because I'd had a strong revelation.

At some point I was going to have to shove myself out into the real world without hiding behind my family or Samantha or my studies. I decided that the next time I saw Yarb I was going to talk to him, like *really* talk to him. Maybe my long, drawn-out fantasies would come true, and he would jump through all the hoops to try to get to know me. Either way it was time to let people in and let Omega out.

I came out of that bathroom a new woman, as melodramatic as that might sound. I felt like I was powerful enough to tackle the winter, all the tedious courses, and all the troubles of living on my own. The next step would be easy. Yaya must have noticed my blooming pride, because she quickly asked me to take out the leaky trash bags.

The chance to speak with Yarb came sooner than I'd expected.

I decided to let Samantha in on my new self-appointed mission, without the added details that a boy had motivated it. Her reaction seemed as if she'd been waiting months for me to bring it up.

"Darlin', don't you know that we're basically the same size? I have so many things that Momma sends me that would look way better on you than they do on me! So many boys ask me about you, and you know, I never say nothing, but everyone's wondering if you got someone back home or if maybe you're..." Sam stopped herself abruptly. I immediately thought that *everyone* was talking about me being a virgin, that I didn't know anything about the opposite sex. I didn't, but I also didn't want people talking about this personal fact of my life. I had barely kissed a boy, but that certainly didn't mean I didn't want to.

"What, Sam? What did they ask?" I tried to restrain the little shake in my voice while I asked.

"Well..." She leaned in closer and whispered, which was fairly dramatic considering we were in our dorm room alone. "Heather thought maybe you were having an affair with one of the professors because you're always going to office hours."

I laughed out loud, from relief and the ridiculousness of it. Of course Heather would couple me with Professor Johnson, the only black male professor on campus. Sam laughed too.

"Actually I've never done anything with a guy," I confessed. "I never had a chance to at home, and I don't know anyone here." I felt better now about letting Samantha in on the truth. She seemed to want to help me, and despite her being attuned to all the campus gossip, I thought she'd likely keep my secret.

"That's no big deal, Mega," she said. "Most of the girls don't know anything either—they just talk as if they know all about it. Although Heather, I hear, is a bit of a go-around. I think she asked me about you and a teacher to blow off the fact that she might be messin' with a TA."

The two of us continued to gossip and laugh late into the night, all the while devising a plan to get me out of the dorm and into impressionable hearts, or that's how Samantha saw it. I just wanted to impress Yarb the next time we happened to run into each other.

We started out simply. Samantha introduced me to her pop-up closet, which took up half of her side of the dorm room. At some point in the first semester, I'd pulled back the floral curtain once or twice just to have a small peek. Sam hated wearing the same outfit twice, which meant she needed a large selection of pieces to group and match together. It also meant steady trips to the local mall, after which she would return exhausted, her hands full of bags and spouting complaints about the returns she'd have to make if she saw another girl with the same outfit. It was a luxury I wasn't familiar with, but I noticed a glazed-over look of addiction and excitement whenever Samantha suited up for a shopping binge.

Opening her closet and sorting through the possibilities finally made me understand why she had that look to begin with.

Every day the next week, I'd borrow a blouse or a pleated skirt. Samantha would make me spin around, pose in front of the mirror, and switch my accessories until she felt it was perfect. Then she'd shove me out the door. She even forced me to wear her tennis attire, which meant constantly pulling down tight spandex skirts while trying to compete.

I had a few moments when I imagined what my mother would have said about the whole transformation. Mom would have criticized how much leg and chest I was showing. She would have scoffed that I was taking charity from a rich white girl who was just using me like her own personal, living, breathing Barbie doll. More important, Mom would have hated that I was dressed in such a way around boys my age. It was just the kind of subtle sin that she hated. Even though I wasn't physically doing anything, the suggestion of anything scandalous would have been too much for her to handle.

However, I didn't live with Mom anymore. Samantha had become one of my closest friends, and I didn't feel as if she were using me or taunting me. I pushed away the nagging voice of my mother and focused on the mission at hand. I didn't have much time to be bothered by it anyway because between school, work, and tennis, I didn't have much time for anything else.

I purposefully didn't bring Yarb up again to Samantha. I didn't wander around the dorm to figure out where his room was, although I considered it every day. I did stare at the students walking by the diner at night, wondering if he'd venture inside, making the bell on the door and my heart ring at the same time. I knew it would happen eventually. Fate had some kind of amazing plan for me to fall into his arms, and I intended to be prepared for it. I practiced my cursory laugh and all the smart things I would say. I would will myself not to be nervous. I wanted to leave him flustered, instead of vice versa.

After midterms I was starting to feel the weight of two semesters of intense study, work, and early-morning tennis practice. I'd started a habit of napping in the medical library. By pulling together two wide reading chairs to face each other, I was able to create a temporary tweed-upholstered bed. I would drape my heavy red wool coat over me and rest my head on top of my bag then pass out for about twenty minutes. There was never anyone in the medical library compared to the general library, which was always full of my classmates, and all the reading chairs usually were taken.

It was an afternoon in mid-March, and I was fast asleep in my little makeshift cubby, when someone squeezed my arm and whispered my name.

"Hey, Omega."

I turned over a little surprised and looked right into familiar eyes.

Smiling, Yarb was leaning right over me, touching my arm through my wool coat.

"You were snoring a little bit," he whispered. He chuckled then sat on the wooden armrest of the chair.

I sat up promptly. I started to pat down my hair and took a quick glance at the state of myself in the nearest reflective surface—a library window. I was a little tousled, my hair sticking out all over my head. I was sure I had puffy eyes and creases from where I'd laid my face across my bag. I noticed I was drooling while I napped and shamefully pulled the coat up to my face to wipe it. As Yarb looked at me, I couldn't help feel flustered. *All that prep out the window. I must look crazy*, I thought.

"I was reading. I must have fallen asleep," I replied quietly and pathetically.

"Yeah, you look tired."

Great.

He looked relaxed and handsome sitting there. He also looked as if he weren't going to leave, so I was trapped.

"I've been working a lot. And tennis. And midterms. And now finals," I replied.

He nodded along. "I think they run us ragged to get rid of the bad freshmen." He picked up an open book that was lying in my lap. The closeness of his touch made me warm all over. The wool was becoming too hot and heavy for me. "The team just made the time trials to compete in nationals," he continued, "so now we all have midterms and extra practice."

Although I'd heard this news earlier in the week, I made a face as if I didn't understand what he was talking about. *Okay, Omega. Play it cool. You don't know anything about him or his life. You haven't been listening intently whenever someone mentions him.*

"I'm on the rowing team. Not varsity, but we still have to stick to the same schedule."

"Oh, okay. Yeah, that sounds like a lot."

A shushing noise was coming from behind me, and I turned around to see a librarian with a book cart standing a few feet behind us.

Yarb rolled his eyes and stood up. I started to gather my things and push the chairs apart. I was slightly relieved to have him move farther away while also being angry about the interruption in our conversation.

He waited for the librarian to wheel away before he spoke again. "Hey, Omega."

"Yes."

"There's a party Wednesday night to celebrate the team making the time trials. It's off campus. You should come."

It amazed me how easily he said this, as if the thought didn't rattle any part of him. Meanwhile I was dancing and jumping inside my head.

"Um, I guess..." I started to say.

"I mean, I'm not sure if you're working, but if you can make it, that would be pretty cool." After saying this, he reached out and brushed the side of my arm. He let out a smile along with it, and my hands shook from nerves.

"Yeah, maybe." I said, instantly congratulating myself for such an aloof response. Maybe all that practicing really had helped.

"Okay, cool. See ya later," he said.

With that he turned and left the library, leaving me standing there dragging the wool coat in my hands across the worn-out carpet. I waited for a moment to make sure he was gone then let out a huge sigh and plopped down on the chair.

A flood of thoughts, ideas, and questions rushed into my head. I had to go find Samantha. She probably already knew all about the party but would be excited to know about my personal invitation. She would make me replay every detail of the encounter. We needed to go through her massive pile of dresses. We needed to figure out where the party was. I needed to call Yaya and fake a cough. We also needed to go over exactly what would happen at this party, because I'd never been to one. Not once. I had no idea what to do with myself.

Four

There was only one class I didn't dread showing up for.

I had chosen to double major in finance and communications because it seemed like an impossible feat, and I apparently was developing a taste for self-destruction. While filling out my freshman course packet, I sifted through my options for minors and decided on art history, thinking it would be easy to just stare at pictures and talk about the starving artists who had painted them. It turned out to be an incredibly difficult and detailed class. And I loved every minute of it.

We all sat at ancient desks every Wednesday at 6:00 p.m., staring up at overhead-projected images of one famous work after another. The room smelled of dust and mildew. Our instructor was a visiting associate professor from a university in France, École de something or other, although she had a slow, crisp Scottish accent. When she listed the French terminology for technique and form, it was as if the Scottish brogue washed away from her for a brief moment. She would say each romantic term with perfect pronunciation. She was young and could have been mistaken for a Bond girl if she didn't dress in the same gray or brown tweed pants suits every day.

Mentally I couldn't place her on the streets of Paris, where she had studied and worked before coming to Dartmouth. I knew very little about France before the class, but once we started to focus on the Impressionists, I fell in love with my idea of the City of Lights. I saw tall, iron lampposts against deep, blue starry nights, or the pinks and reds of sunsets on the Seine. The short, battered buildings on Parisian streets were adorned with a mastery of mason work. Between the grout and pillars, gargoyles and gods rested. They watched over the facades on the street and those who wisped in and out of the buildings lining it. This imagery didn't match with my professor's eternal gray wardrobe scheme.

Samantha had traveled to Paris with her family more than once and described the coffee and men as "divine." I couldn't imagine my professor sitting in a café exclaiming anything was "divine," although she might have described the coffee as "espresso, from Colombia, with a hint of hazelnut." She didn't scoff at the art, but neither did she glorify it. She approached each work like an investigation and instead broke down the psyches of the artist. It seemed the more troubled the soul, the greater the art. Within the context of death, war, or poverty, the colors were brighter and the forms more disturbing. I later was shocked to learn my instructor was a specialist of counterculture performance art and had once had a brief stint of following John Lennon and Yoko Ono around New York, which explained why the ballerinas and bridges of French Impressionism weren't all that exciting for her.

However, I couldn't get enough of it. I'd never set foot in a museum at that point in my life. The projected slides on our class-room wall were often the first time I had seen anything like that before. Maybe I had seen the images in textbooks a few times, but they never were large enough for me to really "get" them.

Tonight was the rowing-team party, the night I'd actually have to attend the event and be around Yarb for more than ten minutes. I wasn't giving the lecture my usual amount of attention due to my anticipation, so instead of looking up at the projections, I was drawing circles in my notebook. My mind was wandering between what to say and what not to say at the party, who might be there and what might happen.

"Ms. Bouvier."

I snapped my head up to my professor, who was standing behind the podium at the front of the room.

"Could you tell me what this woman is doing in this piece?"

I recognized the painting projected next to her, but I was drawing a blank as to the name of it. There was a naked woman in the forefront, sitting with two men on the grass. I looked back and forth from the painting to my professor, trying to think of an answer. In a moment of brilliance, I remembered the name of the piece: *Luncheon on the Grass.*

"Um, she's having lunch."

"Accurate, Ms. Bouvier, but not correct. In the moment this painting represents, there is no representation of anyone eating," she responded.

I heard a chuckle at the front of the room. Everyone snapped to look in its direction.

"Mr. Ashby, what is it that you find amusing?" Professor Graham stepped toward the chuckler.

The guy was one of those students who rarely showed up to lecture. When he did, he was likely napping. It was the first time I'd ever heard his name aloud. The back of his head was sandy blond and perfectly disheveled. That was all I had noticed of him until now. Looking over, I saw details about him that instantly spawned dislike. He was too big for the desk, his legs stretched out in an overly casual manner and extending into the aisle. There was no bag or book on his person, so it was obvious there was no effort being made on his part. Not to mention that he'd laughed at Professor Graham. He seemed like a careless rich kid.

"Well, it looks like one of those dudes just ate *something*," Ashby said, continued to chuckle at himself. A few in the class joined in.

Ms. Graham reacted with a raised eyebrow. "What exactly are you implying?"

He sat up then said, "Naked woman in the park. The dudes all have their clothes on. Plus the woman sitting there really looks like she's asking for it."

Professor Graham stood right in front of Ashby's desk. She let out a small, pained smile, one of the few I'd ever seen from her.

"Asking for what?"

"To get banged," he said, as if it were strikingly obvious.

The other students stayed quiet; maybe they were shocked. My mouth had dropped open when he'd answered. He was clearly trying to get a rise out of the class, talking about sex and naked women. My dislike for him grew even more.

Fine art was for the venerable, educated people of society, those who understood epic poetry and romantic languages. Art represented the deepest parts of love, war, and death. This blond, boneheaded frat boy was turning beautiful works of art into the stuff of *Penthouse Forum* letters. I was sitting on the edge of my seat, waiting for the professor to let him have it. I thought she would at the least send him out of the room, if not flunk him for the entire semester.

The painting projected in the dark, dusty room was stunning. The greens and browns that surrounded the characters were in motion, as if a breeze were settling into the park with them. The men wore draped, refined suits. A blue cloth was delicately wrapped around the woman in the foreground. She was graceful and healthy in the way that all painted nude women seem to be. It was a still moment but captured a time when wearing a tie to a picnic was normal. The more I communed with the painting, the more I loved it.

Yet as I studied it, sitting there with this guy's rude words swimming around in my head, I felt discomfited by it. There was something about the expression of the woman in the middle. If this had been a photograph, it might seem as though she and the photographer were complicit in a good joke. But it wasn't a photo, which meant the model was looking directly at Manet as she held that look. It felt as if she were looking at me, challenging me to do or think something. It was a knowing look—a wanting look—and it started to change the meaning of the painting for me. I felt a little ashamed looking at the exposed woman's body.

"Great deduction, Mr. Ashby," Professor Graham said, "although I would say it's likely the woman already has engaged in said 'banging.' These are women of the night. Prostitutes. However, Manet places them in broad daylight, in a public place. We should acknowledge that the woman in the middle is obviously unashamed of her position in society." She walked back to her podium. "This is a large canvas. It was quite scandalous when first put on display, which was obviously Manet's intention." She paused and looked over at the screen. "I find it rather mischievous. Anyone want to comment on the use of color?"

I felt my skin heat up. It was one thing to be wrong when the instructor pointed me out, which I hated, but it was a whole different thing to be outdone by a guy like Ashby.

I felt betrayed by the woman in the painting. She knew many things I didn't. Her smirk started to feel like a taunt. She was the kind of woman whom men chased down. She got what she wanted and had the bravery to parade around naked in front of them. When Ashby looked at the piece, she looked right at him and whispered, "Hey, there, big boy." But when I looked into her face, she seemed to say, "Aw, poor, scared little thing." Of course, Manet was a philanderer and an alcoholic, like most of his fellow Impressionist painters.

I left class fuming! I knew I could have studied and memorized every painting, painter, and method, but I never would have seen the true message of *Luncheon on the Grass* as clearly as that guy did. Ms. Graham was so pleased with Ashby's interpretation and didn't acknowledge the fact that he was never in class and probably didn't even know Manet was French. However, art isn't about facts. Nor is it about refined nature and beautiful images. Sometimes art is about primal feelings of need, anger, and love. Sometimes art isn't romantic or beautiful. Sometimes art hurts. But I didn't think of this then. I didn't understand at the time that the woman's face was radiating seduction, because those thoughts never had crossed my mind.

I pushed aside the frustration of the lecture and focused on the night ahead. I charged toward the residence hall, knowing Samantha would be there already, primping herself for the rowing party. For a short while I had forgotten about the whole thing, but walking in the cold reminded me of the heat I felt around Yarborough. I was incredibly nervous, but then there was a small, persistent image in my head of the woman on the grass. She was daring me. It seemed crazy, but it was as if I were being teased and dared to do something about Yarb by a bold figure from a long time ago. Honestly I wasn't sure I was up for the challenge.

After I got to the dorm and rushed to change into something perfect for the evening, Samantha and I took her car and drove to a residential part of town, where students would rent a five-bedroom house and fill it with thirteen roommates and regular parties. Familiar silhouettes moved across the orange-lit windows of the house. Sam and I walked up the driveway to knock on the large wooden door. No one answered. She knocked harder, huffing and holding her coat close to her. The sky was white, and it looked as if it might snow over the course of the night.

The door flew open, and a hand waved us in. There were people standing in the hallway leading to the living room, people stacked on couches and chairs. It was crowded and smoky inside, with music streaming from all directions. I recognized a few faces, but mostly it was a sea of students holding drinks, laughing, talking, and moving together. It was exactly how I expected it to be, but it also shook my confidence.

"Don't worry, Mega. He's here somewhere. Why would Yarb invite you to a party he wasn't going to come to? Plus I saw a few rowing guys wandering around." Sam was quickly drinking the beer that had been offered to us as we'd entered, so I started to chug my own, just to feel like I was keeping up. I didn't really like the taste of it, but it gave me something to do other than stand in the corner and stare at everyone.

Samantha was at ease, as usual, leaning over to whisper to me about people at the opposite end of the room. I was forcing myself to be patient and relaxed. After a little while, I almost was.

"Well, hey, you two." A familiar voice was at my side, and its low roll gave me chills.

Samantha's face perked up, and she looked over. "Hi!"

"Interesting class today, wasn't it?" He was standing too close. He was wearing a rowing jacket and a smug look. It wasn't the boy I'd been looking for. It wasn't anyone I wanted to see at all. Blond and still disheveled, Ashby stood next to me, glass in hand, taller than I'd expected.

I nodded, trying to hide the scowl crawling onto my face. Samantha jumped in to introduce herself. Ashby ignored her immediately and continued to speak directly to me, even as I looked away.

"Omega, right?" he said then took a sip of deep-brown liquor from his glass.

Muscles in my back tensed and twitched. I couldn't have been more disgusted by his manner, but in a confusion that only an eighteen-year-old could feel, he was also too attractive to disregard entirely. For Samantha this factor certainly fueled her behavior.

"I'm Sam, Omega's roommate. We're in the freshman dorms. Ew!" She laughed alone but genuinely and then continued to try for his attention. Eventually he turned to her and let out a smile that made me uncomfortable.

"I'm going to the bathroom," I said, interrupting them. I walked between them and around the corner. I made a note to tell Samantha later how I knew Ashby and to clarify why I found him so off-putting.

I located the bathroom next to the kitchen, where I saw a long line of people. This was in the early days of casual cocaine use, and it was difficult to know whether the other girls in line were there to powder their noses or "powder their noses." I looped back through the house and decided to try upstairs. I was at the bottom of the steps, chastising myself for not being more dismissive of Ashby, when a group of guys bounded down the staircase, coming right at me. They were roaring with laughter. My chest tightened. At the back of the group, laughing along with them, was Yarb. I kept still, looking on unnoticed, and then he looked right at me. He smiled. I couldn't move from my spot.

"Omega!" He followed behind the group toward the bottom of the stairs. "You're here! Where you going?"

"Um, the bathroom. The line—"

"Oh! There's a bathroom upstairs." Hyped up and smelling sweet with alcohol, Yarb grabbed my hand and pulled me away.

Once I was in the bathroom, I tried to breathe more slowly and calm myself as I stood alone at the sink. All fantasies aside, this was just a normal night, wasn't it? Yarb still created a heat across my skin that I couldn't fight, but I could keep my mouth and my brain under control. No, I wasn't the woman on the grass. I was Omega, on my own and figuring it out. I wasn't going to be scared or nervous. Finished at the sink, I dried my hands and opened the door.

I walked into the hallway, where he was leaning against the wall, waiting for me. It was a moment I'll always remember, because it was the first time the flutterings of love crossed through my head. It made me dizzy to look at him, and I was excited to spend any amount of time with him, whether it was just a few seconds in that hallway, for the rest of the night, or for the rest of forever. I'd never felt a real crush before, and this one was hitting me heavily. Forget the fact that he was white, and I'd never dated a white guy before. Crap, I'd never dated anyone before. But none of that mattered to me at the time, and I was open to having a new experience. I loved his preppy style, the folds in his sweater just so, and the sincerity of his voice. I couldn't believe it while it was happening, but it was a feeling I knew I'd secretly always wanted to have.

I later would cherish these first few flutterings, as I would have them over and over with men, lovers, and friends. It was the warm, fun part of romance, which we all first encounter and never want to let go. However, I also would learn that these warm, shaky nerves weren't the feelings of true love. That was a deeper feeling that ached in your stomach and could tear you up. Love wouldn't warm my skin or make my heart speed up. The truest kind would sit in the core of my stomach, making me feel like I never had enough, making me want to work every day for more. In the hallway there with Yarb, I was just starting. And that first bit felt so good!

We moved from room to room together, getting closer to each other as the crowd grew. Yarb seemed to know most of the attendees, giving away hugs and handshakes. He made an effort to introduce me to each one we passed. Some of the girls appeared nice and smiled sweetly, but I did receive a few raised eyebrows casting some shade, which I'd expected. Meanwhile the guys occasionally gave Yarb a wink or nudge of approval. His enthusiasm was infectious, and I was becoming at ease with my surroundings. The challenges and judgments faded away for a few minutes while I stood with him. It could have been the fuzziness in my head, after I finished a drink or two, that had put me in such a giddy mood. At the time it didn't matter, as the night was playing out in the most perfect way.

In those moments I forgot all about Sam. I looked around, trying to spot her bright-blond hair, but I couldn't make her out anywhere. Next to me, Yarb was carrying on with his teammates about match worries.

I tugged on his arm. "I need to find my roommate," I said.

"Who?" he replied.

"My roommate, Samantha. I came here with her."

"Okay." He looped my arm with his, and we made a lap of the room.

The more time that passed without finding her, the more worried I became. She often came to these parties on her own, so I didn't have much reason to think something was wrong. However, I remembered the chill that had traveled between Ashby and me, which made me regret leaving her with him.

"When did you see her last?" Yarb asked.

"We were in the big room. Then I left for the bathroom and found you."

"She wasn't in there?"

"No. When I walked away, she was talking to this guy from my art class, Ashby."

Yarb stopped walking then asked, "Henry Ashby. On the team?"

"Yes."

"Oh," he said. He let go of my arm and looked down.

"Why? Is something wrong?"

"I haven't seen him around either, so they probably left together."

I looked at him, confused. "They don't even know each other. Why would they leave together?"

"I don't know. That guy likes to make it with a lot of girls. He's kind of…"

"An asshole?" I said, crossing my arms and feeling angry.

"Yeah." Yarb shrugged.

"I need to find her." I heard the bite in my voice.

The front yard was dusted in snow. The air dipped into the collar of my coat, bringing in cold and more worry. Yarb walked ahead of me, weaving between the parked cars. I wasn't sure if we would find the two of them at all, but I already had images washing over me of my best friend in a bad situation. I knew little about Samantha's relationship with men. I had a feeling that she had much more experience than I did, but it was possible that everyone did in comparison to me. It might not have been my business to find her. Ashby may have been exactly the kind of guy Samantha would chase after. The cold was stealing away a little of my bravery, but I followed Yarb to a long black car parked on the street near the house.

It was obvious from the windows and the silhouettes that the car was occupied. Yarb got there first and tapped on the window. I stood a few feet away.

The door on the other side opened up, and then Samantha appeared from behind the trunk. She walked to me, hugged me immediately, and leaned on me as if she couldn't stand on her own.

"Hey, Mega." She sighed, and I smelled the liquor on her breath.

"Are you okay?" I asked.

"Yeah." She gulped and leaned in more. "I might be sick."

I took her back into the house and into the unused upstairs bathroom. I sat on the side of the tub as she lay across the cold tile. Yarb hadn't followed me into the house. He had been halfway inside the car as I walked away, talking to whom I assumed was Ashby. I didn't expect him to come after me, as I was choosing my friend over him.

When Samantha and I finally made it back to the dorm that night—or I should say that morning—I had a hard time falling asleep. I kept replaying the night's events, thinking I'd ruined my chances with Yarb by being the boring, responsible friend. I'd gotten in the way of myself again, and I almost regretted it. Having

Samantha snore and talk in her sleep next to me gave me a little comfort, and I finally dozed off.

"Omega! There's a note! He left a note!" Sam ran toward me down the dorm hallway with an envelope.

It was a full week after the rowing party, and I had chosen to push it all out of my head. The morning after, with a raging headache and hunger for pancakes, Samantha had explained to me what had happened with Ashby.

"Oh, he was too drunk to get it up anyway." She laughed while eating. "But he was also too hot to say no to."

I'd learned that Sam and many of the girls in our building were sleeping with boys. Lots of them. All the time. No one was dating. She claimed it wasn't that big of a deal, and while rumors flew about who was with whom, it turned out everyone was trading off and pretending it wasn't happening. Everyone was doing it? Not me! What about unwanted pregnancies? Or worse, unwanted STDs? Call me a prude, but I never could see myself being so promiscuous.

That morning I'd realized that I was all right with how the night had turned out. I couldn't justify the way Samantha and her friends were allowing themselves to be treated by Ashby and all the other guys. While I believed Yarb was different, I wasn't sure. I wasn't going to be caught in a steamy car with a guy I'd just met, and for once I became proud of this fact. So I turned my focus back on classes and work. I started to consider study-abroad programs for the summer. Then a week later, Samantha handed me a letter from Yarb as she ran toward me in the hallway.

Hey. How are you? I hope you don't think I'm a total loser for getting drunk at that party. Is your roommate okay? Do you want to go out with me sometime?
—Yarb

It was simple, but it turned my whole world upside-down. It re-granted my faith in everything that had happened before with him. Laughing, Samantha and I jumped around in the hallway.

A blissful few weeks followed. Yarb picked me up for our first date. He bought me dinner. He made me laugh. He took me home on time. He called me the next day. He told me I was smarter than he was, which I laughed at, but it also made me feel more important than I ever had before.

We held hands on campus and created jokes for just the two of us to laugh at. We took long walks and had picnics in the park. He recited works by his favorite poets, E.E. Cummings and Shakespeare, and I recited poems by mine, Langston Hughes and Maya Angelou. We played tennis together, and I taught him the latest dance moves. Yarb always surprised me with how quickly he learned. While I was spending less and less time with Samantha, she still bothered me for details and answered all my questions about sex.

The topic of sex was moving into the foreground of my life, because holding hands with Yarb and admiring all of him in tattered jeans was inciting feelings within me that I'd never felt before. He wasn't pushy and never asked me about it, but I knew sex was on his mind; I could tell by the way he kissed me.

One night he pinned me to the door of my room. His mouth was rough, and he pressed hard against my lips. I felt as if I were being devoured, just like I'd imagined that night in the diner when I first saw him. It was hot breath between our lips and little space between our bodies. He moaned roughly and fell against me, which made me want to stop but also badly want to keep going. I put my hand on his chest, applying gentle pressure, and he backed away. This was where we left it for now, and again I worried about being a different girl from the rest.

It was finally warming up into spring. Everyone was talking about traveling for spring break, but I knew I'd be staying on campus. One night I was studying and napping in Yarb's dorm room while he watched *Miami Vice* on TV. His roommate was gone, and we were moving back and forth between snuggling on the twin bed and lying on the carpet.

Yarb landed another kiss on me that sent me spinning, except this time we were lying down. Before I knew it, he had his hands all over me, and the warm touch kept me from saying no. My body was reacting to him by wanting more, but I still was holding back a little. The bolder he got, the more I wanted to pause. I finally pulled away, breathing heavily, and looked right at him.

"I can't."

He huffed loudly and sat up. He said nothing in response.

"I'm sorry, Yarb. I just can't."

"I know," he finally said.

The topic wasn't brought up again.

Two weeks later Yarb came back from a spring break trip to the Outer Banks in North Carolina. He confessed that he'd had sex with a girl on the trip. She was from another school, as though that made it all right. He said he was very sorry, but he wasn't sure if I was serious enough about him. I cried at the luncheonette booth we sat in while he told me the story. I blamed him and was filled with anger. I ran home to Samantha, who spent the rest of the semester referring to him as "that sleazy jerk."

I never truly had fallen for Yarb, even while I lusted after him. It was the first time I learned that men have needs. These needs are wild and strong, but a real man can tame them for a woman he loves. Yarb was still a boy, and I quickly forgave him as time passed. I did remember the pain of it and made a solemn vow to myself that in the future I would become more and more careful with my heart. It was a vow I would keep until I met Zion.

Five

Miami, 1991

I sat at my desk and looked across the open-plan office to the wall on the other side—stucco, the most common building material to be found in South Florida. And here I was surrounded by it as I worked at my desk, my job consisting mainly of fielding calls on behalf of my agency's clients.

One year had passed since I'd graduated from college, and this was my first real job, if you didn't count all the odd jobs I'd held while working my way through Dartmouth. This was the first job where I got in a car and commuted to an office and spent long hours there before finally dragging my tired ass back to my car and driving home, where I collapsed on my sofa, poured myself a glass of wine, and dozed off for a half hour or so before preparing a single girl's dinner for myself—usually a nice salad with some kind of protein added to prepare me for starting the daily grind all over again the next day.

Now don't get me wrong. I loved my job. And maybe *grind* wasn't quite the right word. But I did find it exhausting, what with the long hours and keeping clients happy and going to endless meetings to woo potential clients to our agency.

I was working in public relations for one of the largest firms in Miami. Our clients ran the gamut from professional athletes and movie stars to corporate CEOs and those who had gotten their names in the paper for reasons they would rather forget (and sooner have everyone else forget too, which is where we came in).

I was paid a decent salary for someone fresh out of college and thought my work was exemplary enough to guarantee a Christmas bonus at year's end. In the meantime I was living in an apartment right on South Beach, which, in the past several years, had become one of the hottest vacation destinations in the world. I found myself surrounded by an international babble of voices, accents, and languages. The only thing they had in common was the fact that the voices usually ushered from bodies, both male and female, who were young, tanned, and at the peak of physical perfection.

I lived in an apartment building situated at the intersection of Collins Avenue and Lincoln Road. On hot days, which was practically every day in Miami, waiting for the light to change at that intersection was a little like standing in a frying pan whose heat source was the sun. But the apartment building itself, which was a little south of the intersection on Collins, was an oasis of shade in a desert with no relief from the heat.

The building was large, and most of those who lived there were Cuban émigrés who had fled the island right after Fidel Castro's takeover of the country. Most of them had been in the United States for more than thirty years, yet very few of them spoke English. There was also a smattering of other types, young teachers who liked the idea of living so close to the beach (which was right behind the building; I could see it from my window) and bartenders who worked at the various drinking establishments that had sprung up along Ocean Drive and Collins Avenue. The bartenders spent their days sunning themselves by the pool at the back of the building or, walking a little farther, going for brisk swims in the warm waters of the Atlantic. The teachers tended to use the pool more in the early evenings and on weekends. As for me, I was almost never at the pool or in the ocean, as I was too busy with work to be able to spend much time there.

Working in public relations is a little like being a doctor. I know how pretentious that sounds. PR people don't save lives—that's true. But we do save careers, which can also save a life or two. We're like doctors because we never know when we're going to receive an emergency call that's going to force us to spring into action. And I guess this might sound pretentious too, but here goes. PR people are also like firefighters because we never know when there's going to be a fire that needs to be put out—and pronto!

That seemed to be the case right now, as the phone on my desk rang, shattering my daydream about what my life was now like. I picked up the receiver and spoke my name firmly, as I'd been trained to do my first week on the job. We were to be firm in whatever we said, to give the impression to our clients that we were always on top of things, even when that wasn't the case—*especially* when that wasn't the case—as had been drilled into us by our supervisors.

"Omega, please come to the office right now."

The voice belonged to Sophia, the secretary to Mr. Abrams, one of the firm's three partners (the firm being Durand, Abrams, & Sifuentes, which highlights how many ethnic bases we covered here).

"I'll be right there," I said, as I hung up the phone. I opened a desk drawer and took out a small mirror to make sure I looked okay. Hair in place. No lipstick on my teeth. Makeup not smeared. Looking down, I checked to make sure my stockings had no runs in them. It might seem silly, but in PR the way you look is as important as what you say. You have to be impeccably dressed at all times. There can be no flaws in the face you present to the world. And while my eyes were focused on myself, I stopped for a half second to admire my legs. All that tennis in college had given me well-toned, shapely calves, about which I'd been complimented on more than one occasion. After putting away the mirror, I got up and walked across the open-plan floor in the direction of Mr. Abrams's office, which befitting a partner, was a large corner office that overlooked downtown Miami.

I was greeted by Sophia, whose desk stood outside the door to Mr. Abrams's office. She was a slightly older Cuban woman who'd been part of the Mariel boatlift some ten years back. She spoke English with only the slightest trace of an accent, which mainly came out in moments of stress. But Sophia was such a cool number, commanding what seemed to be huge a reservoir of self-possession, that I could count on one hand the number of times I'd heard that accent put in an appearance. She was the perfect executive assistant to Mr. Abrams. (There were also rumors that she was sleeping with her boss, but you didn't hear that from me.)

"She's here," Sophia said, looking up at me while holding down the intercom button and speaking into it. The wall between us was glass, and I knew Mr. Abrams could look out at us without any trouble, but Sophia was just following the agency protocol here: all visitors must be announced.

"Send her in," said Mr. Abrams's voice on the intercom, even though he could have shouted out at us through the door, but things weren't done that way here at Durand, Abrams, & Sifuentes either. Low voices in the office had to be maintained at all times.

"Go right in," said Sophia.

Mr. Abrams rose to greet me and led me over to the sofa along one wall of his office. It was quite a space, I must say. The walls were lined with photographs of him shaking hands with practically every famous person who ever had passed through Miami. A quick glance and I spotted Mr. Abrams with Don Johnson, Philip Michael Thomas, Will Smith, Martin Lawrence, Madonna, and a hundred other celebrity names you saw in the gossip columns. There were also pictures of him with the rich and powerful and the movers and shakers who had made Miami the place it was today, a hub for those who wanted to be at the forefront of what was happening in film, music, art, or the art of just hanging out and enjoying life.

The decor was functional and sleek, made to impress. And impress it did as I ensconced myself in the buttery leather of Mr. Abrams's office couch. He sat kitty-corner from me in a chair that seemed to be made from the same material. I pulled at my skirt to make sure I wasn't revealing too much and waited with bated breath to find out the reason I'd been called here.

Mr. Abrams looked briefly at a file he had brought with him to the chair then looked up at me and said, "How are you, Omega?"

"Fine, sir," I answered, giving him the usual Durand, Abrams, & Sifuentes affirmative response.

"And refresh my memory. How long have you been here?"

"Coming up on ten months."

"Very good. And how do you like things here?"

This was a trick question for which there was only one response. "Mr. Abrams, this is the best job I've ever had."

He looked down at the file before saying, "I see this is your first job since graduating from college. So you might say this is the only job you've ever had."

Smiling at him I said, "Yes, but it's also my best. I can't imagine working anywhere else or doing anything else."

Mr. Abrams listened to what I was saying and nodded. "Good," he said, then paused before continuing. "Omega, I have a special job for you."

I sat up straight on the couch. My stomach gave a little lurch as I waited to hear what this assignment could be. I ushered up a silent prayer. *Please, God, let it be something I can't screw up.*"

I looked at Mr. Abrams as he continued. "Omega, are you familiar with the TV series *Miami Blue?*"

"Yes, sir," I said, trying to hold back my enthusiasm. *Miami Blue* was one of the hottest shows on TV and probably the most talked about locally set TV series since *Miami Vice*, which had gone off the air two years before. The city needed something to fill the vacuum left by the loss of *Miami Vice*, and *Miami Blue* was conveniently there to fill the bill. It was a nighttime soap that revolved around the goings-on of the Gonzago clan, which was heavily involved in the production of pornographic films, hence the *Blue* of the title. The family was split by two young sons, one who wanted to maintain porn as the family business, while the other tried to steer the clan into leaving porn behind and going straight. Mediating between them was their grandmother, the matriarch of the Gonzago clan, played by Academy Award–winning actress Rita Moreno in a turn worthy of Joan Collins on *Dynasty*. The only problem was that I'd never seen the show, not one episode. I was either out on business the night the show aired—Wednesday—or was too tired to watch it when I finally got home from work. I'd faithfully recorded it on my VCR and had stack after stack of back episodes to view but sadly lacked the time to get around to them.

"My wife tells me it's great, but I've never seen it," Mr. Abrams confided to me. I knew one of the reasons he didn't watch it was because Wednesday was his night to be with Sophia (but again you didn't hear this from me). "But that's neither here nor there," he added with a dismissive wave of his hand. I noticed his nails were manicured, but I'd gotten used to this trend among older men who plied the PR trade. His nails were actually in better condition than mine. Then again I don't know when the last time Mr. Abrams had been called upon to use an IBM Selectric.

"At any rate, Omega, the guest star in this week's episode is one of our clients, and we need someone to look after him for one night."

"Which one?" I asked.

"Danny Trubo," he said then sat back and waited for my reaction.

Danny Trubo, I said to myself. I couldn't believe it. He was a living legend. A Cuban émigré, he had come to the United States with a trumpet as his only possession. But with the way he played, it wasn't long before he had wrested his fair share of the American dream: penthouse apartments, fast cars, and faster women. Danny Trubo had played Cuban jazz before an adoring public. Men and women loved him—especially women—and he quickly had developed a reputation for cutting a swath through the female population of wherever he happened to be performing, whether it was a smoky jazz club in Harlem, the blueblood-attracting Newport Jazz Festival, or the hippie-attending Monterey Jazz Festival.

That was all behind him now, at least the jazz-performing part. An irate husband didn't like the idea of being cuckolded by Danny and gave him a solid punch to the lip, which never healed properly and denied him the embrasure he needed to make those sweet seductive sounds on his trumpet. Fortunately fate arrived in the form of TV producer Michael Mann, who had loved Danny as a jazz trumpeter and cast him as a once-famous, has-been jazz musician in an early episode of *Miami Vice*. By virtually playing himself, Danny managed to revive his career by reinventing himself as a character actor and was now, thanks to that *Miami Vice* episode, in constant demand for movies and TV series.

I knew this because I had diligently read up on all the agency's clients, staying late at the office to do so. It was the only way I knew to get ahead: be more prepared than the people you worked with. Of course there was a downside to this philosophy, such as not being able to watch *Miami Blue* when it aired or not sitting around the pool with the bartenders and teachers who lived in my building. But I was determined to get ahead and establish a name for myself, and if it meant making some small sacrifices for my career, then so be it.

The other thing I knew about Danny Trubo was the one aspect of his life that hadn't changed, the only constant in his life. He still loved to party. And he still loved to drink and drug. To excess. And I guessed this was where I came in.

"As you know, Danny Trubo is a client," Mr. Abrams said. "Or rather he's the spokesman for Bimini Rum, which is our client. Today's Danny's last day of shooting on the *Miami Blue* set, and his babysitter is sick. So we need someone to keep company with him for one night and keep him out of trouble. Is that something you feel comfortable doing?"

I'd learned a long time ago never to say I couldn't do anything or express an iota of doubt or uncertainty when it came to work. So of course I answered, "Yes."

"Good," Mr. Abrams said, rising. "Check with Sophia, and she'll give you all the details. He's flying out early tomorrow morning, and I want to make sure he's on that flight on time. Understood?"

"Yes, sir," I said, rising, then smoothing my skirt and heading for the door.

Looked like I was going to spend the next eighteen hours in the company of a movie star with a weakness for liquor, drugs, and beautiful women. And I was going to have to keep him away from those three things this city had on tap twenty-four seven.

Miami Blue was shooting a scene in Espanola Way Village, a small Cuban community that had been carved out of the larger international community of South Beach. The scene being shot was a flashback that took place in Havana. Because it was too expensive to shoot there—not to mention the fact that the island was still under embargo by the US government—the company chose to shoot here, where, with a minimal amount of set decoration, the street could be made to look like a *calle* back in Viejo Habana. That was where I was to meet Danny.

Espanola Way was only a few blocks away from my apartment building, so from the office, I decided to stop off at home and change into something more suitable for squiring Danny Trubo around the city. And while I was at it, I decided to wear something that wouldn't give this well-known Casanova any ideas. I did, however, have a very strong fashion sense, so I stopped short of an outfit that would make me look like one of the nuns in *The Sound of Music*. I put on a simple blouse and blazer, cropped pants, and low heels—perfect for a night on the town in a city that gave new meaning to the word *casual*.

I drove from Collins to Espanola Way and parked near the shoot. It looked like the crew was winding down for the day. I went up to a production assistant standing by the craft service table and asked him where I could find Danny Trubo. He pointed to a trailer parked on the street. I went up to it and knocked on the door.

"C'mon in," said a voice from the other side.

I opened the door, and there he stood, Danny Trubo in person, wearing nothing but a pair of white boxers with red hearts on them. I quickly shut the door. I just stood there, trying to get myself under control. *Come on, Omega*, I told myself. *You can do this. You've handled drunken students in their frat houses and stared down amped-up rowers at their boathouses. You can handle an old man who's seen better days.*

I knocked again.

"Come on in."

"If it's all the same to you, Mr. Trubo," I called out through the closed door, "I'll wait out here until you're decent." About fifteen minutes later, the door opened, and Danny Trubo stood in the doorway to his trailer, looking ready for a night on the town in a very shiny suit. I decided to ignore our first meeting and give things a fresh start. I stuck out my hand and said, "Omega Bouvier. Very nice to meet you."

He took my hand and, to my surprise, turned in palm down and leaned over to kiss the back of my hand. When he released it—after holding on to it a moment or two longer than necessary—he looked up at me and gave me a smile that would have given pause to a shark sizing up its next meal. But I knew what he was all about and swore that this was one minnow Danny Trubo wasn't going to swallow.

"Very nice to meet you too, Miss Bouvier." I noted the "Miss." Danny was entirely old school. I bet he didn't even know what "Ms." stood for. "Or may I call you Omega?" he asked.

"Omega will be fine."

"Wonderful. And you can call me Danny," he continued. "How are you tonight?"

"I'm fine."

"Yes…you are *fine*. Mm, mmm, mmm!" he stated with emphasis.

Shaking my head at his ridiculous comment, I knew I was in for a long night. I turned around and led Danny to my car. He gave it an appraising look, and I could tell from his glance that my car wasn't sporty enough to suit him. Well, too bad! My agency wasn't about to spring for a sports-car rental and give me the chance to escort him around in a Ferrari or a Porsche. He would have to make do with my little old Fiat, which was all I could afford on my entry-level salary.

I asked him where he wanted to go, and he gave me an address that was right on Ocean Drive. So it looked like we weren't even going to be leaving my neighborhood. To my complete lack of surprise, the address turned out to be a club, one that was trying to look like a nightclub in Havana at its most debauched. I shook my head and tried to steer him to a restaurant next door, which had a much more sedate scene going on. But Danny was not to be denied. He took me by the arm and hustled me into the club, where he was treated like a regular, which he likely was whenever he was in town.

The big room was dark, crowded, and cave-like, with lots of shadowy areas to cover up a multitude of sins perpetrated by patrons. Danny tried to steer me in the direction of a table in one of the shadowy areas, but I wasn't having it. I sat myself at the nearest table and refused to budge. He had no choice but to join me. But even though I had spoiled his efforts to get me alone, he plastered a big smile on his face as he sat down next to me. "You'll like this place," he said.

I'll see, I thought.

The waiter came and took our drink orders. Danny ordered a rum and Coke—typical. I'd been told that it was okay for him to drink, as long as he did so in moderation. So I began a mental count of the drinks that he would consume throughout the evening. As for me, I ordered a club soda. I had the feeling I was going to need to have my wits about me at all times, and it wouldn't do to have my judgment clouded by alcohol.

For the next hour or so, we made polite chitchat. He asked me how I liked the agency. I asked him how he liked working on *Miami Blue*. Danny had nothing but praise for Rita Moreno, saying she was still as sexy as when she'd played Anita in *West Side Story* back in 1961. Several times I felt a pressure on my knee or the area slightly above it and knew it was his hand exploring my leg through the fabric of my pants. Every time he did that, I immediately—and conspicuously—took his hand and dropped it in his lap, like a mother chastising her mischievous little boy. After several attempts he got the message and left my knee alone.

During this time a small jazz combo came out on the stage, which our table happened to border. This drew Danny's attention away from me. As the band went into its first number, a rapt look appeared on his face. The music seemed to put him into some sort of trance. Maybe he was dreaming about his glory days on the stage in Spanish Harlem.

"That song is 'Ran Kan Kan,'" he informed me. "It was made famous by Tito Puente." I nodded, not knowing Tito Puente from Marshal Tito.

But I liked the music for two reasons. It had a beat that made you want to move, even if all you were doing was sitting, as I was. I also liked that it was keeping Danny's mind occupied so that he wasn't busy ordering drinks or fondling my knee.

After three numbers, the bandleader looked down at our table then up at the audience and announced, "I see we have a celebrity in the house." He paused for dramatic effect then said, "Ladies and gentlemen—Mr. Danny Trubo!"

The audience applauded. Danny stood up, a beaming smile on his face, gave a humble half bow to the room, and then sat down. The applause continued.

"Danny, if it's not too great an imposition, we'd love for you to join us for a number." The bandleader looked down at Danny, who continued his humble act and made a motion of objection.

But the bandleader persisted. He stood there and continued to try to coax Danny onto the stage. The audience members assisted him by chanting, "Dan-*ny*! Dan-*ny*! Dan-*ny*!"

Finally, like the true showman he was, Danny stood, bowed in my direction, and then joined the bandleader on the small stage. One of the musicians stepped forward and handed his trumpet to Danny, who took it, blew into it experimentally, and then nodded to the bandleader. He was ready.

On the downbeat the combo swung into "Mambo Caliente," a wild number made even more raucous by Danny's intense style of trumpet playing. Sure, his lip injury might have prevented him from playing to perfection, but that night, for the length of that one number, he ruled the stage and had the audience in the proverbial palm of his hand. I was impressed. Here I was thinking I was hanging out with some dirty old man, but he instead turned out to be a musician worthy of his once-legendary status.

When the number was over, the audience broke into a huge wave of applause that washed over the stage. Danny reluctantly relinquished the trumpet to its owner, bowed to the musicians, and shook hands with the grateful bandleader, who would now have an undeniably great story to tell his children—"The day I jammed with the great Danny Trubo"—then rejoined me at our table. He was sweating, and his face was flushed from the exertion of playing his heart and soul out.

He looked at me, and I nodded in approval. "That was wonderful," I told him.

"Thank you."

We sat and listened to the rest of the set. At one point Danny leaned over to me and said, "Little boys' room. I'll be right back."

He picked the one place where I couldn't follow him. But I was so in awe of his performance that I decided not to give him a hard time and just let him go by himself to the men's room.

I sat there, grooving to the next number when suddenly I heard a commotion from the far edge of the room. Before I could pinpoint where it was coming from, Danny appeared back at the table, an uncomfortable look on his face, and said, "I think we'd better go."

I looked questioningly at him.

"Now," he said rather adamantly.

I had no idea what was going on, but I quickly gathered my things and headed for the exit with Danny. On the way we were stopped by a beefy white-haired man who seemed to be on an interception course with Danny. Then the man tried to hit Danny. But showing moves worthy of a welterweight boxer, Danny bobbed and weaved in place, causing the man to overbalance and crash into a waiter who was carrying a tray of drinks to one of the nearby tables. The tray overturned, and the patrons were showered with the contests of their drinks. A white light enveloped us, and I realized a photographer had just enshrined this scene for eternity or at least until it hit the front page of the tabloids.

I knew what had to be done. I took Danny by the arm and led him out of the club and to my car, which, fortunately for us, was parked nearby. We got in, and I pulled out into traffic. Luck was with us because, for once, there was hardly any traffic along Ocean Drive, and I was able to get us away from the club before the man who threw the punch at Danny could follow us.

As I drove Danny back to his hotel, I asked him what had happened back there.

"Oh, that," he said as casually as he could. "It was nothing. There was a woman who heard me play and wanted my autograph. It was hard to hear what she was saying, so I took her into an alcove where we could talk. She had a pen but nothing to write on. I suggested that we improvise. The woman liked my suggestion and raised her skirt, saying I should autograph the inside of her thigh. As I obliged, a man appeared. How was I to know he was her husband?" I assumed that was a rhetorical question and didn't answer; I just let him get on with his preposterous story. "Well, I guess the man mistook what was happening between me and his wife and decided to go after me. Good thing we got out in time."

"Yes, good thing," I said through gritted teeth, mentally kicking myself for not having escorted Danny to the men's room. I should have known this incorrigible ladies' man was incapable of not making a move on anything female with a pulse.

We drove in silence until we reached Danny's hotel. Just as I feared, there was a mob of reporters and paparazzi outside the hotel's entrance, just waiting for Danny to arrive so they could get the story from him. This was something I simply couldn't allow to happen. So I drove past the entrance, made a right, and headed for the hotel's back door, thinking I might be able to smuggle him in through the kitchen and upstairs using the service elevator. No such luck. Some enterprising paparazzi also had parked themselves outside this entrance.

I sped past the back door and mentally itemized my options. With a sinking feeling, I realized there was only one. I turned the car around and headed back in the direction of South Beach.

When I got back to Collins, I drove down the ramp that led to my building's underground parking garage. Danny was strangely quiet, and I thought I knew the reason. "We're here," I said after I parked, and led Danny to the elevator, which quickly brought us to my floor and my apartment.

"Please wait here a second," I said, as I put the key in the lock and opened the door. I stepped into my apartment, leaving Danny in the hallway. I quickly ran from room to room, making sure the place was neat and ready for a guest (just the way I'd been brought up by my Mom). I gathered my office clothes from the floor, where I had thrown them in my hurry to change; shoved them into the hamper; then returned to the door to let in Danny, who gave me a look like that of a fox who'd been invited into a henhouse. *What have I done?* I asked myself.

As I turned on some lights, I said, "You can spend the night here."

"But where will I sleep?" he asked, looking around my apartment.

"Here on the couch," I said, taking out some spare sheets and blankets and turning the couch into a makeshift bed. As I did, Danny looked around the living room of my one-bedroom apartment. He spotted my prized possession on the wall and walked over to examine it closely. It was a print of Manet's *Luncheon on the Grass.*

He whistled, and I guessed he was admiring the naked woman in the painting.

As I finished tucking in the sheets and placing the blanket over them, Danny turned to me and said, "This woman, do you know who she is?"

"No idea," I said, hoping to put an immediate end to the conversation. "Someone long dead and beyond your reach."

Danny thought that over and made a face, as though no such thing was possible or it was something that never would occur to him.

"Well, good night," I said, retreating to my bedroom, wishing I'd installed a separate lock on the door. "I'll wake you in up in enough time to get you to the airport."

"But what about my things at the hotel?"

That was a good point. "I'll call the hotel," I said, "and have the concierge pack up your belongings and send them to the airport. We can sort things out when we get there."

And with that I slipped into the bedroom and collapsed on the bed with barely enough energy to wriggle out of my clothes. Thinking about the man in the next room, I changed into the unsexiest nightgown I could find then fell back into bed and into a deep sleep, from which I was awakened what seemed to be minutes later.

When I felt light nibbling on my ear and neck, I thought I was dreaming. I opened my eyes and was shocked to see Danny sitting on the edge of my bed, gazing at me through lust-driven eyes.

"Danny, what are you doing?" I asked, trying to maintain my calm when all I really wanted to do was shout, "Rape!" at the top of my lungs.

"Thanking you for coming to my aid at the club," he said, trying to make it sound like sitting on the edge of my bed and getting ready to fondle me in my sleep was the equivalent of writing a thank-you note.

"Get out of here right now!" I screamed into his ear, which was way too close to my face.

I must have frightened him, because he slid off the edge of my bed and hit the floor.

"Are you okay?" I asked, meaning it despite the anger I felt.

Very slowly Danny rose to his feet then rubbed his butt. "Yes, I'll be fine. Nothing's hurt but my pride."

With that I got out of bed and escorted him back into the living room and onto the couch. As I did, he caught me in a surprise embrace and tried to kiss me. At this point it was nothing but pure reflexive instinct, and before I could stop myself, I slapped him in the face, connecting with him the way the man in the club couldn't earlier in the evening.

"Grow up, Danny," I said. "There's nothing romantic about rape or taking a woman while she's sleeping, which amounts to the same thing. Is that how you got your reputation?"

Danny looked around the room, letting his eyes alight on anything other than my furious face. But I was so wound up that I found I wasn't finished. "I was ordered to look after you, not sleep with you. If that's what you want, I'll take you to someone. It isn't hard to find a hooker in Miami Beach."

With the last shreds of his dignity, Danny gathered himself up and said, "Danny Trubo has never paid for it in his life."

"I doubt that," I said, feeling an embarrassing need to get in the last word.

I watched as he crawled back into the couch and pulled the blanket up over him. Covering his ego, no doubt.

"Now stay," I said, "and I'll wake you in the morning."

I walked to the bedroom door, stopped in the doorway, turned back to Danny, and said, "Stay!" like a dog owner giving a command to her pet.

The next morning I woke up early and drove Danny to the airport. He was unshaven and looked a little worse for the wear. In the apartment and in the car to the airport, no words passed between us. When we arrived at Miami International, I checked to make sure Danny's bags were on his flight. I stood at the departure gate, and we shook hands.

"Thank you," he said simply, starting to kiss my hand then thinking better of it before disappearing down the Jetway.

Good-bye, Danny Trubo! I said to myself. *And while I'm at it, good-bye, career.*

I drove to the office and entered it like Marie Antoinette waiting to be called to the guillotine. I knew I was washed up in PR. There are some things in this line of work you don't do, such as slap a client in the face or tell him off or accuse him of being a rapist. These rules aren't written down anywhere, but they don't have to be because it's just plain common sense.

I sat in my cubicle and went through the motions of doing my work, waiting to hear the wheels of the tumbrel coming for me. It was a relief to receive a call from Sophia, saying Mr. Abrams wanted to see me in his office—at once.

It was a short distance from my cubicle to Mr. Abrams's office, but it felt like the longest journey I'd ever taken. *Dead woman walking*, I kept saying to myself, as I put one foot in front of another until I arrived at Sophia's desk.

"Go right in," she said, and I was grateful my agony wasn't going to be prolonged.

Mr. Abrams was already on his feet to greet me. I looked around for his executioner's mask, but it appeared well hidden.

"I just got off the phone with Danny Trubo," he said without any preamble.

Danny must have called the agency from one of those new sky phones.

"Mr. Abrams," I interrupted, hoping to head things off at the proverbial pass and save him the embarrassment of having to fire me.

"Please, Omega," he said, "I know you're enthusiastic. But just wait to hear what I have to say."

I just stood there, waiting for the blade to fall.

"I've just spoken with Danny Trubo, and he had me on the phone for the last half hour, praising you to the skies. You've done Durand, Abrams, & Sifuentes proud. I see a raise and promotion in your near future, young lady."

The rest of the conversation I can't recall. He shook my hand and ushered me out the door. I returned to my cubicle, but I couldn't tell you how I got there. I sat down at my desk and smiled. I had thought I was done for. But now it looked like I would be rewarded for speaking truth to power. I smiled to myself. You had to hand it to Danny Trubo; he was a real class act.

My phone rang. With a sigh of relief, I put my feet up on the desk, picked up the receiver, and prepared to field my first call of the day.

Six

White lines. Miami was defined by its clean, lean lines. A white sandy strip of beach that ran between the city and the Atlantic. The thin clouds that sat against that thick blue line of water. Crisp tan lines on tourists crowding the beach. A drug-culture euphemism of white lines that fed the underbelly of the city at night. The exoskeleton of high-rise condos, shooting up above Miami and Brickell Avenues. Each terrace and wide window was framed with white trim, trapping in the cool, conditioned air. Docks spread out at the feet of the towers, segmenting their own tiny slice of ocean.

I sat up in bed inside my downtown Miami condo in the Bristol Tower building on Brickell Avenue and watched as the bright strips of sun slid through my vertical blinds, crawling up the side of my sheets.

I was late, and it was going to be a long day.

One café con leche later, and wearing my favorite Versace sunglasses, I was walking into the lobby of my office building. The familiar gush of the cold air hit my face when the glass door swung open to greet me. The doorman wore a suit with a Hawaiian-patterned tie, and I thought, *Only in Florida.*

Bouvier Public Relations and Media resided on the twenty-seventh floor, and as the CEO, I made it a point to be in the office every weekday before any of my staff arrived. However, some days would slip away from me. Megan sat at her desk looking as perky and awake as usual.

"Good Morning, Ms. Bouvier," she chirped as I walked in.

"Megan, did I have any calls before nine?" I pushed my sunglasses back onto my head and dropped my briefcase onto her desk.

"Um…you mean, this morning?" she asked.

I sighed and picked up her notepad, which was resting next to her hand. "Yes, Megan. Have I had any calls this morning, since the open of business?"

"Yes! Three. I wrote all the messages down on the…ah…" She looked over at the notepad I was holding.

"Okay, yes. I got it." I turned toward my office, reading over what she had put down, then stopped myself and turned around. "Thank you, Megan," I said, although I admit not sincerely.

"You're welcome, Ms. Bouvier." Despite my obvious attitude, she continued to smile and speak lightly. I had to give her credit for trying to be professional.

Over the last few weeks, I had considered letting Megan go— that is, ever since she misspelled a client's name in a press release.

I'd been referring to it as the "Anabelle hiccup." One misplaced *l* and Megan had turned an average duty into a publicist's worst nightmare. Bless her heart; through the storm she tried her best to spin a positive outlook, as a PR person always should. I almost felt guilty for chastising her, until the seventy-six-year-old

Anabelle Cruz herself, doyenne of Miami high society, screeched at me for nearly an hour through my conference phone.

For the time being, Megan was a good enough assistant, as long as she was only dealing with me. Or, the UPS guy. Remembering my early days in PR, and wincing at some of the mistakes I'd made, I'd decided to give Megan a second chance.

None of the messages she'd collected were related to the grand opening later that night. That was a good sign. I needed the event to go well, mainly because I was garnering a reputation for my own firm. Also I was over budget with the client's original plan, and I wanted to prove that all the little extras were worth it.

A blue garment bag was hanging on the back of my office door, which meant my dress for the opening had been delivered to my office instead of my condo. I would figure out a way to train Megan eventually. She wasn't dumb, just…spacey.

A large manila folder was open on my desk, fanning out its contents of logo graphics and invoices. At first glance all I could make out was little reproduced images of the same biceps.

Jonny Bali was known to bring the pain. He had started his career as a boxer turned personal trainer, which led to specialty gyms and workout videos. A few infomercials and two fitness books later, and Jonny Bali had grown an empire, without even seeming to work up a sweat (which was the opposite of his exercise regimen).

Based in Miami, Jonny was working on expanding to the rest of the country. As a client he was fun loving and energetic but stubborn. He rarely took my advice regarding business decisions and occasionally threatened to invite a journalist into the boxing ring. Jokingly of course.

One venture that Jonny fell into, despite my objections, was a Latin-salsa club and restaurant on Collins Avenue. The location was fantastic. Locals and tourists would happily drop money there, based on the well-established nightlife and proximity to hotels and resorts. Unfortunately Jonny was investing with his brother and friends from back home. He was financing most of the business expenses while allowing his friends to make most of the business decisions. They were all Venice Beach boys who had spent much of the '70s longboarding and getting high and had little experience running a business. Not to mention they had absolutely no knowledge of salsa and the Latin-Caribbean culture.

I wasn't sure where to start either, but luckily I knew the right people to call. I finally was able to coerce Jonny into including some local investors, one of whom was a good friend of mine, Santiago, a Venezuelan artist I'd met at Dartmouth when we were both students there.

After six months of preparation and headaches, La Matadora was scheduled to open that night. I was excited to see the fruits of my labor but terrified at the prospect that everything might fall apart.

The day started to progress the way I'd expected—quickly, with little room to maneuver. I ate lunch at my desk while I was on the phone. Megan ran frantically up and down the hallway in high platform heels.

I went over the guest list, music schedule, and menu. I tried to visualize every moment during the club's opening, anticipating oversights and possible mistakes. I was thorough. Exhaustingly thorough. I worked best with certainty, not luck.

The phone rang again, like it just never wanted to stop.

"Hello. This is Omega."

"Hey, chica! I have a quick question." It was Jonny Bali, sounding out of breath. In the middle of the day, he was likely in the middle of some kind of extensive workout (or, knowing Jonny, working out on top of one of the attractive females with which he staffed his gyms).

"Go ahead, Jonny."

"I know tonight is a fancy event, but I was wondering if I could make some alterations to my suit."

"It's your party. You can show up in a Speedo if you'd like. It just depends on what kind of impression you want to send your guests."

Jonny laughed heartily. "Me wearing a Speedo would leave a great impression! You know you wanna see that." I could imagine him winking after this comment. He was being a hapless flirt as usual.

"What kind of changes were you thinking?" It occurred to me that, despite all the stresses and concerns about the event, Jonny was going to look over all the minor details and just get drunk on his own dollar. He was a hard worker but also a notoriously hard partier.

"I saw this guy on MTV the other day wearing a full suit but with the sleeves cut off. I was gonna wear a suit to the party, but I figured won't it be, like, gnarly hot out? This is Miami. So if I cut the sleeves off, I would be cooler. And I could dance more."

"Jonny…you can't be serious." I sighed into the phone.

He laughed again. "Yeah, I'm not. Really I was just calling to see if we had room for a couple more guests."

Relieved, I said yes and wrote down the extra names.

"I have to get the list to the security company in an hour," I told him, "so if you want to add any more, make sure you call me before then. Otherwise they'll be left out in the cold. Or I guess the heat."

Santiago had reached out to the many South American consulates in the area, managing to confirm invitations for a few dignitaries and celebrities. This also meant heightened security, which was one of the many reasons I was over budget. Their attendance, however, meant support from the community and publicity coverage that would span beyond the local Miami papers.

After getting off the phone with Jonny, I leaned back in my desk chair. Finally the phone was silent. I closed my eyes and tried to do a reality check of my life.

I was running my own boutique PR firm with a skeleton staff. After five years of climbing the ranks quickly at Durand, Abrams, & Sifuentes, I had made the risky decision to leave. Instead of aiming for partner, I wanted to run a business my own way. There were some ethical reasons that made me leave the firm (including being drooled over by some of my older, less-than-noble colleagues), but mostly I started my own firm because I believed I could do it on my own. My resolve for this was often challenged. Yet here I was, just twenty-seven years old, standing inside the lead office of my firm, calling the shots. Sometimes it's easier to move the dirt beneath a stubborn mule than pull on its reins (something Samantha would've said). Plus there's a pleasant freedom that comes with independence.

Moving to Florida wasn't the easiest transition. Originally I imagined the sunshine and city life would be a welcome change from the chilly Northeast. However, the work at my first job was nonstop and enveloped much of my life. When I finally left, I still hadn't yet learned the landscape of Miami and often found myself lost, driving around looking for the personal life that I was supposed to be having in my midtwenties.

The city was a mosaic of different cultures and people. Each street and neighborhood was vastly different from the next. One wrong turn, and I'd find a hidden world within a few minutes of my office or apartment. Another turn later, and I'd be hauling at high speed on a newly built concrete overpass.

There were no ancient, massive trees to dwarf construction. No cobblestones or prewar buildings. No brick to speak of in the city. Everything was shiny, new, and pastel colored. Most signs were written in Spanish, a language I'd rarely encountered growing up. I was finally starting to pick up important words and phrases in *Española*. I felt so removed from everything I knew. It was exciting, of course, but also lonely.

I moved from my rental into a beautiful condominium that was within walking distance from my office. Bristol Tower was much grander than I'd imagined, and I knew this was where and how I wanted to live.

I made it a point to take time to travel around the city on the weekends. I wandered into Little Havana, eating food from bodegas and discovering what made a real Cuban sandwich. I drank rum with mint and champagne, trying to find the best bench from which to people watch. Old men sat on the street, playing dominos and yelling at their grandchildren. Music seemed to ebb from every corner. I grew to love the sounds of salsa and a Catalan guitar.

Working in PR, I was well read on the who's who of Miami. Between gossip, scandal, and burgeoning trends, I had an encyclopedia in my head of the names that frequented the Miami papers. On the other hand, I had yet to experience the heart and soul of Miami. Discovering the pulse of the city was teaching me how to represent the names and personalities that started to fill my client list.

I was starting to feel like a local. The woman who ran the Chilean restaurant on the corner would get my coffee ready in the morning before I arrived. The doorman in my office building would stop me to ask about the latest tennis match. There was a place for me forming in the city, and my business was fully supporting my position.

The phone rang again, pulling me from my thoughts and back to my long task list.

I left for my salon appointment to prepare for tonight: nails, hair, facial. I was ready for the warm night and dancing. Finally, back in my condo, I looked over this version of Omega in my full-length mirror.

The dress was Oscar de La Renta, a Bal Harbour purchase. It was blue and purple, reminiscent of a dress worn by a flamenco dancer, which I thought was perfect for the event. My shoes were vintage Chanel. I had bought them at a consignment store in

Coral Gables. The look was elegant but not overdone. I was there to promote—but not detract attention from—my client, who was the evening's most important figure. However, I had to admit I looked pretty amazing. I gave myself a nod and thought of how playful Jonny might get after a little rum. He was good-looking, but it was a work relationship, which I made a point to keep separate.

Collins Avenue was busy, usual for a Friday night. Megan was waiting outside when I stepped up to the front of the club.

"Ms. Bouvier!" She ran up to me, waving. "Everything looks so good!"

"Oh, did they let you in already?" I replied. It was still early in the evening, and I had planned to walk through everything before the guests arrived.

"No. I was looking through the window. It's all set up, and the band just pulled up to the back." She was smiling and giddy. I could've guessed that she'd never been to a party of this size before. Her enthusiasm made me smile.

"Well, let's go check it out. Maybe they already have some hors d'oeuvres ready. I'm starving."

After sampling the array of delicious hors d'oeuvres and getting my fill, I felt refueled for the evening. As I double-checked and ran through the list of possible disasters, I realized everything was coming together so far. Santiago arrived shortly after with a few other investors, along with various business partners. The six-piece band set up their horns, African drums, and bass guitars. It would be Caribbean-style jazz with salsa classics laid in, a format I had learned quite a bit about during my experience with Danny

Trubo and the fateful night that had accelerated me up the corporate ladder.

Jonny walked in through the kitchen door, his voice echoing in the large space. I perked up to catch up with him.

"Decided to wear sleeves, Jonny?" I asked.

"I flip-flopped a couple times. But I wanted to impress you," he said.

There was no suit, but he wore a pressed linen shirt and dress pants. Tribal tattoos wrapped around his thick arms like snakes slithering up a tree. His size and power were intimidating, along with his ability to go toe-to-toe for twelve consecutive rounds with the toughest middleweights, but he was more likely to throw around jokes at a party and spare the punches.

"You look great. I'm sure I won't be the only person you'll impress tonight." I placed a hand on his massive shoulder and added, "The club looks amazing too."

"Thank you." He smiled back, letting some of the flirtation fade. "No business talk tonight. Let's get a drink to celebrate. Champagne?"

"Sounds great."

A few flutes down, and Jonny wandered off to greet and humor the incoming guests. The place quickly filled up with bodies. The band coursed between classics and original songs, all of which were popular on the dance floor. The professional dancers I'd hired blended well with the guests and helped jump-start some excitement on the dance floor. Santiago pulled me onto the floor for a little while, whispering gossip in my ear. We laughed and twisted around, half caring who was in our line of vision and half carrying on with our own fun.

Weeks before I personally had picked out the performers. This required scouting bands and dancers from events and festivals from around the city. The music was intoxicating. The tempo was heavy and quick, with the horns section supporting the depth of drama in the sound. Occasionally the beat would stop; the instruments would burst at the climax of the song; and I'd feel suspended. It made me want to dance the entire night.

There were still a few more things to do and people to meet, so I parted with Santiago to leave the crowd. I spun away from him and felt something pulling me from the dance floor.

As I walked I looked toward the tables and saw a man sitting and watching me. He looked at me for a few moments, glaring, then slowly turned to talk to the woman next to him. She was slender and beautiful, leaning over to touch his arm. Ignoring his glance I headed toward a faraway barstool to cool off.

I turned around in my seat, cosmopolitan in hand, and sighed in relief. Tonight looked to be a whopping success. As I contemplated this, the man who had watched me on the dance floor walked toward me. He locked eyes with me and smiled. I shifted my legs underneath the sheer material of my dress and felt the fabric fall from my thigh, much more aware of this action than I'd been a few minutes before. I wasn't sure if I liked how he was looking me over.

He walked up to the barstool next to me and ordered a drink from the bartender then nodded and sat down alongside me. "I'd like to offer you a drink." He sounded friendly and relaxed, even though his statement confused me.

"I already have a drink." I lifted my cosmopolitan.

"I noticed. I'll wait until you're ready for another." He remained nonchalant.

"You do know it's an open bar?" I replied.

"I also noticed that. The offer still stands. You should say yes."

I sent him a skeptical side-glance. "Oh, really?"

"Yes. Don't rush." He paused. "I'm enjoying the time in between." He hit me with the same smile.

"Excuse me. We haven't met. I'm Omega Bouvier." Feeling slightly flustered, I reached out my hand. He took it and kissed my knuckles, which sent a chill up my arm.

"Lovely to meet you, Omega. I'm Zion Bram."

"Hmm," I replied, puzzled by his introduction.

"Something wrong?"

"No. I'm just curious why you're here."

He looked surprised. "Oh?"

"Yes. You're not on the guest list. I printed it this morning."

He laughed. "How do you know I'm not someone's plus one?"

I looked him over. He wore a custom-made Italian suit. His leather wing tips were peeking out beneath perfectly tailored slacks. I would've bet his cufflinks were made of onyx and white gold, which conveniently matched the custom Rolex cozied around his wrist.

"You don't look like somebody's plus one," I answered.

He shrugged and sipped from his drink.

I doubted the woman I saw him sitting with earlier as his tagalong was on the list either. Zion was a strange name but a powerful one. The way he stood, drank, and spoke was powerful too. Not intimidating, like Jonny. This man clearly was used to getting what he wanted, without force and with an obvious patience. I may not have seen his name on the list, but he certainly wasn't here as someone's accessory.

The longer he sat next to me, the more I felt his presence. It made me tense, which made me uncomfortable. It made me want to adjust my dress. Pull it down or pull it up—I couldn't decide which. A few feet stood between us, but he felt much nearer.

"So I'm going to guess you work for Jonny Bali's publicist," he said after the short silence.

"I am his publicist," I said.

He squinted at my response and said, surprised, "You can't be."

"Yes. I am. Bouvier Public Relations. I'm Omega Bouvier." I tried to deliver this without smugness, but he was making it difficult.

"Well, I guess I'm the fool then. I'm very impressed," he said, not letting that gorgeous smile escape his face. "You seemed young and beautiful, with enough naïveté for me to charm you. I'm starting to doubt that."

Normal, nonchampagned Omega would have responded professionally. Yes, I was in charge of this affair and all the press surrounding it. Yes, I was successful for my age. Yes, I wasn't a fool to his charms, like the woman he was previously sitting with.

But…there was something about the space between us. A feverish sensation kept me from sticking to my professional demeanor.

It could have also been the way the tops of his thighs looked in those custom pants: muscled, broad. Or the way his dark chest hair peeked out of his slightly unbuttoned shirt. Or the sexy smell of his cologne. I was spending too much time noticing it.

"I guess we'll see when I get that second drink," I said.

Zion laughed comfortably, not taking my comment too seriously. This made me relax a little, and we moved on to the topic of why he was actually attending instead of his ability to charm me. Still I should have known I was brewing up trouble.

A few minutes later, as I was on my second cosmopolitan, Zion and I were leaning in closely, watching the other guests.

"So you snuck in?" I asked teasingly.

"Not completely. I'm good friends with the man who runs the security company you hired. Some of my clients were invited, so he let me know. I'm in wealth management and development, so I'm always curious to know what they might stake their money in," he answered, then listed a few names I recognized. He mentioned Jimmy Conway, which I grew excited about. Then he pointed him out on the dance floor.

"Wealth management? That sounds…" I trailed off, thinking it sounded complicated. I immediately associated him with Wall Street.

"Boring?" he asked. "It can be at times. But a certain excitement comes with it too."

"Well, crashing parties and following around sports stars seems like fun," I said.

"True." His eyes ran over me. I should've disapproved, but I didn't. "I do love meeting new, very impressive people."

I let myself lock with his gaze. His skin was bronzed, his dark wavy hair complementing his hazel eyes. At first I thought he might have been Latino, as was much of the population of Miami. Then again his features could have been attributed to any sort of multiethnic background. This was as difficult to interpret as his intentions with me.

I didn't focus on the thought of where he came from or why. I started to feel the energy that emanated from him, making my heart race. He broke our eye contact calmly, leaving me lingering and I took in a deep breath I hoped he didn't hear.

"We should dance," Zion said, setting his drink on the bar and standing up. He reached out to gently touch the skin of my forearm.

For a moment I hesitated and was taken aback by his forwardness. Then, in the next moment, I found myself sliding off the seat and into his arms.

Our bodies were pushed close together. The floor was much more packed than when I was dancing with Santiago, and Zion didn't pause to give me room to move away. He moved with the beat, guiding me with him. He spun me around a few times then brought me in closer. I followed his lead with each step, hip movement, and turn. We were completely engrossed in our movements and in the manner in which we flirted with each other on the floor; I could only imagine us doing other things. He was a great dancer, and I didn't doubt it was something he likely had learned growing up. His clothes and swagger said he had money, and the way he danced meant he enjoyed it on the finer things.

Despite the seemingly innocent dance, Zion was smiling and kept his attention only on me. I had no intention to hide from it. He was surprised by how well I could dance salsa, especially since I wasn't a Latina. I was enjoying the way he appreciated me. There were thoughts that faded in and out, telling me this was a man who took what he wanted and probably cast it aside just as easily. I ignored them while we moved. I forgot about my worries while he had his hands on me. All I could think was that I wanted more.

The lights were dimmed, and the air was hot. I was engrossed in Zion, the smell of his shirt, and the faint cologne. My taste buds were tingling from the vodka and lime of my drink, and I gulped while I tried to keep up with him.

We both were panting and moving together seamlessly. He guided me, but I somehow knew where he was going to put me next. I wondered if it was a result of his dance skills and mine, or if we were flowing together naturally in a way I couldn't explain.

I was light-headed. I was out of breath. There was a beating in my chest from my heart, and it matched the beating of the drums in the band.

Zion spun me away from him at the last blast of the horns, which finished the number. When I stopped I spotted a bit of yellow in the distance. It was the woman Zion had been sitting with earlier. She wore a long, yellow, tight dress. She was standing at the edge of the dance floor, staring at me and at him. And she looked thoroughly unhappy with what she was watching.

Something inside me clutched, and I turned to Zion's unshakable, charming smile. "Thank you," I said. "That was lovely. But I need to get back to my other guests." I forced a smile and stepped away quickly. I didn't give myself time to see the response in his face.

I walked outside onto Collins Avenue to get some air.

Zion was certainly the kind of man who would rope in and let down beautiful women. I had just watched it happen. It wasn't something I needed to involve myself in. He wasn't the kind of man I should be allowing into my life.

I reeled in the winded, unhinged Omega. *It was only one dance. With a man you just met. You aren't the kind of woman to be rattled by one conversation and one dance.*

I felt better and grounded. I had to go back inside and return to my job and the event I'd been working on with Jonny Bali for months. It was going extremely well, and I needed to go appreciate that. I took in one more breath of the sea air, loving the breeze that picked up late in the night. I pushed thoughts of Zion from my mind and brought my focus back to the matter at hand.

When I returned to the party, I made a point not to look for him but instead sought out potential clients. I met quite a few of them. Many were shocked upon meeting me and learning about the expansion I'd provided for Jonny's company. I ran out of business cards to give to those who asked. Instead I would spell out my name, knowing I was the only Omega Bouvier in the Miami PR community.

Eventually I found Megan, who was stuck to the side of a staff waiter. He was a younger surfer who seemed just as enamored in the moment as she was. Feeling magnanimous I told her to expense the cab ride home and be safe. Then I ran into Jonny, behind his own bar, keeping up with the demand and working hard. I thought I'd find him fallen over on one of the barstools, but seeing him yelling, slinging, and laughing with the guests gave me more confidence for the business.

After a while I concluded that it had been a successful night, and it was time for me to head home. I hadn't seen Zion since I'd walked back inside. I didn't intend to avoid him, but I'd expected to see him again when I'd returned. When I didn't, I guessed the woman he was with had dragged him away. I had reacted correctly by casting him off. He wasn't a man I needed to set my sights on. A cocky, unattainable bachelor didn't fit into my life at the moment...or ever.

I walked into my building lobby at 2:30 a.m.

Once I was in my condo, I stripped off my dress and stepped into the shower to wash off the adventures of the night. As much as I tried to fight it, I couldn't help think about Zion's hazel eyes watching me from across the room. I thought about how he had looked over my dress while we were sitting. I could almost feel the way his hands sat on my hips. Naked in the shower, I closed my eyes and thought about that touch and how he had moved with me. If I were another woman, I wondered if he would be there in the shower with me, showing me another way to move.

It had been a long time since I'd felt that way for a man. I barely could remember what it felt like to be touched in that way, skin to skin and not through a dress.

I was alone now. Safe in my own apartment—away from cool, collected, professional Omega.

Slowly imagined in my head, my hands merged into Zion's. I focused on the rushing noise of the water and my short, heavy breaths. I ran my fingers over my breasts, brushing my nipples and gasping. They crossed over my flat stomach and down the side of my thighs. The gathering steam made me feel heavy, and I moaned into the sensation.

Zion's wicked smile was hidden between my thighs. I slid my fingers where I was dreaming his mouth to be, and I was ever so ready there, wanting for him. I drew little circles with my fingertips as I threw my head back and gave in. I rode the hot, tortured wave of my orgasm with my eyes closed, seeing his face but being too scared to say his name out loud.

After the shower I slipped into a silk nightie. It wasn't what I normally would wear to bed, because long days in the office made me crave cotton and long sleeves. Yet I was feeling accomplished and proud. I felt sexy, which I was trying to pretend wasn't because of the man I'd met. I thought of how I might have been seen in the silk nightie if I'd been another woman.

Exhausted, I crawled into my bed. I dreamed of pulsing music and jazz trumpets. I saw flashes of hazel and tasted lime on my tongue. I slept deeply, dreaming fluidly well into Saturday afternoon.

I spent some of the weekend at the beach. I had dinner at my favorite restaurant, eating oysters and sea bass. I walked down Lincoln Road, buying a few antiques from booths propped up during the late morning. I got a phone message from Megan, saying she had made it home fine and had lots of fun at the event, as well as calls from Jonny and Santiago but no lingering conversations—only quick congratulations. I almost had forgotten all about the feelings coursing through me after that night at La Matadora.

Monday morning I walked into the office expecting quiet but was surprised to see Megan eagerly answering the phone and jumping up and down as I approached the front desk. She put a call on hold and smiled.

"Ms. Bouvier! We've had five requests for proposals [RFPs] in the last hour. A whole bunch of people who attended the party and their friends have been calling, asking if you're taking on more clients!" she yelped.

I was shocked. Baffled, I took her stack of messages and headed toward my office. I sat at my desk and laid out the names in front of me. One of them was a tennis star, the latest sensation on the courts.

Megan came and stood in the door a few minutes later, taking a break from the phone to tell me about her weekend date with the waiter she had met at the opening. I smiled, listening and warning her not to become too involved too quickly. She had a big career ahead of her. She blushed at this and agreed.

"Oh! I almost forgot," she said. "A woman called this morning three times, asking to speak with you."

"A potential new client?" I asked.

"Yes, she represents some big company and says they want you to head their current PR team immediately."

"Wow. I don't know if I'm up to handle that." I looked over the messages again. "Which company is it?"

Megan walked over and sifted through the papers. "Oh! It's this one." She picked up one of the messages and handed it to me.

I read it a few times before it really registered.

ZB Financial Services.

Seven

Parts of Miami seem to always possess a flamboyant glamour, which can only be rivaled by Las Vegas. This fact always had the tendency to make me feel underdressed a good part of the time. Today in particular I was feeling out of place.

A woman with a silk Hermes scarf around her head and neck rushed past me, shoving me to the side as she made her way out of the extravagant hotel lobby. I walked in and out of massive, Romanesque pillars that jutted into the high ceilings and framed huge crystal chandeliers. The space was filled with bright colors and velvety furniture. A far wall was entirely covered in gold leaf.

I was walking through the center of the Fontainebleau Hotel, trying to find my way to the pool. Simply dressed in a white blouse and black pencil skirt, I followed the bellboys in tasseled uniforms as they walked quickly past me to keep up with their silk-scarf-wrapped guests. I walked up a large, elaborate staircase only to find myself in a small coatroom. Finally I noticed a man pushing a cart full of folded, pressed beach towels and followed him outside.

I moved past the bronzed, sunbathing guests to a cluster of tables and umbrellas, where patrons were enjoying cocktails and finger food. Or so the man with all the towels claimed.

"May I help you?" a waiter stopped me and asked.

"Yes. I'm here to meet someone for lunch." I gave him the name, and he directed me to a table nestled under a palm tree.

Ms. Margaret Rathburn had flown in from LaGuardia Airport that morning. She was in town for one day, to meet with only me regarding a proposed contract between Bouvier Public Relations and ZB Financial Services. I should have expected that she would be gorgeous. She had short dark hair to match her olive skin and wore all black. She looked as out of place as I felt and also read "New York City" all over.

"Hello, Omega. Have a seat. Coffee?" She was curt in her greeting but not unpleasant.

I ordered and pulled a few folders onto the table.

"Oh, no, we don't need to look over paperwork right away. Let's talk about the job a bit first," she said.

I put the folders away and answered, "About that, I'm not sure exactly what you'll need from my firm. We're not built to run a PR department for such a large company. We can take on assignments for certain campaigns and ventures, but it's a small staff."

Margaret sipped her coffee and looked me over, pausing to take in my comments. "Yes. I understand. I've looked through your firm's work as well as some of the work you did at the first PR firm you worked for in Miami."

I sat up, surprised. "Well, then I suppose I need a better definition of what's being requested."

Margaret's smile was soft and disarming. I didn't know what her title or position was with ZB Financial, but I was beginning to see why she had personally flown in to meet with me. She clearly had the hard skills to negotiate whatever was necessary.

"You." She paused. "What is wanted for this project is really just the involvement of you. Not your firm in particular."

"Me?" I remained confused. "Am I being recruited?"

"No. You'll be contracted in a consultant capacity." She stopped to accept coffee from the waiter, placing a hand on his arm to say thanks when he arrived. She was smooth and collected. "Mr. Bram is impressed with your ambition and knowledge so early in your career. He doesn't always like to use tried-and-tested methods. He's a risk taker and go-getter, and he looks for that in those he hires. He's asked me to work with you to create a role in ZB Financial for you—one that will allow you to expand and learn while maintaining the growth of your own firm."

"He wants to hire me as a PR consultant?" I asked.

"He wants to hire you and have you on his team. What the stipulations are of your position and role in the company—well, that's mostly up to what you and I think will work within the parameters of the company." Margaret's tone remained calm and confident. She spoke as if the offer were slight and not out of the ordinary, but it was a situation I'd never imagined happening so early in my career.

As I looked out toward the Atlantic, a line of questions ran through my head. My week had been exceedingly busy, with new offers and work lining up based on the success of Jonny Bali's account. I was taking on a full workload for the quarter, one that made Megan and me stay in the office late every night. I was curious about the meeting and the offer. I'd been excited about this meeting regarding ZB Financial for much of the week, but I couldn't imagine how I would be able to handle such a large-scale job.

Then again, during the busy week I'd also been thinking about Mr. Bram himself, wondering why he had sought to contact me, even after that night on the dance floor. I was positive that a man of his nature had numerous women to follow and entrance, including the one in the crowd at the opening and the one sitting across from me at the table right now.

I had concluded that those few weak moments in the shower that night were the greatest effect I ever would have on him, and I'd just remember it as a hot Miami night. Then the message from his company came in, and now I was sitting at a meeting to become involved with Zion Bram's business.

"To be honest, Ms. Rathburn, I don't even know one detail about ZB Financial, much less where I would fit in. I met Mr. Bram casually. Please don't find me rude, but I don't understand where this offer is coming from," I finally said.

She laughed, placing her coffee on the table with a delicate clink, then said, "Please call me Margaret, and don't be so flustered. Yes, it's an incredible deal for you, but I'm also sure you live up to your professional reputation." She leaned in, continuing with her comforting nature, which started to bring down my nerves about the situation. "I've been working for Mr. Bram for years, and I'm never really sure what motivates most of his decisions. Like I said, he's a bit of a renegade. However, he's very smart. Every directive I've followed through for him has turned out to be the correct one. He's talented, and he's good at recognizing talent, so just think of it as being in good company and garnering success from it."

Smiling, Margaret reached across the table and rested her hand on mine. "I see you're skeptical. Don't be. You have nothing to lose from this offer. Say yes, and then figure out a way to use the deal to your advantage."

I felt a rush of excitement, thinking the opportunity would lead to more experience and business opportunities. It was the answer to what I'd been craving from my career, and while I wasn't so certain on the details, it was still thrilling to consider. I was on my way up, with lots of work to show for it, and I thought that if I didn't take the opportunity, or at least feel out the details, I would regret it.

I also felt a rush thinking about seeing Zion again. I didn't want to admit that the thought of being in close contact with him made my head warm and my heart beat hard.

"I guess it does sound like a great opportunity," I said.

"It is, Omega."

"Could you have the contract sent to my office today so I can review it? I'd like to sleep on it before deciding."

"Of course. In fact I already sent it to your assistant this morning. Megan, I believe? She sounds just adorable over the phone." Margaret called the waiter over and ordered two glasses of champagne. "Shall we celebrate? Even if I'm jumping the gun a little?"

I nodded. The Brut was delicious, with a strawberry floating on the top.

Margaret spent the rest of the sunny afternoon telling me about ZB Financial Services and her own role at the satellite office in midtown Manhattan.

Apparently Zion had a hand in many different fields of financial services. His company spanned from New York to Miami and even into banking centers in London and Zurich. Margaret pointed out that most of the projects were unremarkable, with numbers and stats that interested only a small percentage of bankers and financiers. However, Zion's passion project was advising his clients in wealth management.

Margaret emphasized how Zion wanted to expand this aspect of his company. His clients were wealthier because of him and happy with the results of his work, but even though they had deep pockets, there were relatively few of them. Zion wanted to focus on people who might not consider wealth management. His goal in the project was to empower people, particularly people of color and the disadvantaged, who normally wouldn't embrace the methods and strategies traditionally practiced by the wealthy. She expressed this passion of his as being philanthropic.

"There are old-school, simple ways in which people can invest their money and create their own wealth," Margaret said. "However, many from underprivileged backgrounds don't have access to—or are unaware of—these techniques and miss out. Mr. Bram wants to help empower people financially to make their lives better."

I understood the concepts she was referring to and agreed. My own background was very fortunate, but after attending Dartmouth, I noticed the higher levels of society possessed a real sense of security and wealth. Living off dividends and equity allowed many of my classmates to secure lives that didn't require them to hold real hourly jobs. Not having economics as a stronghold allows more freedom of choice and a varied life of experiences.

"So he'll need help promoting this program?" I asked.

"Yes, exactly."

"But couldn't he hire someone from New York or here to help? Or a firm with much more experience in financial public relations?"

Margaret nodded, then answered. "He could, of course. But much like the people he wants to help advise, he wants those working for him to be from a different background—the kind of people who have to work their way up the food chain to find success versus having it presented to them on a silver platter."

As Margaret spoke of empowering people of color and different ethnic backgrounds, I couldn't help wonder about her. She dressed in couture, though subtly. She was articulate and highly cultured. I must have looked confused by her comment, even though I didn't mean to show it.

"You're wondering why he hired me," she stated smugly.

My face must have given it away. "Oh, well, I'm sure that's none of my business," I said.

"I'm a tattooed lesbian from an Orthodox Jewish family in Brooklyn," she stated. "Despite my having an MBA, there aren't many finance firms who would consider me, until I met Zion. Now I work on hedge-fund row in a better position than most men my age, much less any women."

I was stunned and impressed. It occurred to me that Zion must have sent her here not because of her skills of persuasion but because she exhibited a quality that he also saw in me, and he knew she would be able to convince me. I started to respect his offer more. For a moment that week, I'd thought the offer was just a way for him to contact me after our heated encounter at the party. I wasn't interested in being romantically courted over false professional pretenses, which also fed into my apprehension. However, after talking to Margaret, I was beginning to see Zion's philosophy and his offer in a different light. It was something I could also be passionate about. It was something my business could benefit from. If he was really allowing me to write my own role into the project, I couldn't think of a good reason to say no.

I said my good-byes to Margaret, truly hoping I might see her again. As I headed down to the office, I considered a contract that already seemed too good to be true.

By dinner I carefully had reviewed the whole packet, line by line. I thought perhaps there would be at least one reason to send it back for revision; a perfect contract is rare to come by. I searched for excuses that would make me understand why the offer was being extended to me but came up with none.

I sat down at the large wooden table in my condo. It was meant to be a dining-room table, but more often than not, papers were laid out across its surface.

I turned the black business card for ZB Financial over in my fingers. The surface of the card stock was smooth, embossed, and somehow warm to the touch. There was no name, no title. Only a Miami number. A voice in my head told me to pick up the phone and dial it. Maybe the decision would come to me based on who picked up the other end. It was probably a generic company number, and since it was after hours, I could leave a message. I thought this would prove me to be interested in the position and reliable, even if I hadn't really decided yet.

The phone rang twice; then halfway through the third ring, it was picked up. A scratchy voice came through the line.

"Hello," it said.

It was a man's voice, and there was no introduction about who was on the line or where I was calling. Caught off guard I stuttered a bit as I answered.

"Hi. I'm looking for ZB Financial." I thought briefly that I had misdialed the number.

"Who is this?" the voice answered. It was a chilly, serious voice. The man on the other line didn't sound upset or suspicious, but his tone gave me a shiver.

"I'm Omega Bouvier. I'm calling for—"

"Hold on." He cut me off, and I heard the phone click. I sat on hold for a minute or so, and then the phone clicked over again.

"Omega? It's Zion." The new voice answered. This one was softer, with a brighter tone, but again I was caught off guard. I hadn't expected to reach Zion directly. The contract and the proposal had come to me through third-party hands. The fact that the number on the business card connected directly to Zion, the CEO, was totally unexpected. Not to mention that his voice brought up the memories of my meeting him only a few nights before.

I took in a breath as I squeezed my fist at my side to calm myself.

"Hello, Zion. I wasn't expecting you to pick up. How are you?" I said.

"Oh, yes. I'm usually at the office late. I'm trying to fix some last-minute issues. How's your night?" he said.

I was working late too, which was common for me. I guessed that accepting the deal and working for him would mean a lot more late nights in the office. Something about that idea excited me more than turned me away.

"My night is well. I'm looking over your offer," I answered.

"Oh, really?" he said. "Are you happy with it?"

Yes, too happy, I thought. *Maybe a little eager too.*

I started to bring up some finer points, detailing the dates of events and seminars to come. Zion listened and answered professionally. There was no flirting during this phone call. Only the serious side of Mr. Bram was showing, which made me more confident about the deal. He was generous with his answers to my questions but still stuck to the point that his business and his concepts came first, which I respected.

"You'll report solely to me. There won't be any other executives to veto your decisions, although there will be plenty of other people involved to advise of course," he said.

"That's perfectly fine," I said.

"So is that a yes, Omega?"

The way he slowly said my name forced me to imagine that smile on the other end.

"I think so, Mr. Bram," I said. "Should I bring by the signed agreement tomorrow?"

"In the morning. I'll have Reesey pick you up. What time works best?"

"I'm sorry. Reesey?" I asked.

"The man who picked up the phone. He's my tennis partner," Zion said.

"Your what?"

He laughed and said, "Well, among other things. Eight a.m.?" I agreed, though I was a bit confused. "Good night, Omega. I'm happy to have you on Team Zion."

After hanging up, I picked up the final page of the packet and paced the floor of my apartment. I looked over the empty spot above my neatly typed name. Below was a name signed in bright blue, with "Zion Bram" typed beneath it. He was already fully committed to the deal. I couldn't turn back now.

I walked out onto my balcony. The air was always salty in Miami, and from high enough up, the noise of the street barely could be heard. The sound of the waves beating at the shore was constant. I sat in a white vinyl lounge chair, still staring over the thin piece of paper. It flapped a little in the ocean breeze.

I'm not sure why, but I'd expected Zion to be flirty over the phone. Actually I hadn't expected him to answer at all, but when he did, I thought I would hear the cocky, sly attitude he'd carried with him at the party. I imagined that whenever I spoke to him about the offer, I'd have to ward off his advances. And I considered I probably would decline the deal because of that.

True enough, our short moments on the dance floor that night had been inspired by a little vodka and heated music. Maybe I was reading too much into the way Zion and I had interacted. I was the one who had run off, filled with sinful ideas. Now that some time had passed, I realized he had only reached out to me professionally. I thought of all the possible motivations for his offer, and I was starting to come up with plenty of reasons that didn't revolve around him getting into my pants.

I felt a little embarrassed thinking that those feelings weren't mutual, and to Zion our dance was just another dance with another woman. He obviously had other options to go home with. I reminded myself that I didn't interact with the opposite sex very much socially. In my career I was serious and polished around my male and female clients, making it a point to act the same with either. Although I was friendly, I was always looking to win business, not a husband.

I hadn't been with a man intimately for a long time, but that didn't mean I was no longer able to read whether or not one was interested in me. Did it?

The idea of love had evaded me over the last few years, and I had replaced it with my ambitions. I was still young and in no hurry. But I didn't have time to fool around with men who weren't important to me in the long run.

Then again I was sitting up late, looking over Zion's curved blue signature. I thought of Megan's excitement almost every Friday afternoon as she told me about her next blind date or potential boyfriend. I thought about how satisfying it was to flirt with Jonny Bali on occasion. I felt confident that I was a beautiful, passionate woman, and I certainly wanted to experience more in my life. I just didn't want to sacrifice what I'd found to be most important.

I glanced at the top of the page again and read through it slowly.

The compensation for the temporary franchise of Omega Bouvier's professional services should amount to no less than _____.

The spot was blank. Previously in the day, I'd assumed that Megan had sent a price breakdown to Margaret or someone at ZB Financial who handled the contract. Then I remembered that they had reached out to us and sent over the contract before I'd met with Margaret.

This was a huge discrepancy that I'd somehow missed as much as I'd gone through it. I berated myself for not noticing it until now, especially after speaking on the phone with Zion and entering into a verbal agreement. Thanks to my hesitation, I had managed not to sign the document.

Zion, however, already had signed it. He had a contract prepared by his own lawyers, with my name, detailing the exact arrangement, but somehow had forgotten to fill in the price? I easily could have filled in any figure, signed the document, and then forced him into abiding by the contact. Notary stamp or not, the document was on his letterhead, and it seemed to be a final official copy.

Some financial advisor he was! Hmmm.

So I left the contract unsigned, arranged everything back together, and slipped it into the manila packet. I wasn't the type of person to take advantage of the situation, although I did consider my options. I resolved to address my price in the morning with Zion before I signed anything.

My confidence rose a little, thinking about the one issue left to handle in the deal. I did find the catch after all—only I wasn't the one at a disadvantage.

I curled into bed, a little later than I wanted but feeling excited about the following morning.

I woke up early and dressed in a simple sky-blue, sleeveless, fitted dress. It was sleek and cinched at my waist, with a V neckline. The dress was a classic design that came right above my knees but accentuated my figure and bronzed brown skin beautifully. I thought that if Zion did intend to flirt and tease me, then I should at least look good when I rebuked him.

I headed down to the lobby, greeting the doorman happily as I walked out. It was exactly 8:01 a.m.

Parked in the lobby driveway sat a black Bentley, with a tall man leaning on the hood. Downtown Miami was still a lucrative area, but my own building rarely housed anything better than a Mercedes. Once he saw me walk through the front doors, the man strode up and stuck out his hand.

"Ms. Bouvier, I'm Michael Reese. Please call me Reesey," he said.

I shook his hand, and he led me to the car door before opening it and helping me inside. The interior was polished wood and leather. The car was already running and heavily air-conditioned. I was in shock at the feel and extravagance of the vehicle.

Reesey turned around and motioned to the console between us. "I have some coffee here if you'd like." He pulled a paper cup up and handed it to me.

"Thank you." I was truly grateful and sipped it while we worked our way out of the building's parking lot.

The coffee was exquisite. There were hints of hazelnut and chocolate, and it was filled with steamed milk. We drove down the avenue softly and peacefully. *I could get used to this,* I thought.

All the elements came together suddenly in my head. The car, Reesey, Zion, the manila packet that sat next to me on the leather seat.

Zion hadn't forgotten to fill in the blank space where my price was. No one with a Bentley and a business that spanned the country would forget such a huge detail. Everything was well calculated and planned. Zion's direct office line was on the card but without a name listed, and I'd met with Margaret at the luxurious Fontainebleau the day before. Reesey's quiet demeanor matched perfectly with the peace and extravagance inside the huge sedan.

We pulled up to one of Miami's biggest skyscrapers, right at the front lobby door. There, next to the soaring glass windows, was a list of the companies located inside. Some companies were listed in small printed clusters; these were the companies that held small spaces in the building. Most were in medium print, while a very few were in large print, with logos placed alongside them. At the top of the list, in the largest print, lettered in frosted glass, was ZB FINANCIAL SERVICES. It was written in the same font and style as the business card that sat in my purse.

Zion was sending me a message in that blank space on the contract.

He didn't have a price limit. Looking up at the tall glass building as I got out, with the Bentley pulling away, I realized Zion Bram was telling me I could have anything I wanted from him.

As long as I said yes.

Eight

As time went on, I would learn many facets of Zion and his complex character. However, I never did get around to asking how he had managed to install rafters in the ceiling of his office.

ZB Financial was located in a brand-new skyscraper in downtown Miami. Everything inside was modern and sleek, almost as if it had been designed in Tokyo. Zion's office was lined with windows and simple furniture, but the ceiling looked as if it were sourced from a European chapel. Nothing else in the room matched the style of the dark wooden rafters. I guessed that he did it just because he could.

I sat in the thin, leather chair across from his desk, waiting. Zion was yelling into his phone. Well, he wasn't necessarily yelling, as his voice wasn't loud. It was *forceful*. It may have been intimidating to his peers, but for me his rough tone had an entirely different effect. I watched his hands shuffle over the desk and through papers. Again I couldn't help but imagine those hands gliding over my skin. This time he was in the room with me, which made the vision even more intense. I gulped and tried to erase the image from my mind—at least for now. He finally hung up the phone and broke my trance.

"Sorry, Ms. Bouvier. How are you today?" he said, sighing through obvious stress from the phone call.

"Fine," I replied.

I could tell Zion was still annoyed by something as he flipped through my contract without looking up. I shifted in the chair uncomfortably.

"So let's talk about your price."

"Okay," I said hesitantly.

Maybe I was remembering a different Zion Bram. After being chased down by his cohorts and dwelling over our brief meeting at the party, along with everything that had happened thereafter, I was now very confused by his reaction to me. He didn't appear to be excited to see me or enthusiastic about the deal he was handing over. I felt like I'd just been fooled or tested. I thought maybe Zion was just playing around, trying to see if I was eager enough to actually come into his office.

I didn't find it amusing to be toyed with or taunted. I crossed one leg over the other and huffed defiantly then tapped my fingers against the arm of the chair. I may not have been as wealthy or important as Mr. Bram, but that didn't mean I wanted to be kept waiting either.

He began to run through the options on the contract. The price was settled on simply. He stated a number quickly, looked across the desk, and I nodded in response. The number he started out with was higher than I'd intended to negotiate for, so the only reaction I could muster was a nod.

I had walked into the building with two things on my mind: my price and the possible reactions to my fee. Once Zion started talking in that monotone way, I forgot entirely about the stupid number. I had begun the meeting thinking I was going to play some kind of cat-and-mouse game, but he was all too serious. The price was right, and so was everything he'd listed out for me. I had no words. I sat still in the chair, paralyzed with confusion.

On the phone the night before, he had been a little playful, and his tone of voice sound as if he were happy to hear me. On the bright, beautiful, life-changing day that I walked into his office for the first time, he was acting like a future boss who already was annoyed and bored with the project. I was itching to get out of the room. I couldn't figure out what had changed, and thinking back on that day, I wished I'd instigated some kind of back-and-forth between us to loosen up the tension.

In a flash we had shaken hands, and I left the room with his secretary. She walked me down the hall to another smaller office, one where I could work if I chose to work at ZB Financial's offices, instead of at my own firm. After I sat down at the empty desk, she brought me a coffee and gave me a pat on the shoulder. It was 9:15 am.

Zion's secretary, Clara, was an older woman with a slight accent. Later, I would learn that she was a grandmother from Bogota, Colombia, who had lived in the Sates for the last thirty-five years. She was gentle and acted like a mother to the wound-up young finance boys who worked under Zion and Reesey. She was the first to show up to the office and the last to leave, except for Zion himself. She brought coffee and food for the office from the market on her street, instead of ordering it from the building's delivery service. She was very capable and organized, with a stack of poetry and novellas on her desk to read in her spare time—not that she had much of that with Zion as her demanding boss. She wasn't like many of the women I would come to meet in Zion's circle. She didn't have an instinct to kill. I could tell this the moment she placed a hand on my shoulder, that first day working for Zion.

"He isn't so good in the morning," Clara said, then smiled and walked out of my new office.

It must have been obvious that I was flustered. I wasn't a woman of fantasy and hadn't gathered it in my head that anything spectacular would happen that day, but neither did I think it would be so empty. I reconsidered taking the job, thinking maybe it was a mistake. I thought that maybe I was investing too much into a job that I knew very little about. My ego was boosted by Margaret's assessment of me, but that was just one lunch, and I was mirroring it off her personality and not my own.

All the moments of the last week flooded together. It had happened so fast, and I had lost track of where I was headed. I took a deep breath and opened the files on my desk. I had a job to do, and that was the bottom line. After all the thinking and guessing and hidden meaning, the reality was that I was in my client's office with a set-out assignment. A hard long-term assignment I was hoping would change my career. The contract price easily could be reinvested into Bouvier Public Relations to expand and become more competitive. I set aside the confusion and misdirection of any ideas I had about Zion as a man and the devious smile that had eluded him this morning, and I set to work on Zion as a business.

A few hours passed, and I was in the groove. I programmed the speed dial on my phone to all my favorite journalists, publicists, and inside men. Clara stopped in for two more rounds of coffee and a break for homemade arepas. I had a list of dates for scheduled events and all the deadlines leading up to each one. I also had a list of strategies for image and marketing. I reached out to hotels, restaurants, and businesses to explore their promotions and venue interests for the seminars and events. Every time I brought up the firm's name, the business almost immediately said yes. Zion must have been making the rounds in town and associating with important clients and their connections in the Miami scene. It was making my job easier but not mitigating my curiosity about him.

I shoved away all the nonwork-related feelings, and by four thirty, I had a huge amount of work to show for it.

Get it, girl, I thought as I sat up. The basis and plans for the project were all but complete in the layout. I scheduled a meeting with Zion's small PR team for the following day to review the plan and develop small tasks for them. I wanted to feel out how they worked as a team before assigning them to long-term parts of the project. I learned their names from Clara and discovered my first real qualified employees, other than Megan.

Cece was a twenty-five-year-old Cornell grad from the Ivory Coast. Frederick had little college education but a talent for selling, or at least that's how Clara described him. Marcus was a Miami native, raised in Coral Gables, with a degree from the

University of Miami. He was an aristocrat who knew every political refugee in the city and how they had assimilated into Miami city politics.

Three young men working for me, most of whom were around my age or older. I wasn't sure how this would work out. In the past, when I had male clients, experience proved that as a woman I had to work much harder than my fellow male colleagues to garner their respect. Based on Clara's descriptions and my impression of Zion's other associates, however, I thought they would be a rowdy, unique bunch. I was starting to love the idea of it.

One of the many things I learned from working for Zion that came to later benefit my career was this method of hiring. Any work I embarked on, or companies I started in the future, were built with this methodology in mind: hiring people from different backgrounds who possessed different skill sets. Forming a group that usually never would work together could induce better results and creative outcomes than the same cookie-cutter group of interns other companies tried to replicate every year. I frequently saw the same pattern—from interns to employees—at firms like Durand, Abrams, & Sifuentes, throughout my career, and I never wanted to compete with what they were doing. I didn't want to create a company to emulate the bigger corporations and firms, because they'd already gathered the best people in the field straight from the Dartmouths of the world. That was where my classmates would end up, and where they would do well. I wanted something different. My main advantage was that my work offered something different, outside of the norm. This was made evident by the people I chose to work alongside.

While Zion had his faults, one of his biggest strengths was his ability to see the very best in people and guide them to a place where they would thrive. He looked beyond the obvious and tried to be radical. I was always grateful for this lesson.

By the time I finally felt I had completed the day at ZB Financial, I sauntered down the hallway to check in with the mystery boss, who had politely cast me out just hours before. He was gone for the day. Clara said he had an important business meeting and started to pack her own things. I felt abandoned.

I went back to my desk and picked up my phone, which was ringing.

"Hola, my beautiful," Santiago said gracefully.

"Oh, how are you, Santi? It's so nice to hear your voice." I sighed and let out a little giggle then leaned back in my chair. I felt the stress of the day lift off me as he spoke.

"Things are hectic, lovely. I'm getting ready for an art-gallery opening tonight in Fort Lauderdale. I love the space and the art, but you know how much I loathe getting on the turnpike." He made an exaggerated grunt.

"Oh, that sounds fun. Who's the artist?" I asked.

"Some man who paints forty-foot nudes. I don't know his real name, and his artist name is some elaborate, elusive adjective, like they all seem to have. I'll just enjoy mingling with those who think they're important, along with the free wine."

I couldn't help but to laugh. Santiago's humor about his work and the people around him was amusing because I knew how much he really loved the nit and grit of it.

"Omega, my beautiful, would you like to be my date?" he asked.

I had planned to go to my own company's office and work for the rest of the evening on projects I had to put aside throughout the day. But I decided to take him up on his offer.

"Sure, Santi. When are you leaving?" I replied, smiling and thinking of a warm, relaxing night with an old friend.

"Whenever we want."

A few hours later, Santiago and I were strolling up and down the New River, which ran through downtown Fort Lauderdale. There were tourists walking along with us, and homeless men sprawled out on the benches along the water. Santi wore a sharply pressed Ferragamo suit, and I was still in my blue dress from my workday.

I ran through everything with him, from the night I'd dance with Zion, to my rather anticlimactic meeting with him that morning.

"He sounds intriguing and dangerous." Santiago ran his fingers over the scruff on his chin, mostly from the five o'clock shadow that he attributed to his distant Italian roots. "I like it. It sounds hot!"

I made an exasperated sound and put my hand up. "Now stop. He's my client, which means it's out of the question. Plus I don't have time for anything like that right now."

"Hmm, a likely story. But the more you say no, the hotter it sounds!" he said, then laughed at himself. He looped an arm through mine as we walked. "You need a little excitement, Mega. You had that one unfortunate fling with that frat boy in college, and now...well, you can't look like that in a dress and not have a little fun. This *is* Miami after all."

I blushed a little from his suggestion. Santiago was far from being interested in women, preferring the French male dancers he usually ran around with, but I still felt flattered by the suggestion. It also reminded me that this was the exact dress I'd worn while I'd sat in Zion's office as he ignored me.

"Technically, this"—I waved my hand in front of me—"is Fort Lauderdale."

"Oh, don't be silly, Mega. South of Disney World, it's all Miami. It's all swamp—a hot, neon, lit-up paradise. It's not New Hampshire or the tiny backward town in Maryland I'm from." He patted my arm comfortingly while they were looped together. "It's the kind of place where a dark, handsome, mysterious man wants to give you the world; crawl into that dress; and try and convince you he's the king." He laughed again. "I say you show him what you're made of."

I laughed along with him but shook my head. "No. I can't. It's a risk to my career. And besides, a man like that can't invest the amount of time that I want. I'm not some girl just looking for a sugar daddy." I paused as Santi raised an eyebrow. "No matter how sexy he is."

"Ha!" Santi yelled out. "Well, at least you admit it."

The next morning, with Santi's words from the previous night still ringing in my ears, I sat down with my new PR team.

Three men sat across from me at the conference-room table with puzzled expressions.

"You want us to cold-call newspapers?" Frederick said, the confusion mirrored in his tone.

"Yes. Start at the bottom," I said.

"Mrs. Bouvier, we have contacts for editors to get articles through, if needed." Cece said respectfully, a little of his French lilt slipping through.

"I understand that. I have a list of contacts as well. That's not the point. And it's *Ms.* Bouvier," I emphasized.

They weren't being overly resistant to their given tasks, but I noted they definitely felt the cold calls were beneath them. It was something that should be done by an intern, but I was asking them to do it for a reason. I also was testing them to see how well they would respond to my direction; so far it was limited.

"Well, then, what's the point?" Frederick asked, leaning back in the chair, acting more skeptical than others.

"We can go over it after we analyze the responses you get. This is what I need you to do for today. It won't take long. I have a script printed here about the seminars." I slid a few sheets of paper to them then sat up and waited while they read them over. They looked at one another and the scripts for a few moments.

"Are there any questions?" I asked.

There weren't. They all got up and left the room. Frederick left his paper behind, so I followed him out with it.

"Frederick? You forgot this." I handed the paper to him through the open door.

"Nope. I read it. I know what it says. I got it," he said, clearly annoyed.

"Fine," I said, then shrugged. I crumpled the paper and threw it on to the table. He turned and left, shaking his head.

I was fuming on the inside. I didn't think they would have welcomed a stranger with hugs and endearments, but they were being dismissive, and I didn't like it—especially Frederick, who irritated me even more because he happened to be the only white male in the office. I tried not to focus on this factor and his rudeness. Instead I walked calmly into my office and shut the door. I picked up the phone to call someone I knew had no trouble taking instructions, even if she might not fully understand them. I needed a dose of Megan's positive attitude.

"Ms. Bouvier! How are you? Are you ever coming back in? Like, what are they doing to you over there?" Megan yelped happily into the phone.

"Hi, Megan. I'm just fine. There's some setup to be done here today, but I'll probably be back in tomorrow. How are things going over there?"

"Oh, great! I mean, it's been busy but nothing I can't handle. By the way, Jonny came in yesterday, looking for you, but I told him about your new gig. Or wait…maybe I shouldn't have. I'm sorry," she said quickly.

I laughed. "No, it's fine. It's not a secret mission. Did he say what he needed?"

"No, he just stopped by to see you."

"Oh, interesting."

"Yep. I think he might have a crush on you!" Megan said this in a singsong way that made me laugh again, and I realized I missed her crazed eagerness during the day.

It was then that she told me all about the waiter she'd met the night of the opening of La Matadora and how he was stringing her along by promising to take her on a date but never following through. We talked through the gossip of the hot but elusive waiter. It gave me a little relief from the morning meeting with my new team. I thought briefly how most of the encounters I'd had in the new office were turning out to be total disappointments. Zion and his crew didn't seem to be taking to me very seriously. And it was only my second day.

One of the reasons I'd opened my firm was so I wouldn't be cast off in such a way; instead my ideas would demand attention. After getting off the phone with Megan, I resolved to handle the new team as if they were employees at my own firm. That was, it seemed, one of the reasons Zion wanted to hire me. Even though I was within his walls, it didn't mean I had to stop playing the game my way.

The afternoon came, and so did my meeting with the guys.

"Well, any feedback?" I asked.

There was some silence until Marcus finally spoke up. "I got through to the *Herald* desk just fine, but they didn't know where to direct me. It's not financial news. So I just ended up talking to the social columnist about the events as if they were promotional parties," he said.

"Yeah, I called the *Sentinel*, and they plain just didn't get it," Frederick added.

"Okay, good. That's perfectly fine," I said.

Their mouths gaped open in surprise; they clearly were unsure what was going on.

"Cece?" I turned to him and motioned for an update.

He looked over a few notes he had jotted in front of him then said, "Yes. The papers I called wanted to focus on the classifieds instead of events. But then another paper transferred me to the lifestyle section."

"Hmm, that's interesting," I said. "The lifestyle section could be useful. Maybe an interview with a well-known Miami business owner could fit in there."

"So I guess we didn't really get anywhere today," Fredrick said with a slight smile.

"Oh, I disagree," I said, turning to look right at him. "ZB Financial is well-known. Recognized for overseeing wealth management for only a certain number of people, and really the only thing the newspapers have ever been focused on is Zion himself bumping elbows with his powerful clients. That's not what we want. That's what your established contacts think this project will be about, but it's not. So we have to start fresh. Where does it fit in? How do we attract interested investors from other places, from previously untapped sources? The question is always how we sell but also where." I turned to Marcus after watching the smug smile fall from Frederick's face. "You're right. This doesn't technically fit in financial news or events promotion. And it's not a classified ad, because the people we want aren't opening the paper to look for a used car. They're people who read the paper, but where? In the lifestyle section? New money trying to discern how to accumulate into a life with more money—money they don't know how yet to invest and manage? Maybe. Maybe not."

I shrugged and waited for their responses. I was feeling very good about the argument I was making, and the best part of it was seeing on their faces that I was right, that they were approaching the situation the wrong way. The practices they had used before to entice wealthy clients were mainly by word of mouth and reputation among the elite. That wouldn't work for this job, and now they were starting to realize it.

They all looked at me approvingly, even Marcus, who gave a curt nod to the points I'd made.

"So then I'd say we have some good places to start. I'll be back in the office on Friday. We'll meet again then, and I'd like to hear some new ideas on the image of these seminars. Not self-help, not wealth management—all-inclusive by economy, with an emphasis on people of diversity." They continued to nod along with my instructions, with Cece furiously taking notes. "You know how Zion rolls, boys. Let's give him something exciting." With this final statement, I smiled and stood up.

They each shook my hand as they left the room, and I told them I was looking forward to their ideas. I finally felt in control again, as if I knew exactly where I was in the project.

When the room emptied, I started to organize the scripts and folders, bending over the conference table. I felt so ecstatic with how the meeting had gone and was in such a completely opposite mood from earlier in the day that I couldn't help do a tiny little cha-cha as I gathered my things with a smile on my face.

"Don't start doing that too often. I won't get any work done."

I turned around, shocked and slightly embarrassed. There he was with that smile.

Oh, shoot. Don't do that, I thought and, *It's about time!* At the same time.

He was leaning against the doorframe, like men in old detective movies do when they know how suave and debonair they are. From his leather shoes, to his gray suit and silver watch, he was sexy all over. I remembered then how I had described him to Santiago the night before and thought I really hadn't done him justice.

"The guys seem impressed with you," Zion said. "You've had a productive couple of days?" The smile stayed, and my heart sped up as he spoke.

The day before his effect on me was silenced from whatever sour mood he had been in, but today he was laying it on full force.

"Hmm. Well, they weren't too pleased at first, but they'll come around," I said.

"I'm sure you'll whip them into shape." He moved to sit at the table.

A subtle smell of him, whether cologne or just body wash, fanned over me as he came into the room. I'd noticed it in our previous encounters, and I'd taken note of how it lingered heavily in my nose.

He leaned back comfortably in the chair and said, "How are you liking it so far? Is Clara helping out enough? If you need more assistance, I'd be happy to bring in a temp."

"No, thank you," I said, standing at the door, holding the papers against my chest. Good thing too, as I felt my nipples begin to tingle and rise to attention in response to the cold air conditioning and perhaps the sexy timbre of Zion's voice, and I didn't want my reaction to him to be so obvious. Darn it! Betrayed by my own body, which couldn't decide if I should rush out of the room, jump him, or stay and have a chat with the man who was making my heart beat too quickly for my liking.

"And the office?" he asked.

"It's fine," I said.

His smile turned down a little. "Do you need any assistance?"

I couldn't tell what he might have been digging for, but it was beginning to annoy me. Maybe it was leftover energy from the meeting or the blood pumping through my veins from his presence, but I found myself getting defensive over his wanting to help.

I snapped my head toward him and leaned in. "I'm perfectly capable of handling this job and your Boy Scout troop, thank you. There's no need to coddle me."

"There she is," he said, so damned sure of himself. "I was wondering where all that sass was."

I pulled back, feeling surprised but also pleased with his reaction. "Well, I have to be sweet sometimes," I said, smiling.

"Just go ahead and save some of that for me." Zion checked his watch then stood up. "Speaking of which, I have dinner plans for us, if you don't already have a date for tonight." He reached out to place his hand on my shoulder as he held that smile on his face. I would always wonder whether it was genuine or riddled with a hidden agenda.

"Dinner plans for us? Let me make something perfectly clear. I don't date men I work with. I don't think it would be appropriate for us to have dinner together alone," I said, as convincingly as possible.

Zion leaned in closer, bringing that delicious smell with him. "I agree. Inappropriate in the most perfect way, no?" He licked his lips then took his hand away. "I meant for all of us. People from the New York office are in town, and we're all going out to meet them. All of us Boy Scouts, that is."

"Oh…" I thought about my plans for later on. There were none. Well, except to catch up on work, but I'd be in my own firm's office for the next few days, and I thought it might be good to see the team in a different setting. "Would you mind if I invited my executive assistant?" It occurred to me that I might need Megan at the ZB office on some days; plus it would pull her away from the drama of the hapless waiter.

He nodded and said, "Of course. Eight thirty. I'll have Reesey pick you up." He pulled the door open and held it for me to exit. "We'll reschedule that other dinner…for now anyway." He winked at me.

I rolled my eyes in response, pretending to ignore the suggestion. If he was serious about it, I was afraid I wouldn't be able to say no.

Nine

I rode the elevator up nearly every morning, the tension climbing with each floor. My steel box moved between the iron and concrete of the massive skyscraper, faster and faster. I felt the basement shrink in size underneath my feet. The ding that announced every floor and the rush of air from passing an opening made my heart pound. Extreme heights made me nervous, and the ride up to the penthouse office was something I never could get used to.

ZB Financial was much like any office in the morning: everyone amping up for the day, saying their hellos, and settling down at their desks. It was a great rush every time I arrived. Lingering inside my head, while I waved to Clara each time, was the thought *Will I see him?*

Zion just wasn't someone to sit still, or so I was starting to learn when working alongside him. There were quite a few mornings when I walked out of the elevator to find out he was in New York. Or France. Or the Caymans. Or Switzerland. Or nowhere, because no one had any idea when he'd be back.

The headquarters of ZB Financial Services was based in New York City, where his team of investment bankers and traders operated. Margaret worked out of that office. Miami was Zion's public relations hub and his main office. He usually didn't leave for more than four or five days at a time and called me in on an occasional Sunday when he was jet-lagged and behind schedule. Still he just couldn't stop from having his hands in everything that would let him. Though tired and disoriented, Zion still was unbelievably charming those weekend days.

He also managed to keep every meeting he'd scheduled with me and even sat in sometimes on meetings I led with the PR team, just to see how things were progressing. I couldn't tell if he was working on the seminar project he had assigned to me, or if he was there to micromanage the team. Some days it seemed like I was the only one making decisions when it came to our project. Then Zion would pop in at exactly the right moment when we needed him. He was an invisible force that everyone acknowledged was there, even when he was in another country altogether.

The money-management strategies Zion was basing his latest project on—what he had termed the "Art of Wealth"—were gleaned from a book titled *The Richest Man in Babylon*. Our team was revamping the next tier of seminars and events, running through the planning of logistics for each location on the tour. Knowing it was going to be a long day, I set up a lunch where the guys and I strategically laid out the agenda for each event location. It was entertaining as we brainstormed ideas for promoting the company's events throughout the country, and the concepts became quite suggestive. Some mocking inside jokes were made, and the meeting wasn't really efficient in terms of producing concrete plans—that is, until Zion unexpectedly walked into the room.

"That sounds like a board game," Zion said, and laughed. He placed a hand on Marcus's shoulder and looked over all the scribbled notes across the table. "So how's it going?"

"We're eliminating the bad ideas," Frederick said confidently.

Zion sat at the head of the table and motioned for us to continue. The guys seemed more reluctant with the big boss in the room, but they still continued with their creative, sometimes over-the-top promotional concepts.

"We want simple, refined, enticing marketing strategies," I reminded them.

Zion was enjoying the back-and-forth of the team, laughing at the most ridiculous suggestions but also encouraging the ideas that didn't completely work. I took notes to mirror the way he casually took hold of the meeting and steered attention to the most important concepts. It was another day of learning from him. He was an eloquent spokesman and a connoisseur of words. I admired how he inspired his employees and earned their loyalty. He had a gift for it. He was gifted in other ways as well, and I was trying not to be distracted by his perfectly fit body, which I couldn't help notice.

He was wearing a thin, teal sweater in contrast to his tailored suit jacket and collared shirt, his usual office attire. His attitude was just as calm and casual as his dress. But I now felt more comfortable with him than I had over the last few weeks.

Multiple dinners had taken place with everyone in the office. Often clients would join, sitting at a long communal table at one of a handful of restaurants where ZB Financial carried a tab. We usually had a private room set up for dinner, with ten to fifteen people sitting and talking business over a five-course meal.

Zion always ordered before we got there. It was one of the many things he did that exhibited his sense of luxury, and he seemed happy for everyone to participate. I also found it to be calculating. After my first few rounds of nights out, I noticed that, depending on who attended, Zion would focus on particular foods or chef specialties that sparked conversations with his clients. Some would fawn over dishes from home that they hadn't tasted in years. Others would ramp up with excitement over tasting something new and exciting they'd never tried before. On one very smooth occasion, Zion ordered rarified Russian beluga caviar, and his foreign guest, being from Estonia, promptly began to talk about Russian oil figures. I couldn't tell whether the information the guest shared was helpful to Zion because I had little knowledge of where and how Zion made his investments. I could, however, see on his face when the previously silent guest started a monologue about the relation of caviar to oil that it was precisely the reaction Zion was reaching for. Zion would listen intently, raise his left eyebrow, and nod with approval while extracting the exact information he was seeking. He was as smooth as butter. And I loved watching him in action.

Being there also meant I was trying new things I couldn't have imagined. Despite my attempts to seem collected, Zion must have recognized this. He would sit at the table and order a bottle of reserve Bordeaux or a seventy-year-old Scotch. Everyone else would wave down the waiters, asking for dry martinis. Without fail whatever Zion was drinking would appear at my side. He would watch carefully as I took my first few sips. Oysters, foie gras, lobster bisque. Caviar with lemon and crème fraîche. If I didn't know how to dress a dish or dismantle a shellfish, I'd pause and watch everyone at the table dig in first. Most of the time, I was the only woman there, as Clara often declined the dinners, and I wished I had the opportunity to observe mannerisms other than those of Marcus and Frederick, who gladly crammed two pieces of sushi into their mouths at once for sport. I would wait, observe, and then follow suit. Every minute that passed, I felt Zion watching over me, waiting along with me.

Despite the presence of so much food, Zion barely ate at these dinners, instead spending most of the time talking or toasting, resembling an ascetic monk—monks don't drink, and they practice silence for the most part. This made me acutely aware of his gaze and disappointed that I couldn't observe him in return. The more divine the food, the more I felt his downcast eyes hover over me. There were times I couldn't help close my eyes and moan in full approval. There are tastes that are too delicious and exciting to have anything but a guttural reaction to; Zion would catch me then flash that sexy smile at me. This was a tiny bit of shared communication, and while the first few times I felt unnerved and on display, after he looked away and responded I'd feel a wave of pride. A voice inside of me said he was challenging and manipulating me, teasing me by placing wine or a delicacy in front of me. I would respond and indulge greedily.

And as time passed, I was beginning to live for those tiny flashes of approval. In the office, however, our interactions were straightforward and professional. Zion's commentary on my work was positive, but he declined to fawn over anything about my presence. Yet in the dim lighting and warm air at these elaborate, crowded dinners, those few times that he winked at me or nodded to me—to sip more or take another bite—I felt more than catered to. But he was reluctant to express anything beyond that. Even so I sensed there was something deeper there.

I suspected from remarks he had made here or there that there was an essential part of Zion that kept himself from falling in love. Perhaps he had been hurt deeply once and was loath to have the process repeat itself. Whatever the case, I felt he needed to hold himself back for fear of being hurt all over again. For me this was the really frustrating part; I didn't know how to take him.

I'll admit that, although it happened rarely, there were a few times when I would come home, fuzzy from wine and dinner talk, when the feeling of his gaze still lingered through me. I'd slip into bed and think of all the ways I'd let him linger over me further. The soft cotton touch of my sheets, bunched in my fists while I thought of him, wasn't quite enough. I would touch myself with just the right amount of coconut oil, call his name in ecstasy, then fall deeply into sleep, wondering just how much longer it would take before he made an attempt to tease me in a more intimate way.

Then in the morning, as I passed him, he'd smile at me quickly and innocently. He'd lean against his office door, relaxed and chatty, holding a coffee closely to his chest. His shirt would be casually unbuttoned again, and I would push the close moments from the night before out of my mind. He almost never came by my office. He didn't leave messages on my machine. He wouldn't call me into to his office for updates. Clara said she would ask him how I was doing. She would relay to me that he approved.

Some mornings I found myself in this in-between space, wondering why I was fantasizing about my boss, unexpectedly finding myself getting turned on at the thought of him, doubting he was instigating but also knowing that those looks from him were fraught with some special meaning. And I would question where else he was casting his stare. Did Zion take other women to the back room of brasseries? Did he watch when they slipped oysters into their mouths? Did he pour champagne in their glasses, letting it spill over their fingers then licking it off? Thinking of this drove me nuts, because on the one hand, I could imagine myself at that table, and then, in the next, it was a long, beautiful woman, like the one I saw him with at the party where we'd first met. How could I feel special treatment from a man who routinely bestowed luxury on others? How could I feel jealous over a man with whom I had no romantic relationship?

Again I'd wash away these thoughts. It was silly to be jealous about something that didn't exist, not to mention that it was incredibly unprofessional given my situation.

So I'd sip down my coffee and try to forget—at least until the next dinner.

All the planning and preparation for the launch of the Art of Wealth seminars had been laid out. We were now ready to put all the pieces into action, and with the name of the project sealed into place, the team was set to go. The seminars needed to be planned to the last detail. The venues had to be booked for the allotted dates. Zion's own schedule had to be locked into place, which I thought might be the most difficult part of the whole equation. Graphics, advertising, write-ups, press contacts, social circles, business sponsors, airline tickets, hotels reserved. Every box we lined up had to be checked.

I became nervous that we were at the breaking point, where the whole idea would just fall apart from failure to achieve momentum. I finally was heading the job that I had signed up for. This opportunity, if I managed to pull it off, would catapult me into the first rank in the industry. Working with ZB Financial carried a great deal of power, and I intended to use my status to elevate my reputation.

Everyone in the room felt a sudden rush of adrenaline, knowing as I did what the next few days would entail. As I headed into my office with a few samples of designs for brochures, I thought of all the ways we could attract new potential clients and investors.

"Frederick walked me through your plan of action for promotion and press interest." Zion was leaning against my doorframe when I looked up from my desk. I couldn't remember another time he had been in my office with me, alone. Mostly the space was filled with floral scents from Clara moving in and out with whatever I needed for the day. Now it was full of the scent of him, and the space suddenly felt smaller.

"I could have run through it with you," I said, highlighting the fact that he didn't interact with me too often in the office.

"True." He shrugged and sat down in the chair opposite me. "Anyway I like the challenge of it."

"Okay. Thank you," I responded.

"I'd like to do more word-of-mouth promotion. Network with *whales* and VIPs in Miami. That's why I put Marcus on your team, by the way."

I thought it over for a moment then answered, "That's certainly still a part of the plan. I just thought we should get a few events underway first, work out the kinks in them, then involve Marcus's contacts."

Raising an eyebrow, Zion asked, "You don't think the events will go well?"

"I'm sure they'll go fine. Especially the way you're able to improvise like you did in the meeting just now." I felt composed, despite the waves of thoughts crashing in my head about him. At this point I had become used to them. I could almost ignore the attraction and heat that lit me up whenever he was around. I was resolved not to let my personal feelings shake me.

"So why wait? We can put in some real groundwork now with important people," he said, seeming skeptical.

"I just want to be sure." I thought through what he was trying to push for a moment then finished with, "You hired me for my ambition and drive, but I hope you also noticed that I'm a perfectionist."

Zion nodded, running his hand over his mouth, thinking about my comment. I wished he hadn't because it only made me more aware of the curves of his lips. I looked at my watch pointlessly, as an excuse to glance away from him.

"Fair enough. I did notice that when"—he looked me up and down—"you were considering my job offer. I guess I'm more impetuous." He shrugged once more then stood up. "I'm excited to see how things pan out. I'm headed up to New York for the rest of the week, so I'll catch up with you early next week?"

I agreed, and he left my office, taking most of his scent with him but leaving a little behind for me to think about.

Something in the tone of the discussion made me wonder whether he really did trust my decision-making in the matter. I cast it off, knowing he'd be out of town and involved in other company ventures. I'd a have a few Zion-free days to get started and spend late nights in the office with the guys. I packed up my things for the day, knowing I needed a good night's sleep.

My office phone rang just as I was heading out.

"He stood me up." It was Megan, and before even getting to a greeting, I knew from her sad tone that she was referring to the elusive waiter.

She barely paused to breathe while she related to me the events of the night before, from the outfit she had picked out to the type of place he had chosen to meet her. I cringed a little to hear that she had waited for an hour and half before leaving the restaurant in tears. She was sweet and didn't deserve that kind of embarrassment. I almost regretted not going into the Bouvier Public Relations office, knowing then that she had been there alone all day. She had even waited to call me until the end of business day to tell me. She was slowly becoming more useful and confident professionally since I'd been leaving her to managing the office by herself, but her social life was an absolute disaster.

"Meet me at my condo, Megan. We're going out," I said cheerfully.

"Okay," she slowly replied. "It's not like I have any other plans." She couldn't disguise the note of self-pity in her voice.

I hadn't planned to be out for the night, but it would be the first time without Zion and the elaborate dinners. As I was leaving, I ran into Cece at the elevator. Chitchatting, he explained there was so much of the city he had yet to see since moving to Miami and working long hours at ZB. A spark of an idea lit up in my mind.

"Come out with me and a friend tonight," I said, almost as a demand. He looked rattled by the invitation at first, but then he agreed.

A few hours later, Megan and I were sitting at an outdoor café in a bustling part of Little Havana. Musicians were playing on the street corners, calling out with their voices and horns while a crowd gathered around them. The restaurant was packed and filled with plastic, bright-red tablecloths and plastic silverware. The margaritas were a little tart, but they were perfectly refreshing after the weeks of perfectly placed crystal settings I'd become used to lately.

Cece was planning to meet up with us a little later on, so Megan and I were able to cover a little needed girl time. We had established that the waiter would have to be forgotten, because Megan was a career woman who needed to date men with the same sensibilities. After this we moved on to my imagined affair with Zion, or at least that's how Megan had begun to view the situation.

"So he, like, flirted with you that one night. Then he gave you a job, and now he totally ignores you?" She waved her drink around dramatically as she spoke.

"He doesn't ignore me. It's just all very professional," I said.

"Men just can't decide what they want. That's the problem. I mean, like, was he drunk or something the night you met and doesn't remember?"

"I don't think so. I'm never really sure what his motivations are." I looked around at the other patrons, who were laughing and enjoying the night. It was hot and balmy, just like most nights in Miami. After spending weeks in the vortex of ZB Financial's office, I was glad to be out and remind myself where I was. I made a note to myself to do this more often. All work and no play make Jill, as they say, a dull girl.

"You know, it's so weird that he has that guy as his secretary," said Megan.

"What guy?" I asked, confused, thinking of Clara and wondering if she had a very deep voice over the phone.

"That big creepy guy. The one who always answers the phone and comes over to pick up things you need from the office."

She was referring to Reesey, who was in no way Zion's secretary, but I also couldn't really describe how he fit in. The number Megan had for the office must have been off the original business card I'd been given, which must had Zion's direct line on it. Or maybe it was Reesey's.

"He has a secretary, but she stays in the office. I guess Reesey is…something like his personal assistant," I said.

"He looks like he could be his bodyguard," she added.

"He may be that too. It's a strange situation. If he bothers you, I can ask to have someone else come and pick up things from the office. I'll also get you Clara's number."

Megan dismissed the matter as not being important, but it led me to think about Reesey's presence a bit more. He generally was so quiet that I didn't notice how frequently he lingered around the office. He had no desk of his own but instead followed Zion in and out of the big office to off-site meetings, on trips to New York, and I assume, anywhere else Zion traveled. He acted as if Zion were his superior, so the idea that he was Zion's full business partner didn't seem to match up. It almost seemed as if, in his former life, he had been a part of the Secret Service or some kind of military unit, like SEAL Team Six. "Bodyguard" seemed like a more accurate assessment of his position, but again I also knew he had hands in much of the company business.

Finally Cece joined us, finding the table right away and pulling up a chair to join us. I quickly found out that he was a very different kind of man than those I normally did business with. He was conservative and timid, actively listening to the conversation between Megan and me even if it had little to do with anything he knew about. He asked thoughtful questions and seemed shy during moments when we asked him about his own life. He was well educated and refined. I also noticed how he became instantly enthralled with Megan. They'd been introduced maybe twice before at ZB dinners, but among the flurry of guests, I don't think they'd taken much time to notice each other. Now, in this informal setting, they paid close attention. I hadn't planned for any connection between them, but I thought he might represent an example of a nicely put-together man next to the sad example set by her waiter. I didn't expect anything else from it, but as I watched Cece lean in to Megan, I knew something else was brewing under the surface between them.

Megan was being entirely herself, talking a mile a minute and laughing at her own awkward observations. She even tried out the story of the night before on Cece, who was very sympathetic to her. He made her laugh a few times, and eventually the two told stories of why they had moved to Miami and their dreams of a bigger and better life.

There was chemistry between them, and I was happy to see it. I did, however, wonder how things could possibly pan out. After all, Megan was a young blond girl from a small town, whose previous history with men told me she didn't have fantastic taste. Cece was notably African and culturally very different from her corn-fed upbringing. It was too early to tell if it would lead to anything, but I hoped it would. Maybe it was the romantic in me that thought it could be something more than a good night out with friends.

"I thought Marcus and Frederick were the lucky ones tonight. This is more fun," Cece said, pulling me back into the conversation.

"What do you mean?" I asked.

"Well, they're at the Miami City Ballet. Mr. Bram gave them tickets," he said.

"Oh, I love the ballet! I used to take classes when I was little! Then I started gymnastics," Megan added.

"That's interesting. Does the firm have box seats?" I asked, curious. It didn't matter much what the team members did in their time off, but it did seem interesting that Zion was involved in it. Something in my gut told me there was an ulterior motive there.

"No. There are many Miami business people there. Some Marcus knows but Mr. Bram doesn't," Cece answered.

"Wait," I said. Cece was repeating the information as if I'd already known what was going on, which meant the ballet tickets were a well-known fact around the office, yet I hadn't heard anything about them. It was a minor detail, but because of the discussion Zion had had with me earlier in the day, I wondered why I'd been left in the dark. "Does this have anything to do with the Art of Wealth project?" I asked.

"Oh, is that the name? That's catchy," said Megan.

"Yes. Of course. Mr. Bram asked them to mention it if they ran into certain people. He gave Marcus a printout," Cece said. He looked confused, as if I should have already known.

I was furious. I understood that ZB Financial was Zion's company. Yes, he could do whatever he wanted with the Art of Wealth project because he owned it. He could ask his employees to do any task relating to it because he paid them. I understood it was perfectly within his realm to ask that of Marcus and Frederick for the night. But I didn't like it.

He had gone over my head and outside of my lair. I said nothing else to Cece. Instead I squeezed out a smile and excused myself to the bathroom. I needed a moment to calm down. I couldn't believe Zion had gone over my head. It might have been his company, but this was my team. And I'd be damned if anyone would lead it except me.

I paced inside the small bathroom like a caged animal looking for a way out then returned to the table. I was calmer now, but the giddiness of the fun evening had been sucked out of me. I left Cece and Megan alone to enjoy the rest of their night and returned to my condo.

I changed as soon as I got home and went straight to the rooftop gym. I ran out the aggression I had built up from the situation and thought through how I would approach the new information.

In my head I played out every angry response I wanted to throw at Zion. I even thought of actually throwing things at him the next time I saw him. He might have thought I would just lie down and accept whatever he wanted to do, like everyone else in the office. He might have thought I wouldn't challenge him. He was wrong. It wasn't about the money in the contract or the big opportunity. I would quit if it meant getting my point across. After this Zion would either be out of a PR director, or he would know never to mess with me like that again.

I could wait patiently for him to return from New York to give him my opinion of his decision to go outside of my control. I would even direct Marcus and Frederick to use any information or contacts they made to benefit the project. But I wasn't going to feel any less irritated.

Zion owned the playground and therefore thought he could always get his way. Unfortunately he didn't know that bringing me in meant he would have to play fair. If anything came at the expense of respecting my leadership over the team, I was going to make sure that arrogant, cocky—albeit sexy—man was going to have hell to pay with the not-so-timid Omega Bouvier.

Ten

Monday I woke up before the sunrise. My irritation had simmered into a burn of determination.

While it was still cool, I went for a run. I passed through the parking lot of my condo, where the concrete retained the cold night air, and along the road toward the beach. My feet were pounding against the asphalt and onto the sidewalk. When I reached the sand, I felt such a satisfying pace in my stride.

On the horizon huge construction cranes and front-end loaders aligned the beach area near my condo. Erosion had pulled away too much of the Miami sand, so the iron monsters were hauling sand from the Atlantic trench and renourishing the shoreline of multimillion-dollar properties.

The massive machines appeared rather beautiful, silhouetted in the sunlight's pink hues. From a distance they looked like toys along the expanse of the Florida coastline. Up close they were like slow-moving conquerors. I imagined Zion fancied himself as one of these machines, making big footprints in the Miami sand. Besides my private thoughts about him being a smart businessman and a well-rounded leader—and having a sexy ass in dress pants—a new image was forming of him over the last few days. If

I'd had a punching bag, I probably would have taped a picture of his fine-looking face to it.

Two things happened on the Monday after Marcus and Frederick went to the ballet. One was that I sat down with them, taking notes and highlighting who had attended the event and with whom they had spoken. We assessed the biggest charitable contributors to the ballet production. Frederick even spoke with the performance director, presenting the Art of Wealth as an event sponsor. There were several Caribbean and African modern dance companies in Miami that would be eager to perform, and it was a terrific initiative to enhance the image of ZB Financial.

The second event transpired with me alone. I was brainstorming, doodling on the big dry-erase board in the conference room, when I had an epiphany about boosting media attention and membership for the Art of Wealth. I smiled and did a little dance! It wasn't a groundbreaking idea, but it was something ZB wasn't doing when it should have been. I did more research throughout the day and felt confident.

Later that day I made it clear to the team that any PR-related ventures were to be cleared with me first. Zion may have been my boss, but I was theirs. They initially seemed a bit reluctant, but I trusted their promise to keep me in the loop. After some conversation I discovered they assumed I'd known about the ballet, so I didn't get the impression that it was a deliberate attempt on their part to line up with Zion behind my back. It was simply a matter of miscommunication and something that shouldn't happen again.

Friday afternoon I was hanging out around Clara's workstation, talking to her about her plans for the weekend. I was trying to decompress from the week, and hearing Clara talk about her grandchildren always brought me a certain level of calm. She was positioned in the middle of the office floor, near the elevator, so she could easily accept guests. Sure enough, the elevator door beeped around 3:45 p.m., and we both peeked around the corner to see who the visitor might be. I tensed up a little, thinking Zion might have headed back early from New York. I wasn't mentally prepared to ask him about his stunt before he'd left. I planned to mull over my approach with a few glasses of wine over the weekend.

Fortunately it wasn't Zion strolling down the hallway. Instead a woman in impossibly high heels and a skintight black dress walked up to Clara's desk. Her long black hair landed at her waist, and I had the idea that she looked familiar; perhaps she may have been a model I'd seen in a commercial or magazine layout. Then again, she didn't carry the sleek, elegant look of most models. The thickness of her makeup seemed more suited for a seedy nightclub near the strip.

"Excuse me." Her voice was lightly accented, and she pulled her Gucci sunglasses up as she spoke to Clara.

"Yes, how may I help you?" Clara asked.

"I need to leave something for Zion Bram," the mystery woman said, sounding almost annoyed.

"Well, you're in his office," Clara retorted. I'd never heard anything but kindness in her voice, so my eyebrows lifted as I listened to the exchange.

The woman sighed and said, "Well, anyway, I'm only dropping off his Corvette. It's in the parking lot. He let me borrow it for the week." She pulled a set of keys out of her purse and set them on Clara's desk.

"I'll make sure the car is returned to him. Thank you, Ms....?" Clara said, with still a little bite.

"Simona Borghi," the woman answered.

"Ah, okay. Well, have a nice day," Clara finished.

Simona sauntered out, leaving a wake of thick perfume as a frustrated look set on my face. Clara blew off the encounter and put the keys in her top drawer then continued our conversation as if the scene never happened.

It was one thing to fantasize about the endless possibilities between Zion and me, and true enough, perhaps I'd grown too attached to them, thinking I owned him in some way. However, the sense of entitlement and the strong persona of the woman who had just waltzed into the office shook me from fantasy to reality.

I felt a small pang of jealousy because I thought, even after the weeks that had passed, there was still some kind of connection between Zion and me from the first moment we met. I couldn't explain it; it was unspoken, but it was something there. I had to remind myself that it was better for me to keep things professional. I ignored my jealousy and focused on the fact that I had nonromantic matters to attend to with him.

Without the boss in the office all week, the place felt empty on a late Friday afternoon. I found myself sucked into some work that had piled up from my private-practice accounts. I was spending almost no time at my own office. Jonny Bali's nightclub and fitness business were earning gradual profits and notoriety. I'd ignored a few smaller accounts for a few weeks running, and while I easily could have gone home to wash off the intensity of the week, I quickly was becoming a workaholic. The skies were dark by the time I left the building, but I was satisfied with everything I'd accomplished.

Sleep came easily to me once I reached home. All thoughts of Zion and his long- legged Italian drifted away. I had an entire two days off to myself. I had an appointment at the hair salon and planned to meet up with Santiago for lunch and a bit of shopping. It had been a while since I'd seen him at the art exhibition, and I was excited to catch up with an old friend. If all else failed, I would walk down to the beach in a big hat and tight bikini. After all, I had moved here to look for and acquire the perfect Miami lifestyle.

My plans were completely rearranged and quashed at 10:00 a.m. when the phone on my kitchen counter rang three times in a row.

"Hi, Omega. I hope I didn't wake you." It was Reesey's voice, so I didn't believe the forced sincerity.

"It's fine, Reesey. What do you need?" I sat on a stool in the kitchen as I scrambled eggs for breakfast.

"Well, Mr. Bram would like you to come in today to set up a new event," Reesey said dryly.

"Okay…" I scrambled lightly and folded in some vegetables, anticipating a full, nourishing breakfast, as compared to my usual two cups of coffee and an oatmeal bar.

If Zion wanted to tack on another event between dates, it could wait until after the first event, which was scheduled for the next week.

"What time does he need me there?" I asked, toying with the idea of saying no altogether, based on the fact that my eggs smelled so good, and the planning really could wait until Monday.

"As soon as possible. He wants to hold the event tomorrow," Reesey said, again with little excitement.

My mouth dropped open, and a series of questions lined up regarding the when, where, how, and why he would want to do something so…stupid. It seemed rash and something we were totally unprepared for. I also didn't feel like abandoning my fully planned weekend for such a poor idea.

"Is he serious?" I said without thinking.

"Yes, Ms. Bouvier." Reesey wasn't moving on the topic, which annoyed me.

"Fine," I said. "I'll be there in an hour. I need to finish my breakfast."

I showed up precisely at 11:00 a.m., and I had an attitude of a woman none too pleased during the entire elevator ride up. The office possessed a warm, quiet feeling on a Saturday as I made my way into the corner office with the illustrious rafters. Zion was on the phone and waved for me to come inside. I flopped down heavily in the leather chair, crossing my arms across my chest while I waited for him to finish his call.

"Good morning. I appreciate your coming in. Did you miss me?" He smiled, sitting there, looking comfortable and not at all stressed that he wanted to do the impossible on a day's notice.

"Zion, we're not having an event tomorrow," I said flatly and not giving him any sympathy.

He opened his mouth to reply but stopped and looked confused, as if not hearing what I'd said right away then giving himself some time to process my response. I leaned back, sitting there confidently. All the thoughts and arguments I'd had a few days before came back to me. However, instead of letting them loose, I decided to allow Zion to lead.

"Omega, it'll be very small. Just a starter for me to approach some people I connected with in New York. It won't be as big of a deal as next week," he said softly.

"No," I replied, not too harshly but assured.

"No, we can't do it, or no, you won't do it?" he asked.

"No, I won't do it. I can do it, but I won't because it's not in the set plan, and I think it's a bad idea," I explained.

"So...you're not going to do it?" Zion asked, clearly confused.

"No, I'm not," I said, finishing with a smile.

"Interesting." He put his hand up to his chin, stroking the little bit of scruff that had grown in since I'd seen him last. "So there's no persuading you?"

"No," I said, and shrugged. "Why don't these connections just get invites to the events already planned?"

"Because they won't be in town next week, Omega. They're important investors. I can't treat them as if they should sign up just like everyone else," he said, the frustration building in his tone.

"That seems to defeat the purpose of your message, doesn't it? Allowing the common man to access investment strategies of the wealthy?"

He pulled his lips together into a frown but didn't answer my question.

"Also," I continued, "I don't have time today. I have other plans, which you're currently interrupting." I stood up, pulling my purse up onto my shoulder. I figured if I left early enough, I could make my point and leave him with little response. "I'll see you on Monday, Zion. I'm happy to see you made it home safely."

He stood as I headed toward his office door and moved behind me. As I tried to open the door to leave, he rushed next to me and shut it with his hand. He leaned in, obviously angry. "You're being really difficult right now, Ms. Bouvier," he said.

While I could feel the frustration in his voice and body language toward me, there was something else in the way he looked at me. The room became warmer, and I suddenly noticed the space between us was more like the night we'd spent dancing than any time we'd spent together in the office. I felt my heart beating faster with the smell of him so close. I was still angry from the pressured request and the entitled way he was behaving. I stood still, as immovable as he was, looking directly into his eyes.

"I think I'm being completely reasonable. It is, however, difficult for me to execute the project you've assigned me when you won't allow me to follow the set plan—the plan you and I both agreed upon," I said, trying again for the door handle.

"It's *my* project," he said, his jaw tightening as he held the door closed. It was powerful to see him so worked up over my refusal. He didn't make any aggressive movements toward me but stood stubbornly with his hand on the door.

"Then you can take care of it and go ahead and lead the team without me. You've already started," I answered, trying to maintain a sense of calm.

Zion looked confused for a moment, then, realizing the reference, said, "Oh, I see. I thought you might be upset about that. Again it's my project and my team."

"Then you can go ahead and handle it," I said slowly. "I don't want any part of your half assed, fly-by-the-seat-of-your-pants events. That's not how I operate, Zion. Now please excuse me!" I said sternly.

Zion refused to step aside from the door and remained unmovable. I don't know how long the silence lasted, but he stared at me, his jaw twitching and his hand stuck to the door. I stared right back at him, watching his nostrils flare and his breathing quicken. Yet he still didn't move. I mirrored his stubbornness.

I had nothing left to say and was waiting for a response when his gaze traveled from my face downward. I instantly felt the air shift in the room from a standoff to an energy that pulsed between us as he slowly and deliberately looked me over.

In my rush to get out of the house and into the office, I'd thrown on a simple halter-top sundress. The fabric was sheer, because I knew I'd be walking through the heat of the afternoon. I didn't try to dress for a business meeting but instead for a relaxing weekend to make the point that I hadn't planned to do any work that day.

His eyes traveled down to my cleavage, which slightly peeked out from my dress, revealing just a hint of me, while admiring how it hugged my small waist. I knew the kind of thoughts that were going through his mind. I could read them on his face, and they mirrored the few I was having as well.

Then the stillness broke.

Staring deep into my eyes, he reached an arm underneath me and pulled me in close to him. I gasped. Before I knew it, he leaned in to kiss me. I expected it to be rough to match the anger brewing between us, but the pressure of his body against mine registered as needy. He touched his lips to my lips—closed but hard against mine—and he sighed in relief. I closed my eyes and let myself lean back as his arms wrapped around my middle, holding me up. I responded, getting lost in the passionate kiss.

I let it happen; I was just as eager as he was. I fell into the feeling for one hot moment. Then my sense of what we'd just been talking about and the fact that we were in the office came back to me. I pushed against his chest, and he unwrapped his arms and moved away from me, gasping for breath as he detached himself.

I put my fingertips to my lips and watched him.

"I'm sorry," he said, looking remorseful and avoiding eye contact. "You were mad and you looked so…"

I placed my hand on the doorknob and took a moment to collect myself from what had just happened.

"I'll talk to you on Monday, Zion," I said, and walked out.

All weekend long, I replayed in my head those few intense minutes in his office. I had moments when I thought maybe I'd been too hard on him. Other times I wondered why I hadn't immediately slapped him in the face and quit my job!

Our brief dramatic interaction had confirmed a few things in my mind. Zion knew he was taking a risk in his decision to talk to Marcus and Frederick without me. He felt as if he could go over my head to gain control over the project, or at least he thought he could before. And it was no longer just my imagination playing out some kind of chemistry between Zion and me. It was real.

For a while I'd been able to pass off my fantasies as being unreciprocated, thinking the slight flirtation between us during dinners was just Zion being Zion. Since I was consumed with my work and building a career, the slight perceived romance was just an interesting facet of my limited personal life. Plus I had a rule for myself that I wouldn't get involved with men I worked with.

Now the fantasies had leaked into reality. Zion's quick breaths and tense body against mine for those few minutes brought back a flood of all the feelings of the night we'd met. And all the fears that accompanied those feelings.

I had calmed down by the time I returned to ZB Financial on Monday morning. No matter how much I thought it over, I wouldn't have been able to predict what I would be walking into.

Placed in the center of my desk was a bouquet—two dozen bright yellow and white roses, calling attention from people walking by in the hallway. I quickly put my purse down and walked over to examine them.

I hoped this wasn't some semblance of an apology. There was no way I would accept flowers from Zion as a way to handle our argument and our encounter in his office. The thought of it already was making me furious again, until I pulled out the card and read it.

Have a happy birthday, Omega!
Love, Jonny

I'd forgotten. I knew what day it was exactly. I had to know the date in order to plan the project and continue with my work. Maybe I was spending my time considering the date as a countdown instead of reality. Or maybe, just maybe, because I grew up not celebrating birthdays in my family, I'd become accustomed to it being just another day. I still couldn't believe it. I was so caught up that I had forgotten my own birthday!

I sighed and plopped down in my chair. I was grateful to Jonny for remembering and for taking the time to send the gorgeous floral arrangement. I had to call and thank him. In light of everything else going on, I gave myself a moment for reflection and gratitude then placed the vase with my new flowers on the windowsill. After that I was able to slip into work mode.

I got on the phone quickly with a new idea that would increase the projected membership requests for the next few seminars. The calls went well, and I was surprised by how much interest I was garnering in the project. Of course there was more time and work to be put in, and I wanted to introduce the news to the team on Tuesday. I was in the groove again, focused in with laser-like intensity on what I did best, and was blowing through the morning.

"Those are beautiful. Where did you get them?"

I looked up. Zion had walked in from the hallway and was wandering over to the flowers. He caressed a few petals between his fingers, looking at them then out the window.

"They were here when I came in." I kept my voice cool. I knew we would have to continue a working relationship, no matter the implications of what had happened over the weekend.

"I see." He sat on the ledge of the window and looked directly at me. "So I think we should talk about Saturday."

I sat up and matched his stare with one of my own but couldn't think beyond his gaze. Instead I just waited for him to go on further, knowing he had more to say. His face was set seriously. He pushed his hands into his pockets and gave me a small smile.

"We didn't have an event yesterday. You were probably right about being our being unprepared."

Probably right? I thought but stayed quiet.

"We're all very excited about our event. I intend to—"

The phone rang, which made me jump. I quickly picked it up and turned away from Zion.

"Hi ya, lovely." It was Jonny, who had just returned from a tour around the country for a fitness video he had made. I had forgotten about that too.

"Hi, Jonny. How are you?"

"Good. Happy birthday!"

"Oh, thank you. The flowers are beautiful. What a lovely surprise! How did you know?" My tone lightened as I felt more at ease on the phone with Jonny.

"Megan mentioned it. I just called her to check in. Thought I'd tell you about my trip," he said.

"Oh, okay. Can I call you back later on today?" I asked, trying to think of when in my schedule I'd be able to get in touch with him.

"Better yet, how about you let me take you to dinner tonight, and I'll tell you all about it?" he asked.

"Um…" I couldn't think of a reason to say no, other than wanting to avoid my birthday altogether. Then again, it would give me an excuse to catch up on Jonny's account, which I'd been neglecting due to my intense devotion to Zion's project. "Yes, okay. I can do dinner. Is seven thirty okay?"

"Perfect. I'll pick you up at your condo."

We said quick good-byes, and I turned to see Zion pacing in my office. His face and demeanor had changed from relaxed and sincere to irritated.

"Sorry about that," I said, "It was another client."

"Hmm," he said, crossing his arms; "I'm sure it was." He stood there for a minute or so, as though waiting for an explanation from me.

Well, I wasn't going to provide one, as it really wasn't any of his business. It may have been hopeful for me to imagine that his sudden irritation was out of jealousy.

"Anyway I'll be stepping into your team meeting tomorrow," he said. "I hope that's all right."

"Yes. You're welcome in any time you'd like," I said graciously. I should have stopped there, but I couldn't help add, "After all, it *is* your company."

Zion nodded curtly then left the office. I felt a little victorious after the encounter and felt justified about the decision I'd made in the office on Saturday. I went about finishing my work and getting ready for my impromptu birthday dinner.

Jonny and I were just about as close as you can be with a client. The dinner was casual, and he actually did want to tell me about the business specifics of his trip. We laughed over crab legs, ripping them apart and sipping up loose buttery bits. As it turned out, his trip had been very profitable, and he had more ideas about expanding La Matadora into a franchise operation, opening a few more locations in a slow rollout. He wanted to start in LA, his hometown. We talked out the logistics of this. It was a long ways away, but as always I enjoyed thinking through it and planning. It was later than I expected when we finished our dinner.

"Jonny, thank you. It's been a wonderful evening, and it's so great catching up with you. But," I told him, "tomorrow's a workday.

"For me, too," he said.

He drove me home and delivered me to my doorstep, planting a chaste kiss on my cheek and enveloping me in a warm embrace. Jonny was a true gentleman and was becoming a good friend. As I opened the door and entered my apartment, I kicked off my shoes, walked into my bedroom, and tossed my purse on the chair. I took a good, hard look at the lady in the painting that hung above my bed, the same woman in the park who'd been taunting me for years. The glimmer in her eyes and the smirk on her face was whispering something different to me now: "Leave him wanting for more…"

On that note I prepared for tomorrow's meeting. I laid out the perfect outfit to wear. And I had a surprise of my own in store for Mr.…Zion…Bram!

Eleven

At the team meeting the next day, I had plenty of news to deliver. I felt good, and I knew I looked amazing in my new Diane von Fürstenberg purple wrap dress, paired with my gold strappy Jimmy Choo heels that I bought last weekend while shopping with Santiago.

"So it looks like we've filled the seats and sold out the first five seminars," I said. "I'm thinking we can possibly squeeze in a few more. There's time to arrange smaller events for those who may have bigger contributions to make."

The team members' faces brightened up, especially since this was the first they'd heard about the full sales of the events. Zion in particular looked impressed at the mention of these new events. I didn't mean it to mock him, as there was a need for smaller events based on the news he'd brought me over the weekend. But if he thought it was a secret dig, then so be it.

"That's amazing!" said Cece. "How did you manage that? I heard from the venue rep that we'd only sold tickets for half the capacity."

"Well, yes, that's where we were then," I replied. "But I took another tactic and contacted a few church leaders in the city—some politically based and others who mainly head up large, black community church organizations. They were very enthusiastic, and after speaking with a few people in their congregations, I got a huge response. So now we're at capacity." I smiled fully for the first time in a few days. The team was returning the sentiment. Even Zion managed to break out in a grin, nodding at me when we locked eyes. I'd almost forgiven him. Almost.

We were all itching for the next day, when the project would really start in full. It felt like it had been so long since the days when I'd first started at ZB Financial, when I was intimidated and overwhelmed. I was able to conquer those feelings and make it my own, despite the obstacles on the outside and within.

That afternoon Zion walked into my office again, silently, and pulled at my birthday flowers once again. "Ms. Bouvier, you've done an incredible job. I had high expectations, but I'm very impressed."

I was riding on a cloud and happy from the day, but I still held back from showing him my complete enthusiasm. "Thank, you, Zion," I said.

"I'd like for you to go over my presentation with me later on…and some other points of the seminar, if you can."

"Of course. In here or your office?" I asked.

"My office, but not for a bit. I have some phone calls to make beforehand. Would it be all right if you stayed later?"

"Yes. I suppose that's fine," I said, slowly and skeptically.

"Unless you have dinner plans." He sat down in the chair across my desk, bringing his eyes level to mine.

"I don't," I said shortly.

"I know you're upset with me." He kept eye contact with me, leaning forward in his seat. "I can be very…stubborn."

I raised my eyebrows but didn't reply. I'd been upset, yes, but it had worn off. I respected how demanding and driven he was. I'd made my point about working with the team and veering away from the plan. After that I felt as if Zion and I had a solid agreement. As for being mad about the kiss in his office, I couldn't bring myself to be angry about it because a part of me had wanted it too. But I wasn't going to tell him that just yet.

"Zion…" I whispered his name, preparing to tell him that I appreciated his attempt to apologize, but before I could, my phone rang. We jerked to look at it. In the next moment, Frederick walked into my office. He glanced at Zion, then at me, then at the ringing phone, looking as if he were brewing with something to say.

Zion nodded and finally let out the smile I was starting to love to see. He stood up, patted Frederick on the shoulder, and then walked out the door.

The rest of the day was a rush of double-checking, making final calls, and pulling team members into the office one by one to go over questions. Everyone received guest lists and last-minute changes. Clara ran around continually from the Xerox machine to my desk.

In the back of my mind, I wondered when I would be pulled into Zion's office to help him review tomorrow's events. As the clock ticked away and gained speed toward the end of the day, I was starting to doubt we'd have time. The office stayed busy until after six, and ultimately, when we were satisfied with my team's last-minute reports, I sent everyone home.

The skies through the floor-to-ceiling windows were purple, shifting into night. I walked through the quiet cubicles and hallways to Zion's office to see if he needed anything, to say good night, and maybe just to see if he had more to say from earlier.

His office was empty, the lights shut off, and still. I really thought he would have been there later, but maybe he felt he needed to rest. I shrugged and thought I should head home too, even though I was still pumped with energy and excitement.

When I turned to leave, Zion was walking toward me down the hallway.

"Omega, hi." He stopped a few inches from me, looking comfortable with his shirt unbuttoned at the top and his tie missing, "I thought we could work in the conference room...spread out a little."

I nodded and followed him. There wasn't much in the room in the way of work, except for a stack of cards that held his prepared speech notes for the next day. In the place of work, there were plastic packages and a few bottles of wine, with matching china and stemware.

"I thought if I kept you late, I might as well feed you," he said, standing behind me at the door, close enough that I felt his breath tease at my ear.

I recognized the logo of the restaurant on the side of the packages. It was one of the places we frequented with the rest of the firm. I thought of all of those dinners and the way he had watched me during them. I wondered how intense it would be without anyone at the restaurant to distract him.

We sat across from each other. Zion opened a bottle of Sancerre and unveiled a few starters of PEI mussels in a tomato base. I had forgotten to eat for most of the day and was famished. As I watched the steam rise from the dish, I licked my lips in anticipation. Zion chuckled softly as he served me. He must have known how hungry I would be. The wine was smooth and perfect, and I barely paused before digging into the food. It never even occurred to me that Zion's choice of meal opener also had a reputation for being the perfect aphrodisiac.

"I'm impressed with how you filled up the events so quickly. I didn't expect them to pick up for a few weeks," he said, all business.

"There was a whole segment of the community we weren't reaching out to. I'm surprised I didn't think of it earlier." I sipped more wine, my head feeling lighter. "I sold it as a positive-feedback loop. If the congregation invests and makes more money, it feels more secure, and the congregation will contribute more. The church can grow and accomplish more. With growth they'll have more attendees, and so will we. It's win-win."

"You're absolutely right. I've always made use of connections I made at synagogue but never thought too much about involving the temple leadership. That was a great sell, Omega," he said, then raised his glass in my direction as I mirrored his action.

"Also it's nice to think that while we're helping people who are settled and doing well for themselves, if you incorporate the church, then you're helping out in charity work as well. We could consider getting more involved for tax write-off purposes," I suggested, finishing off the last spoonful of sauce.

"True. I'll run that by our accountants." He stood and walked around to my side of the table, removing the plate and setting down a small plate of bruschetta and fresh vegetables. As he did, his arm brushed against mine with a subtle charge of electricity. I found it so sexy how he served me casually and comfortably while standing tall and commandingly over me.

"Did you grow up involved in church?" he asked, sitting back down.

"I did. We were a large family, so the church was one of the few buildings that could hold us all comfortably."

He laughed at my response. "How many children did your parents have?" he asked.

"Ten."

His eyes widened, "Ten? That's incredible!" He slipped a small bit of bread into his mouth then said, "I'm guessing you're the oldest, considering how organized you are."

"No, I'm the last one. That's the significance of my name—Omega."

"Oh. Well, then your name makes perfect sense."

I nodded, not wanting to go into any additional details about my name or religious upbringing. It was enough information, and fortunately he didn't ask further. He continued, "I was an only child. Which probably explains why I'm so stubborn and demanding, or I'm sure that's what my mother's therapist tells her." He laughed to himself.

"That must have been lonely, I'm guessing," I said, not thinking over it much. His face drifted a bit into confusion or reverie. I thought for a moment that maybe I'd struck a difficult cord, but then he let his smile return.

"It was a little bit…save for all of the nannies I tortured," he said.

This time I laughed, imagining his angry furrowed brow as a child, expecting to get his way in impossible situations.

We continued on to the main course, talking through stories of college and his career. We laughed often. I could tell he was surprised by how quickly I kept up with his wit. We'd never been so comfortable around each other, and it was intoxicating to carry on a conversation with him. His life was luxurious from start to finish, but he seemed to have a true appreciation for it. He was sincerely interested in my tales of college, my roommate, my moving to Miami, and my working at Durand, Abrams, & Sifuentes. I even retold the story of the incorrigible Cuban trumpeter I once set straight.

"After getting to know you, that doesn't surprise me at all. I'm sure he deserved everything he got," Zion replied, as we moved on to the main course of roasted veal in a red-wine jus. We were on our second bottle of wine now, this one an Italian red that gripped at my tongue.

"So should we actually go over your presentation for tomorrow?" I said, pointing my fork toward the stack that had been moved farther and farther down the table as we went on.

"Honestly I tend to just wing it at these things," he said.

I stopped eating and cocked my head to the side, looking him over.

"Don't worry. I won't go off message. I just may use the cards as more of a guideline. I'm good at this," he attempted to reassure me.

"Then we don't need to go over anything?" I asked.

"Um…no."

"Then why…?" I put my hands in the air.

"Because I wanted to get a chance alone with you that wouldn't be interrupted." His voice sounded a little annoyed. He breathed in deeply. "I really wanted to talk about what happened on Saturday. I wanted to apologize."

I swallowed, surprised that he'd brought up the subject of our kiss. I said carefully, "It's fine. No apology needed. It was a heated moment. We were both behaving…outside ourselves." I looked down at my plate and continued to eat, trying to remain calm.

After a moment of silence, Zion said quietly, "Every single moment with you around is heated."

I looked up. "What does that mean?" I asked, maybe sounding somewhat accusatory.

His face looked stern and serious this time, without the playful smile. "It isn't obvious? You drive me absolutely insane."

"Excuse me?"

"Those flowers on your desk made it increasingly worse. I don't know if you're seeing anyone, but if you are, I hope you won't rub it in my face and—"

I interrupted. "I don't understand how that would make you crazy."

"Well, because…I want you, Omega. I want to be with you. I want you to be my woman, and I want to be your man," he said, his face still, his eyes searching mine.

I felt shocked, although wasn't that what I'd been thinking about all along? Wasn't this the moment I'd been waiting for? I'd just assumed I was another good-looking woman in his presence, not that I was someone with the ability to make him crazy.

He sighed and continued. "After Saturday…I didn't regret it. I was taking what I wanted. Maybe it wasn't the right way or the right time. Then, yesterday, you ignored me. Made plans to go out to dinner right in front of me. Today you were aloof. I'm sorry if I'm making you uncomfortable. I realize in our current situation this is bad idea, but…I can't help it."

My heart was beating again in a now very familiar way. I thought back to Saturday again and through the last few days. I had imagined there was something going on but nothing like what he was explaining to me now.

"What about…Ms. Borghi?" I asked, trying to collect my feelings.

"Who?" he asked. "Oh, Simona. You met Simona?"

"Yeah, she dropped off your Corvette last week."

"Simona's an interesting woman," he replied, "but there's not a single trick she has in her snare-the-man playbook that keeps me from thinking about you."

His response shocked me. He was acknowledging that he and this woman, Simona, were intimate. Then again maybe he thought of her the way I did and kept her around just to pass the time. I didn't particularly like that idea because I didn't want to be that kind of woman to him. But it seemed as if that was exactly what he was saying. I was different than her. I was something he wanted so badly that it made him crazy.

We dropped the subject briefly and moved on to dessert—chocolate mousse with strawberries. Simple and delicious. We finished it off with some Prosecco. This time, when he moved the dessert in front of me, the smell and warmth of him settling over me felt so different. He was tender in how he moved and how he interacted with me.

In that moment I admitted to myself that I was falling for him, which scared me. Before Zion had been just a distant crush—a shower and late-night fantasy—someone I'd had spent a few intimate moments but knew it would never amount to anything. Now we had worked together, butted heads, built the project together, and shared our stories. When we weren't battling over getting our way, we worked well together, and the team responded to our leadership. At dinners with clients we bounced ideas back and forth respectfully. Now that we were alone, it was even more apparent how easy it was to be around him and how hard it was to ignore our attraction for each other.

There wasn't much talk after his confession, and we finished the Prosecco during the pause. He looked defeated.

"Zion, it's all right. I appreciate your candor," I finally said.

He stood up and cleared all the leftover plates and glasses off the table. "Thank you," he said. "I hope I didn't make things difficult."

"Oh, you do. Every day. Very difficult," I said, laughing.

"How so?" he said, standing next to my chair.

I stood up to face him. "You switch back and forth between flirty and aloof. There's no way to know what you meant by that kiss. I just assumed you were a player." As I spoke I ran my fingers over his lapel, adjusting it. I watched his breath quicken in his chest.

"True." His voice was lower. "I've had my share of women."

"I'm sure you have," I responded.

"But none of them were like you," he said, finishing off with a low rumble in his throat as I dropped my hand, trailing it down the length of him. I looked up to find him hungry, despite the meal we'd just finished. He was standing completely still, staring down at my lips.

He whispered, "I'll never try to kiss you again if you don't want it, Omega."

I did want it, though. I knew right after he said it that I wanted so many more of those kisses. I wanted more than just that.

I leaned in, feeling his breath against my lips, my eyes locked with his. I felt the buzz of the wine through me, and I had a moment when I thought I could pull away and stop, but I didn't. I was so close to him now, our bodies inches apart.

He stayed still, tense, unmoving as we stood there. He was resolved to leave me in control, and I knew it was driving him crazy to be so close without contact. It had the same effect on me.

Finally I rested my lips against his, reaching up on my toes to get there. Once I did, he released his body and wrapped his arms around my waist, pulling me against him. I felt my breasts hit his hard chest, and it caught my breath. He held me tightly and devoured my lips, nibbling and licking my tongue. The breath that escaped our lips was quick and hot. He groaned and squeezed, holding me against him in a rhythm that matched our heartbeats. It was far more passionate than the kiss on Saturday. That one was rushed and a surprise to us both. In my mind Zion had imagined this new kiss for days, resting beneath the surface, boiling to escape. His large hands moved up and down my back, grasping me tightly. They made me feel small and completely enveloped by him. I heard a deep groan between his breaths, and I matched it with a small moan of my own.

For as hard as Zion pressed against me and as much as he pulled and touched me, his lips stayed soft and teased my tongue into his mouth. He led me to the chair where I'd been sitting and he sat down. I sat on his lap, facing him, my legs straddling the chair. I leaned over, and locked my lips to his. He pulled away teasingly.

"You're absolutely breathtaking, Omega," he said gazing deep into my eyes.

His hands were stroking my thighs, and I shifted closer to him. He moved them slowly upward, as he looked into my face, waiting for me to stop him, waiting for me to beg him to continue. When his hands brushed over my breasts, we gasped. He caressed them through my dress, running his thumbs over the skin of my cleavage. I placed my hands over his, urging him to squeeze harder, as the gentleness of his touch was all the more tortuous.

He undraped the top of my dress to reveal my satin lace bra. My hard nipples were visible through the fabric. He bit them through the material of my bra and made me moan. Then he pulled down my cups and sucked my erect nipples one at a time, making them even harder, if such a thing were possible. More moans escaped from my lips, urging him without words to kiss them, lick them, and even bite down on them if that was his pleasure. He could do anything he wanted to them; they were his to enjoy.

He moved his hands down, over my hips, to the hem of my wrap dress. He tugged it up an inch or so as he looked up at me. I saw him plead for permission. I nodded, and he quickly shoved it upwards.

It was a thin purple dress that bunched up easily around my waist. He took his eyes away and looked down at my satin thong underwear. I parted my legs a little and moved closer to him. He kept his hands at my side as I moved. Now it was me who was urging him and asking.

Showing his strength, Zion lifted me up and sat me on the edge of the conference-room table. I felt the cool wood against me. He pushed me slightly, and I leaned back, staying somewhat upright so I could observe what he was doing. I saw—and felt—one hand move much too slowly, down my stomach to the front of my thigh and up again. One of his fingertips brushed the edge of my thong, sliding underneath the strap. Then he lowered his head and playfully pulled them down with his teeth. As I felt the fabric slide down my thighs, leaving me naked in front of him, inches from his face, his hands slowly moved up my legs as he discarded the satin.

"Wait, Zion...We need to be safe," I said as I moaned.

"Don't worry, Omega. I've come prepared," he assured me.

When he finally put his hand between my legs, he placed his thumb against the slit of my lips, parting them and brushing my clit immediately. He used pressure and made slow circles, and I found him to be patient, even as I moved against his hand. I closed my eyes and became lost in the sensation of it, throwing my head back and grabbing his shoulders.

Zion grunted again, moving his hand away and pulling to the side. I opened my legs completely and leaned back, lying across the table amid the discarded cartons, plates, glasses, and note cards. He parted me again with his fingers, exposing every inch of me in front of him, then rested his lips against me.

He licked slowly, softly, stopping over the swollen parts of me, making me buck against him and bite my lip. He held me still at my thighs, continuing with his pattern. My body was reacting more than I'd ever felt before, and I gave in to it, shamelessly running my hands over myself, wanting him never to stop.

After much too long, he finally sped, flicking me fast enough to send me through the first waves of an orgasm. Warmth ran from my pelvis up my spine to behind my eyes, and I shoved my fingers through his hair. It was then that he slid two fingers inside me, finding me wet and tight around them. That was the end of it as I cried out and arched my back until I didn't have the strength to hold out any longer.

It was quick for me, but there had been so much buildup, and it had been a long time since any man had touched me in such a way. In fact I didn't remember a time when my body had reacted like that to any man.

I lay on the table with my eyes closed, regaining my breath, regaining my consciousness.

Zion started to play with me again in slow circles. I was sensitive still, and he stayed soft. He leaned down again to nibble where I was swollen with arousal.

It was too much, so I sat up a little, saying, "Mmm, no more. It's okay. I'm done now."

He looked up from between my thighs and smiled. "But I'm not done." When he dropped his head to kiss me there again, I barely could stand it.

As with most gigantic, monstrous buildings, the one where I worked at ZB was never really shut down or asleep. The windows were darkened but not completely black, as the glow of the emergency lights and hallways seeped through.

The security team paced through the hallways and shafts and tiny spaces, thinking through the silence and finding ways to entertain themselves. The cleaning crews canvassed every floor, preparing the office for the start of business the next day. The action was small and uneventful when night descended on the office tower, but it was still milling around us nonetheless.

That night in the ZB office, in the conference room at the end of the hall, there was a bit more action than usual.

I was left in a languid stupor, my limbs spread across the table, while Zion untied my dress. The smile across his face was satisfied as he looked over what he had done. I opened my eyes briefly to see the cocky smile then rolled my head to the side as he pulled my dress off me and unsnapped my bra, leaving me naked just in my gold Jimmy Choos.

As if inspecting me, he brushed every inch of my skin with his fingertips. When he trailed over my firm nipples, I couldn't help but squirm. He laughed lightly then leaned down to kiss my neck, trailing wet soft touches down my chest and over my shoulders.

He stood up again, and I sat up on the table to follow. He wrapped his arms around me again, kissing me and pulling me against him. I felt his erection through his pants; it was moving against the inside of my thigh, making me crazy again, when I thought I was already spent. I reached down for it, placing my palm against the soft fabric. He pulled away and moaned.

"Oh, God, Omega!" he whispered in a husky voice, pushing himself farther into my hand. I smiled, running my palm over it slowly. I imagined him slipping inside me and went straight for the buckle of his belt.

He quickly unbuttoned his shirt, looking down to watch as I undid his belt. His chest was broad, with soft hair across it. As he kicked off his pants and shirt and stood between my legs in black boxer briefs, it was my turn for inspection. He was well built and athletic, and I suddenly imagined him at home in his own gym, working off the tension between us in the weeks before. He was warm and well endowed, which felt amazing underneath my hands. Then he pulled me to him, our bare skin touching completely, the warmth emanating between us.

I stood with him, and he picked me up, his hands underneath my thighs. He carried me over to the window, his tongue in my mouth during the walk. When he set me down in front of the window, he moved one big hand between my legs again, finding me dripping and ready. He slipped on a condom.

It was scandalous to be sure, standing naked in front of the office window, many stories above the city streets. But I didn't care.

Zion spun me around and dipped his face into the curve of my neck, running his hand all over the front of me. My back was pressed against his chest while he nibbled my skin and grabbed at all of me. He reached between my legs, playing and moaning as I moved my whole body against his.

Finally I bent forward, grabbing on to the cold glass of the window, my palms and fingers spread. He thrust into me, and I cried out in pleasure. It had been so long—years—and I felt completely stretched by him. He stayed slow for a little bit, whispering in my ear how amazing I felt, telling me he couldn't stop. I barely understood him as my legs shook, and I let out a yelp with every thrust from him. My breasts pushed against the glass, and the cold of the window chilled and engorged my nipples.

Bent over, his hand holding up my body, pressed together in sweat and desire, he finished. As soon as he did, with a final hard push, he pulled me against him again. I felt his chest move up and down against my back and the air from his lips against my cheek. I reached back to hold on to his shoulders, and we stayed that way, standing weakly for a minute.

In the distance I heard a small buzzing, like a tiny engine. I thought very little of it until I remembered that I was pressed against the window of the conference room. I remembered that we weren't in a private space—we were in the office.

The cleaning crew had made its way to our floor and was in the hallway, vacuuming their way to us.

Zion and I laughed and sheepishly rushed to the pile of clothes on the floor. I was flushed with embarrassment but still kept a smile on my face. When I looked at him, he was beaming widely as well. We made it out before the cleaning crew even noticed they weren't alone in the office.

Twelve

I climbed to the top of the building and blissfully jumped off the edge.

Falling for Zion was like feeling the descent from many stories up without ever hitting the ground. That night in the conference room, we gave everything to each other, opening up completely.

Sure, it was amazing sex, but afterward Zion spent the night whispering into my ear how badly he wanted to be with me, how much he needed me, how much he couldn't live without the feeling between us. I reciprocated his sentiments, and we spent the night wrapped up in each other's arms.

The next day was the first seminar, and the Art of Wealth was born. I walked into the event feeling lighter and fearless. If it went off perfectly, or even if it hit some obstacles, there was nothing I couldn't handle that day.

Zion was a vision on the stage. He didn't stick to his note cards or any rules really, but he was perfect in the setting. He was a confident, smart salesman. Almost all the attendees signed up for a ZB Financial investment package. I was smiling from ear to ear for the entire day.

Even Frederick, Marcus, and Cece, who had spent years seeing Zion in action, remarked that there was something extra to his swagger that day. He was at his best. Afterward we went out to celebrate a successful day at—strangely enough—La Matadora. I wondered whether Zion had picked the club as a way to signify something between the two of us.

Megan came along, locked in arms with Cece, looking just as happy as I felt. I was at ease around everyone, as they had become my close friends, and I was glad to be celebrating one of the biggest accomplishments of my career with them. We all toasted our successful day with flutes of champagne.

The most exciting part of the night was hiding what was going on between Zion and me from the team. Although we tried to maintain professional demeanors throughout the day, we couldn't help treat each other with more attention than usual. As he stood with the team and clients at the seminar, he'd shake hands and stand next to me, letting his fingertips brush my side. No one noticed the subtle brushes and looks throughout the day, but they left me crazy and craving him.

At La Matadora we sat on the same barstools where we had met, facing the dance floor together, discussing the day with the small crowd gathered around us. He sat so close that I felt the heat of his body radiating onto every part that made contact with mine. The side of his leg met my bare thigh. His forearm grazed my rib cage. It was all one big tease.

As the night went on, everyone went for the dance floor. The salsa music was rippling through my body more than usual. I was full of energy and ready to dance with Zion for the rest of the night.

"Ms. Bouvier, may I?" Marcus offered, putting his hand out for mine.

I looked sideways at Zion, who smiled a little. I accepted and walked to the dance floor with Marcus. We were close in age, and he was certainly a great dancer. We laughed and joked with all the other ZB team members in the middle of the crowded floor. All the while I felt Zion's eyes on me from his seat at the bar. I danced a little closer with Marcus, trying to entice Zion over, letting myself be a little devious.

Sure enough, Zion appeared close by, tapping Marcus on the shoulder. He gracefully pulled me away to dance. It was innocent at first, since we were still in sight of the team, but slowly, as he moved us away and deeper into the crowd, it became hotter. Once we were far enough away, Zion pulled me up against him and leaned down to look into my eyes. He was hard against my thigh, and I melted into him, moving exactly as he did. We were one body with the music, the other dancers pushing us closer together. It was exciting to think that our coworkers were only a few feet away, unaware of how much Zion and I were sweating onto each other's bodies.

I ground my hips hard against his, letting him know what was running through my head. He pushed a hand between us, dipping it underneath my short skirt and finding me eager for him. He almost made me explode right there on the dance floor with his fingertips rubbing against me. The beat of the music pulsated through me, and I was responding to the heat of our passion.

"Let's get out of here," Zion whispered in my ear.

We escaped from the dance floor and slipped out of the club unnoticed by anyone on the team. We giggled at the thought of our scheme and affectionately embraced and kissed as we awaited the arrival of Zion's Aston Martin convertible. Zion tipped the valet, dropped the top, and sped off down Brickell Avenue. The full moon illuminated the sky as we drove down the highway. It was the perfect ending to a most perfect day. I smiled to myself as the wind blew through my hair. I couldn't believe I'd captured the heart of one of Miami's most coveted bachelors.

I woke up the next day in Zion's huge Biscayne Bay home, which was on the water and had too many rooms to count. My head was spinning from last night's celebration. It was hazy to me how we had gotten here, but as I fumbled around, I saw empty champagne bottles and my clothes and his from the night before strewn across the living-room floor. I vaguely remembered being on my knees on the thick shag carpet with Zion standing over me, and with that thought, my legs ached from the acrobatics of the night before.

I found Zion in the kitchen, with coffee in hand and one already set up for me. I walked into his arms and wanted to stay there for the entire day.

Unfortunately, with the Art of Wealth jump-off, we were busier than ever. The days started to blur together, between early mornings at the office running from place to place to make the final arrangements for seminars and handling the new client list, to long nights at Zion's large house. He showered me with even more attention and care now, having elaborate dinners brought to his house for us to eat on the bedroom floor whenever we felt hungry after another round of lovemaking. I hadn't been back to my own condo in such a long time that I had to send Megan to check on the mail.

Sometimes, when Zion left early in the morning for a flight to Europe or New York between events, I'd wake up alone in his house and wander through the long hallways. On weekends, if he was gone, I'd swim a few laps in the pool and lie in the sun, exhausted from how much he'd been working me, professionally and otherwise. I hadn't made it to the gym in a while either, and from all the decadently rich food and pampering, I'd put on just a little weight around the middle. I still looked great in a bikini, and that new red lace teddy Zion had brought home for me, but I had to get back into my routine when things calmed down.

Often I found boxes with my name written on tags attached to them. They'd appear on the pillow next to me, on the bathroom counter, or in my purse. Zion gave me Tiffany diamond tennis bracelets; Dior, Chanel, and Hermes designer dresses; suits; and handbags—a never-ending stream of gifts. Sometimes I'd argue that I didn't need all those gifts, that I had enough money to buy whatever I wanted, that I wasn't a woman to be spoiled because I could buy my own things. Zion would laugh and explain that since I was staying at his place all the time, I didn't have any clothes there. It was the least he could do.

One night, when I mentioned I needed to run home just for one thing or another, Zion wrapped an arm around me and said into my shoulder, "Just bring everything here. I don't want you to leave."

I was becoming used to the feel of his home and even occasionally thought about what it would be like to stay there permanently, giving in to each other's needs all the time. I laughed, thinking I certainly couldn't work for him professionally and maintain what we had personally for long. My leg muscles just wouldn't be able to take it.

Finally we reached the last event of our tour. The Art of Wealth was closing out its circuit with an event at the Ritz Carlton in Boca Raton. It wasn't a large event, but the pockets of those attending were almost bottomless. As with every other seminar Zion led, he was on point and perfect in his presentation.

As he interacted with potential clients, bouncing from one topic to another, weaving a story together for them regarding their future needs and pitching how he could help, I felt my love for him pulsing through me. He would look at me and smile from across the room, and I knew I was head over heels in love with him. I could tell he was just as crazy about me, since he wanted me with him each night, taking care to please me in every way.

This was when I discovered the true deepness of what love could be—how proud you can be of another person and how much it hurts to be away from him. Zion and I were giving each other everything we had in all those moments together. I felt the safest I ever had as I lay between his arms in the morning, breathing softly through the early rays of sun. Every inch of him was perfect, and I couldn't imagine it any other way.

At the end of the final Art of Wealth event, my contract was up. There was talk of rebuilding the tour for a second round of seminars in a few months. The tour would cover more cities in the United States. When Zion asked me to stay on for the second round, I declined. I was ready to take my career to new heights, to expand and learn more in my industry—not to mention that I was concerned about continuing a professional relationship with the man I loved. He was still stubborn and a workaholic after all. And I was ready to be my own boss again.

I had all my things ready to be moved back to Bouvier Public Relations. Clara and the team set me up with a sweet care package on the day after the final seminar. It was bittersweet, but I knew being tangled up in Zion's life meant I certainly would see the team again. I definitely would see Cece more frequently, as he and Megan were nearly inseparable.

After the dinner to celebrate my final day at ZB Financial, the exhaustion of it all hit me. I turned down invitations to continue on for the night and decided to head back to my condo for some much-needed recovery. Zion walked me out of the restaurant and kissed me good-bye on the hot Miami sidewalk. After a hot shower at home, I was instantly asleep in the comfort of my bed, which must have been missing me too, with all the welcome I felt when I fell into it.

I woke up with a man's arms around me. Zion was fast asleep, with a little snore escaping him, in my bed. I was startled and sat up. He shook a little as he woke up with me.

"'Morning, babe. I missed you. I couldn't stand to be alone," he said groggily.

"How did you get in here?" I asked.

"Oh, I know the doorman."

"You couldn't. He's only been here a week. He's new," I said, pushing him playfully.

"Okay, fine. I used the spare key you left at my house for emergencies. Don't you remember?" He was smiling devilishly, and I couldn't help laugh.

I'd completely forgotten about that. But I was more than pleased that he longed to be near me.

"I have a surprise for you," he said, stretching and rolling out of bed. He walked across my bedroom, naked except for his boxers. I admired him as he walked, my heart filling with the same warmness of love that had become so familiar.

"Oh, yeah? Where?" I asked with a playful tone.

He turned around and raised an eyebrow at me. "Not like that. It's in the living room. Close your eyes," he said as he led me out of the bedroom. I followed him with the sheet wrapped around me.

"Okay. Hold out your hand," he said.

I couldn't stand the suspense of it all, but I obediently followed his instructions.

"Okay, open your eyes, Omega."

To my pleasant surprise, in my hands was a beautifully wrapped box. I carefully opened it. Glowing before my eyes was something I'd always dreamed of—an elegant diamond-and-gold Omega watch. It was absolutely stunning and must have cost a fortune.

"This is a small thank-you for all the work you've done, Omega, and a reminder of the time—no pun intended—that we've spent together on the Art of Wealth," Zion said, leaning down to kiss me on the cheek. "Wait, there's more."

Next to my coffee table was a set of dark, leather Louis Vuitton luggage. The pieces were beautiful, but seeing them made me a little confused. I turned to Zion, waiting for his cue.

"Get packing," he said.

I thought over what I'd be packing for. Moving in? Going to New York? I wasn't sure what he had planned.

"What should I pack?" I asked.

"Definitely clothes for warm weather...and some of those bikinis I saw you in at my pool, please," he answered.

By 2:00 p.m. that day, we set out on a short flight to Owen Roberts Airport on Grand Cayman. Zion described it as a well-needed rest from the success of the Art of Wealth. There was no date set for our return, and it would be just the two of us.

The water looked crystal blue out of the airplane window, and the islands below seemed like little patches of land lined with sand. It was gorgeous even from thousands of feet up. Zion read the newspaper on the flight as he sat next to me and held my hand.

He had rented a bungalow on the ocean, right outside of George Town. The weather was hot, with a breeze, and the house was open, with air flowing easily between every room. I set my bags down and headed straight for the beach, reaching the water and dipping my feet at the edge of the ocean. I sat down in the sand, listening to the lull of the waves and watching the water wash over my toes again and again. I sat there for a long time, reflecting over the last year of my life and how I'd ended up on this beach.

It was perfectly quiet except for the ocean. I felt as if I could weep from happiness right there, with my head between my knees. I was on my own in the sunshine, enjoying the peace of it, then heard the crunch of sand behind me as Zion came and sat in the sand next to me, saying nothing. We watched the ocean together.

Later on that night, after a long nap, we went into town. Zion rented a moped to explore the island, so we leapt on and headed out just as the sun was setting. The streets were filled with tourists, decked out in canvas and pastel floral outfits. Locals were lined up on the street selling hats, driftwood, and souvenirs. Others sang as they played guitars or drums. After walking by popular restaurants and shops that mostly catered to European and American tourists, Zion explained that we should get back on the moped and out of town. I was starving.

"All the restaurants are here. Shouldn't we at least get some food to bring back to the house?" I asked.

"We're going to get food, just not here," he said.

We drove along the tiny road that ran along the sound, watching the anchored boats sway in the tide. We ended up in a less-populated part of the island, which was quick to get to, as Grand Cayman is only twenty-two miles long. Set up along the road was a light-blue restaurant. It was small, with a neon sign hanging in the window for Guinness beer. Apparently Guinness is one of the most popular beers on the islands, despite its origin in Ireland, or at least that's how Zion explained it.

A thick smell of fish and spices permeated the inside of the restaurant. Everyone sat at weathered, wooden-plank tables and feasted over paper plates. A shout came from behind the food counter, and a large woman ran around to the front of the restaurant to greet us. She hugged Zion tightly, and he laughed as she did. When she spoke to him, it was musical and loud, but in a language I couldn't understand. I could make out some English words. Things like *Miami, big suit,* and *swordfish* seeped through her sentences. Zion responded in a version of the language she used but more accented with American English. She spoke in what he told me was like Jamaican patois but singular to the Caymans. When she talked to me, it was in heavily accented English, and she hugged me tightly as well then rushed us both to sit down. Crouched over paper plates, we ate an entire fish—including the eyeballs and cheeks—with our fingers.

"Not that it isn't perfect, but what are we doing here?" I asked. It was a strange experience compared to the many luxurious ones we'd had together. I understood now that he frequented Grand Cayman enough to know it so well that everyone around recognized him. It wasn't just quick stops to check on his bank accounts there.

"I guess"—he paused and looked around, considering—"it reminds me of my father."

I had little knowledge of Zion's cultural background or his childhood, and now he was giving me a window to see it. It was a touching, intimate thing for him to do, and I felt closer to him for it.

More people stopped at our table, shaking Zion's hand and tossing jokes around. While he seemed to understand the local dialect, he also continued with other guests in Spanish. He seemed comfortable, much like when he was presenting for work or leading in the office or really doing anything anywhere. I was sitting with a man who could conquer anything or would at least fake it so well that he had everyone convinced. I smiled, because as much as everyone around was doting on him, I remembered how hard he'd been working lately to please me. I smiled, thinking of how addicted I was to it all.

Even at night in the islands, everything was bright and alive. The moonlight was full and lit up everything. There were few buildings and no streetlights to block out the expanse of stars in the sky. The ocean still lulled in the background. Riding on the back of the moped became a perfect moment, as I rested into Zion's back, completely relaxed. The salty air blew past us.

Now that the Art of Wealth circuit was over, our stay didn't have a set end date. Part of me wished that we'd never return, that this would be my new life—riding to our favorite restaurant, walking though the sand and water, without anything to worry about except pleasing each other.

Which was exactly what Zion set to doing when we got back to the house.

The windows were open, with the breeze blowing through every room. He gently tugged at my cotton sundress as he kissed me. I tugged at his belt loops, and we slowly undressed each other, savoring the feeling of the clothes moving across our skin.

I climbed into bed, motioning for him to follow, but he stood at the end, watching me instead.

"Stay there. I'll be right back," he said, and left the room.

I was already turned on. I spread out on the comforter and closed my eyes. I ran my hands over my own body, reaching between my legs and thinking of what Zion would see when he came back to the room.

I was so close to orgasm on my own when I felt something surprisingly cold touch my breasts. I sat up to see Zion holding an ice cube against me and smiling. He pulled my hand away, stopping me. He ran the ice down my stomach and over my thighs. I had chills even in the heat and humidity. As with much of Zion's lovemaking, it was slow and torturous in all the right ways.

The ice melted quickly, so he grabbed another. I heard the clink of the glass when he retrieved it, and it sent a shiver through my body.

He stood next to the bed, tracing cold lines over me, his erection within inches of me. I reached out for it, and he groaned in response. I smiled, knowing I could torture him too. So I did.

After a minute he crawled into bed next to me, not being able to take the teasing any longer.

His motions were slow and powerful. He held my face as he moved in and out of me, his eyes holding intensely onto mine. We rode the wave of an orgasm together and both cried out with it then collapsed.

I fell asleep with his heavy breaths echoing through me. I fell asleep knowing I loved Zion more than I'd thought I could.

We spent four more days on the island. We swam in the ocean every day and walked for miles through the town.

We planned to fly out late in the evening, so on the last day I walked through George Town to do some shopping. In town there were high-class boutiques as well as big shops from designers like Cartier and Prada. Although I was reluctant to leave the amazing island that evening, I was ready to get back to Miami and back to work in my old office. I had exciting plans for Bouvier Public Relations.

Through the crowd of tourists, I spotted a tall figure that my eyes recognized before my mind could pull the pieces together. I stared for a minute, standing still in the road. I was confused for a while, and then I became a little angry about his presence. I returned quickly to the house to find Zion.

"I saw Reesey in George Town," I told him.

"Can't be. He's in Miami," he answered.

"No. I saw him here. Are you doing business here? I thought this was just a vacation for us," I said, getting more upset. It wasn't all that surprising that Reesey was there, since he seemed to have some kind of security ties to Zion, but it bothered me to have him around. He was a generally unnerving guy. Zion knew my feelings about him and hadn't told me he would be there.

"No, babe. He can't be here. You must have seen someone who looks like him. Lots of guys of his type come here."

"Fine," I finished, and decided not to push the issue. I was certain it was Reesey, but I supposed Zion could have been right.

Miami was almost exactly as we had left it, and I was excited to be home. Still I was a little confused and irritated from the conversation about Reesey earlier in the day. I told Zion I wanted to spend the night at my condo. We'd been together almost every minute together on the trip, and while I loved it, I felt the need to check on the life I'd left behind. Zion agreed and explained that he had things to attend to at his house as well. We parted with a deep, loving kiss. I walked into my condo with a huge smile on my face and slept soundly, imagining I could still hear the Caribbean waves right outside my door.

The next morning was like any other. I turned on my coffeemaker and slipped into a kimono then read through the paper. Because of my hectic work schedule, my kitchen counter barely had been used since I'd moved in, but I thought about changing the granite style to match the type the beach house had in Grand Cayman.

The TV was turned to the news, but the volume was turned down low. I glanced up and thought I saw a familiar face but couldn't believe it, so I immediately dismissed it from my mind. Nevertheless I continued to stare at the screen. And still that familiar face was there. My hands shook uncontrollably and I dropped my coffee cup, spilling coffee all over the counter. Very slowly, dreading what I was about to hear, I found the remote and turned up the sound. A third glance at the screen told me I wasn't mistaken. That face was familiar to me for a reason. I heard the news anchor say, "Zion Bram of ZB Financial Services was arrested at nine o'clock this morning on counts of money laundering and securities and investment fraud."

Thirteen

Zion Bram was multicultural before he knew he was multicultural. He was multicultural, in fact, before such a term even existed. In those days, you were just called mixed (and that was a polite term for what you were). Zion's father was of Afro-Caribbean descent, and his mother was of Polish extraction. The two of them met while attending Temple University in Philadelphia. They were married shortly after, and then along came baby Zion, even more shortly after. The two events were so close together that people quite naturally whispered about someone putting the cart before the horse. But it didn't matter because no matter what anyone else said, Zion's parents had married out of love, not expediency.

They were proud of their Zion, who excelled at education and athletics as a youth. One teacher characterized him as a "shrewd student," which Zion realized wasn't totally a compliment but decided to take it as one anyway. He knew the teacher was really saying that he knew just how much he needed to study in order to make it sound as if he knew everything about a given subject. It was a natural ability that would go on to serve him well throughout his life.

Because she was a practicing Jew, Zion's mother insisted he become a bar mitzvah when he turned thirteen. He was indifferent to the ceremony, which marks a Jewish boy becoming a man, until he heard from his friends how lucrative a rite of passage it could be.

Zion loved earning money. That's why he had worked after school at his uncle's pharmacy, where he helped out around the nonpharmaceutical side of the business and also made deliveries to various homebound customers. His uncle also had a store car that he used for deliveries, but Zion was too young to drive it. The vehicle was so battered from all the teenage drivers who used it that it looked like it had seen action in a demolition derby.

Zion studied hard for his bar mitzvah, and when the big day came, he recited his haftorah and Torah portions perfectly, albeit with the slightest Afro-Caribbean accent, which gave a unique sound to the tropes of the Hebrew alphabet.

After the Saturday-morning service during which he became a man in the Jewish religion, his parents held a dinner and dance in his honor at a nearby catering hall. It was a lavish affair, with about two hundred guests, all of them dressed in their finest—the men in tuxes (most of them rented) and the women in gowns (most of them purchased just for the occasion). Zion's father looked handsome in his tux and his mother beautiful in her gown. They were youthful enough so that, if seen in a certain light, they almost could have passed for high-school students on their way to their senior prom.

The event featured a traditional sit-down dinner as well as a nine-piece band that played songs more to please the taste of his parents than Zion and his friends. Zion had invited a mix of boys and girls who danced together despite a basic unfamiliarity with the music being played. The band was fronted by a beautiful woman who looked a lot like Billie Holiday and solidified the comparison by wearing a gardenia in her hair. Zion noticed that she kept giving him the eye, which made him inwardly shiver and wonder whether she was just politely singing to the bar mitzvah boy or had something else in mind entirely, but he chalked up the latter to his overactive imagination.

Zion dutifully spent the evening accepting gifts—the pockets of his suit were stuffed with envelopes containing cash or checks—making speeches, listening to speeches, horsing around with his male friends, dancing with his female friends, and accepting hugs and kisses from his relatives and friends of his parents. It was a wild mix of an affair, what with his father's Afro-Caribbean family and his mother's Jewish family in attendance. What a beautiful thing it was to see the two sides of the family mingling and helping Zion understand what a special day this was for him.

And then there was the singer, whose exotic name Zion never would forget—Gardenia, just like the flower in her hair. At one point she jumped down from the bandstand and asked the bar mitzvah boy to dance with her. The band was playing a slow number, so Zion had no choice but to put his body against hers. He couldn't believe it; he'd never been so close to a member of the opposite sex before. He could feel her shapely body and smell her perfume, and its scent this close to her intoxicated him. He felt dizzy and was afraid he would pass out right there and then. But then the dance would end, which was something he definitely didn't want to happen. So he willed himself to remain functional.

And then there was something else. Zion noticed he was getting an erection from being so close to Gardenia. He felt embarrassed and tried to put some distance between her and himself so she wouldn't notice the effect she was having on him. But instead of allowing him to stay distant, Gardenia pulled him in closer again so that his enlarged penis was rubbing right up against her. This time Zion knew he would pass out for sure.

Fortunately, before that could happen, the song ended, and Gardenia returned to the bandstand for the next number. Zion breathed a sigh of intense relief and looked around. All his friends were staring at him. The boys couldn't believe his good fortune, and the girls decided maybe they should reevaluate Zion as future boyfriend material. Whether or not Gardenia knew, she had upped Zion's popularity with one simple act of generosity.

About an hour into their set, the band took a half-hour break. During this time the dessert, an elaborate affair, was served. It looked delicious, and Zion couldn't wait to eat it. But he never got a chance to, because, out of the corner of his eye, he noticed Gardenia eyeing him from the service door that led to the catering hall's kitchen.

All the guests were so engrossed in eating their dessert that they didn't notice when Zion got up from his seat and approached Gardenia, who stood provocatively in the door to the service hallway.

"Hello," she said in that same breathy voice she used when she sang. Zion could feel it vibrate in the lowest parts of his anatomy.

"Hello," he said, hoping his voice wouldn't break and give away how immature he really was—and how nervous.

"You're a wonderful dancer," she said.

"Thank you."

"Do you have a girlfriend?"

Zion thought about lying, but an instinct that would serve him well in later years told him it would be better to tell her the truth.

"No."

"I don't believe it. A boy as handsome as you? So well-spoken and such a good dancer, and you don't have a girlfriend? Impossible."

Zion smiled. He didn't know whether Gardenia was being serious or lightly making fun of him.

"You know," she said in a hushed voice, "what the girls like?"

Zion had no idea and shook his head, too afraid to speak.

"They like a man with confidence. And do you know what builds confidence?"

Again Zion was afraid his voice might crack if he answered aloud and settled for a shrug.

"Experience," she said. It was one word but freighted with meaning.

Zion nodded, hoping to seem wise beyond his years.

"And do you know how you get experience?" Gardenia asked.

"No," Zion croaked out.

"You follow me," she said.

She moved down the hallway that led to the kitchen. She didn't look behind to see whether Zion was following her. From the way she walked, swaying rhythmically from side to side, as though she were still on the dance floor or bandstand, she knew he was helpless to do anything but.

She stopped about halfway down the hallway, next to a closed door, which she opened and entered. Zion followed, having no idea where he was going but not really caring as long as he was in the company of this dazzling older woman.

He looked around and saw the room was empty, except for coats and other outer garments and empty musical instrument cases. He realized this was the band's break room, except none of the band members was in sight.

In addition to all her other abilities, Gardenia must have been able to read his mind because she said, "They're all outside on a cigarette break. We have this room all to ourselves."

And in such a way that she thought he wouldn't notice (although he actually did), she flipped the latch on the door so no one from outside could enter. She stood in front of the door, her hands behind her back, and gave Zion a frank appraisal with her eyes. Zion couldn't recall anyone ever looking at him this closely before, and it made him feel self-conscious, as though he were standing naked in front of this gorgeous woman with a flower in her hair. The thought of it gave him the chills and made all his body hair stand up, as though at attention.

Zion had no idea where to stand or what to do. Gardenia moved away from the door and slowly approached him, like a predator moving in on her prey. Zion wasn't sure what she had in mind, so he took one step back. For every step forward Gardenia took, he took one step backward. This went on across the checkered linoleum floor until Zion found himself with his back against a counter that ran along one wall of the room.

With nowhere else to go, he was helpless to prevent Gardenia from moving into a fatal proximity with his body, with virtually the same degree of closeness as before, but then they had been dancing, and right now they weren't.

Zion scrambled up on the counter and sat facing Gardenia, who looked him straight in the eye and said, "Today you are a man."

Zion gulped, wondering what she meant by that remark.

A half hour later, the break was over, and the band crushed out their cigarettes and returned to the bandstand. Gardenia unlocked the break-room door, and she and Zion returned to the ballroom but made their entrances separately. Gardenia was now fifty dollars richer, thanks to one of Zion's gifts, and Zion, thanks to Gardenia, could now proudly—and truly—proclaim, "Today I am a man."

Making his way across the dance floor as stealthily as possible, Zion was intercepted by his parents. He wondered whether they would notice there was something different about him and hoped they wouldn't. That would raise too many questions he couldn't even begin to figure out how to answer.

"Where have you been?" his father asked.

Good, Zion thought. *He suspects nothing.*

"We've been looking for you," said his mother. She seemed equally oblivious to her son's change of status.

Zion tried hard to think up an excuse, but his recent activities had fogged his brain to the point where a lie would no longer come readily to his lips. Instead he hemmed and hawed, hoping to buy himself a little time. Fortunately his parents leapt in to fill the conversational gap.

"I hope you weren't out with your friends gambling," his father chided him.

"No, of course not," Zion said, protesting mightily but being careful not to overdo it.

"That's good," Zion's mother said, "because that's a terrible hobby."

Zion didn't care if that's what they thought, as long as they weren't suspicious of his *new* hobby.

He looked at the bandstand. Gardenia once again was cooing into the microphone. She tried to make eye contact with him, but he had a difficult time meeting her gaze. He turned his attention back to his parents. His mother was smoothing down his hair, one of her usual preoccupations, even when there wasn't one hair out of place.

"Your great-uncle, Lester, has been looking for you," she said.

"He has a very special gift for you," his father added.

Zion knew Lester but not well. He was the mystery man of the family. He was Zion's mother's uncle, and he was some kind of world traveler. Nobody exactly knew what he did for a living, but it had something to do with finance and involved him traveling all over the globe. This was why he was seldom at home, except to attend the occasional family event, such as Zion's bar mitzvah. For reasons unknown he always had declared that Zion was one of his favorite relatives.

Zion's mother and father led him to the table where Great-Uncle Lester was seated with the rest of the single relatives (also known as the "outcasts table"). He was sitting there, enjoying the music, but from the look in his eye, he was especially enjoying Gardenia's performance. He sat there leaning on an ivory-headed cane that gave him a distinguished look. In his Panama suit, he looked every inch the world traveler he claimed to be.

"Hello, Zion," he said, leaning forward and taking Zion's hand. For the first time, Zion noticed that his great-uncle's hands were unusually rough for someone who supposedly worked in an office and dealt with money and papers all day. "Mazel tov on becoming a bar mitzvah today."

"Thank you, Uncle Lester," Zion said.

"This is a special day, and I have a special gift for you," Great-Uncle Lester said with a special emphasis in his voice.

Zion waited to be presented with yet another envelope, but instead Lester produced, from seemingly out of nowhere, a wrapped gift, which he pushed across the table at Zion, who just stood there and stared at the gift.

"Go ahead," his great-uncle urged. "Open it."

Zion did so, tearing through the gift wrap that covered a medium-size gift box. And when he opened the box, he saw, to his disappointment, that all it contained was a book. He took out the book and read the title: *The Richest Man in Babylon*, by George S. Clason. Zion tried to hide his disappointment. How could a book be a special gift?

He must have been quiet for too long because his mother surreptitiously nudged him and said, "What do you say, Zion?"

"Thank you, Uncle Lester," Zion said, trying to fake as much enthusiasm as possible.

"I'm telling you, boy," Great-Uncle Lester said, "one day this book will change your life."

Zion was anxious to rejoin his friends. His mother could tell and said, "I'll take this for you." After saying good-bye to her Uncle Lester and giving him a kiss on the forehead, she put the book back in the box and took the box to their table. Zion went over to his friend, who asked him about the old man with the cane.

"Oh, he's just a relative," Zion said dismissively. He looked at the bandstand, where Gardenia had just moved into a quick-tempo number. She was so sexy standing behind the mike and gyrating in place. Zion looked at his friends and saw that they too were captivated by her movements. He wanted to tell them what had transpired with Gardenia in the break room but couldn't bring himself to do so. He felt it somehow would diminish Gardenia's special bar mitzvah gift to him.

One week later, Zion's parents saw that he hadn't taken Great-Uncle Lester's book out from its box. They expressed their disappointment that he hadn't even bothered to look at it.

"It looks boring," Zion said in his own defense. "It looks like a book for school."

"Well, how do you know if you haven't even looked at it?" his mother asked, her logic irrefutable and unassailable. Zion had no answer, so he remained silent. "I want you to read that book… right away. And then I want you to write to Uncle Lester and tell him how much you enjoyed it."

"Yes, Mom," Zion said, capitulating.

That night, after he had done his homework, Zion finally took out the book and grudgingly began to read it. At first it was a boring slog, as coma-inducing as any book from one of his classes. It talked about wealth management and money and how to make more of it. Zion had no objection to being rich. In fact it was one of his secret goals in life. And here was a book that told him how he could achieve it. Once he understood this, he read through the book with a fervor that almost frightened his parents. They'd never seen him so engrossed in a book. And when he read the last page and closed the book, he knew it somehow had changed his life. It provided a map to a hidden treasure. It was an even better gift than the one Gardenia had given him.

The following day, after writing a sincere thank-you note to Great-Uncle Lester, Zion decided to put some of the precepts from the book into action.

The first thing he did, without his parents' knowledge or permission, was withdraw all the bar mitzvah money he had received from his savings account at the bank. The next thing he did was arrange for a wager. His parents had been right: he was incorrigible when it came to gambling.

At his uncle's pharmacy, on a day when he knew his uncle wouldn't be in the store, he approached Philly, a teenage boy who drove the battered store car for deliveries.

"Hey, Philly. How's it going?"

"Not bad. How's it going with you?"

"Okay," Zion replied. "Hey, Philly, I got a question for you. How many deliveries do you think you make an hour?"

"In the car? Three or four. Depends on how spread out they are. Why?"

"I was just wondering," Zion said, then added, "Hey, you up for a bet?"

Philly looked at him suspiciously. "What kind of bet?

"I bet I can make more deliveries in an hour than you can."

Philly laughed. "You? On foot? And me in the car? That's impossible. That's a sucker's bet."

"So if it's a sucker's bet, you should take it."

Philly doubled down on his suspicious look. "How much you got?" he asked.

Zion took out a thick wad of bills and held it up for Philly to see. The size of the wad made Philly let out an impressed whistle.

"So what do you say?" Zion asked tauntingly. "You in?"

Philly reached into his pocket and pulled out an equally thick wad of bills, his accumulated tips as a delivery boy. "I'm in," he said.

With two stock boys acting as judges (and taking side bets from the rest of the pharmacy crew), Zion and Philly made up the rules for the contest. In exactly one hour, they would return to the pharmacy. The one with the most receipts from customers would be declared the winner.

"Five...four...three...two...one...go," the judges said, simultaneously ending their countdown. Philly gunned the store car's engine and took off across the parking lot. At the same time, Zion sprinted out of the parking lot and took off down the street.

One hour later both boys were back in the parking lot. Zion was huffing and puffing from exhaustion. Philly was barely breaking a sweat. They were surrounded by the judges and the rest of the pharmacy crew. Both boys handed over their receipts for the judges to tally. In the end, in the course of one hour, Philly had made four deliveries and Zion had made seven.

Philly couldn't believe it; he could scarcely concede that Zion had beaten him. He looked royally pissed, but there was nothing he could do. He couldn't welsh on his bet, not with the rest of the pharmacy crew watching. Reluctantly he handed over his wad of cash to Zion.

Zion pocketed it and held out his hand for Philly to take. "No hard feelings?" he said.

Philly turned his back on him. "I got more deliveries to make." He got back into his car and pulled out of the parking lot with loud a squeal.

"Sore loser," Zion said to the pharmacy crew as they broke up to return to the store.

Zion made it back to the bank in time to redeposit his bar mitzvah money along with the money he had received from Philly. But before he did, he stopped and paid off the seven boys who'd actually made the deliveries for him and allowed him to beat Philly. That's what *The Richest Man in Babylon* had inspired him to do. It was the proverbial gift that kept on giving, in the words of the TV commercial, as the book the mysterious Great-Uncle Lester had given him would set the course of his life for decades to come.

Fourteen

It was one thing to see your lover arrested for fraud and other charges and taken away in handcuffs making headline news, right in front of your shocked eyes. It was quite another, I considered, as I stared disconsolately through the iron bars at the concrete blocks that made up my jail cell, to find yourself arrested along with him, especially when you weren't guilty of the charges against you.

It was a sad and ironic state of affairs. I was someone who'd never gotten so much as a parking ticket or a jaywalking summons. I'd been scrupulous about never being issued a library fine. I'd led a law-abiding life. And yet here I was, in jail, charged with being my lover's accomplice in bilking clients out of millions of dollars.

Yes, according to the papers filed in Dade County District Court, Zion Bram stood accused of using his company, ZB Financial Services, as a massive con game to part gullible clients from their money. It wasn't bad enough that he had ripped off his wealthy clients, but through the wealth-management seminars that I'd helped to organize and promote, his list of victims included many ordinary people who had put their entire life savings in his hands. And where was that money now? According to the FBI, the SEC, and numerous local law-enforcement agencies, a whole host of Caribbean and Swiss bank accounts in Zion's name had been fattened with his ill-gotten gains.

It had been a whirlwind couple of days since Zion's arrest, and then mine, and the only good thing about being temporarily stuck in this jail cell was the fact that I had plenty of time to contemplate what had transpired, as well as my current situation. The only distraction I had was my cellmates, or "the girls," as I liked to refer to them. "The girls" consisted of several drunks, a drug addict, a prostitute and a shoplifter. The shoplifter, an obvious kleptomaniac, was the only other middle-class denizen of this inhospitable environment, and the two of us clung together for mutual support. The shoplifter—Doris was her name—was from Coconut Grove, a well-to-do Miami enclave. Her husband was out of town, and she was having a difficult time making bail. She was a tasteful lady, dressed in classic Ann Taylor attire, and she stuck out about as much as I did in the Versace dress I'd been arrested in. If there had been a contest for best-dressed inmate of the Dade County Jail, we probably would have tied for the honor. And if we weren't released soon, we'd end up trading in our outfits for the orange jumpsuits all new prisoners were forced to wear. And neither of us had a clue as how to accessorize with that.

In the days following Zion's arrest, I had read through every newspaper I could get my hands on and, from the articles written about him, was able to piece together, in jigsaw-puzzle fashion, a fairly comprehensive picture of what he was being charged with.

Basically the government was accusing Zion of operating a large-scale Ponzi scheme targeting innocent investors, many of whom were African-American and Latino. Although I'd been unaware of this, Zion previously had operated his financial services company in several different states. When one state would shut down his operation, he'd start up all over again in another state, with a new name for his company. In his brashest move, he even had managed to seduce and swindle a sheriff in Charlotte, North Carolina, out of millions of dollars from her own department. Setting up shop in Miami was ZB Financial's latest iteration. But unbeknown to me, the Miami scene had become too limiting for him, and Zion had begun to open up companies in other countries as well.

It wasn't only Zion and myself who'd been arrested. The authorities also had picked up Reesey, who, it seemed, was Zion's bagman. That's why I'd spotted him during my romantic Caribbean getaway with Zion (even though I wasn't supposed to catch sight of him). He had been making a cash deposit to one of Zion's banks. Also arrested were Margaret and several other accomplices in New York and Miami who were members of Zion's team of confidence men, helping to swindle money out of the savings of people who were trying to make better lives for themselves.

The most shocking thing about Zion's arrest was the fact that, in addition to the FBI, SEC, and local law enforcement, he also had been under investigation by the CIA. "They thought he might be laundering money for foreign drug cartels," I muttered to myself, a sentence I couldn't believe had actually come out of my mouth. I seemed, at this point, to be living someone else's life, like a character in a bad telenovela.

Since we had become lovers, Zion had given me many gifts—clothing, jewelry, artwork, even an Aston Martin. After Zion's arrest, then subsequently mine, I had to appear in court for the arraignment and bail hearing. "Embezzlement, fraud, insider trading, money laundering, Ponzi scheme, et cetera, et cetera," were the charges. It felt like the list of crimes was never ending. I desperately tried to separate myself from Zion and the rest of his con-artist cronies. I swore to the judge that I was innocent of all charges and that I didn't want to be referred to as a defendant. Instead the judge decreed that I could be categorized as a respondent. It had the same meaning, but it was important for me to distinguish myself from Zion and the rest of his coconspirators before the court. Despite this, according to an assets-forfeiture ruling, the government seized all of Zion's gifts to me and froze all my bank accounts until the conclusion of the trial. The only thing I was able to hold on to was my condo, which I had purchased well before meeting Zion. When my bail was set, I used it as collateral for my release from jail.

The first thing I did when I got home was take a very long shower in scalding hot water, determined to get the jailhouse stench off my body.

The next day I went to see my new lawyer. His name was Reuben Sifuentes, and he was a cousin of my former employer. I already knew him by reputation. Reuben was one of those old-school lawyers who dressed like an aristocratic dandy. A lot of bold, three-piece, pinstripe suits made up his wardrobe, along with striped suspenders, shirts with contrasting collars, and loud polka-dot bow ties. The color combinations were enough to make you think you were inhabiting someone's psychedelic dream. But from a public relations point of view, I understood that Sifuentes's sartorial choices were more than just mere eccentricity; they were a canny way to set himself off from the rest of his brethren in the legal profession. His beyond-*GQ* suits were a constant advertisement for himself as a gentleman barrister.

Sifuentes was also his own best public relations man. He took on the highest of high-profile cases and was known for giving impromptu press conferences on the courthouse steps, with those reporters covering the courthouse beat hanging on to his every word. He had a silver-tongued gift for florid oratory. Sifuentes was also a master manipulator of the court of public opinion, hoping to impress a potential jury even before they were seated in the jury box. Although he sometimes came off as eccentric, Sifuentes was about as crazy as the proverbial fox in the henhouse, and there wasn't a move he made that wasn't plotted out in advance, like a practiced tactician prepares for a major battle.

Sifuentes's office was located in an older section of Miami, and unlike his clothes, his office was very plain. He chose not to spend money where it wouldn't be seen by the general public. His secretary led me into his office, and I sat down in a chair opposite his modest-looking desk. A minute later Reuben Sifuentes entered from his private bathroom and came over to shake my hand.

"A pleasure to meet you, Ms. Bouvier," he said, as though this were a pleasant social occasion instead of a strategy session to decide how he would keep me from going to prison.

"My cousin tells me very good things about you," he continued, as he seated himself behind his desk.

"I enjoyed working for him," I said.

"My cousin is an excellent judge of character. And if he says you're innocent, I'll take him at his word."

In my mind I offered up thanks to my former employer for believing in me.

"That's very nice to hear," I said.

"Unfortunately," he continued, "my cousin's word has no sway in court. So you and I are going to have to find a way to get you out of this mess."

"And how do you plan to do that?" I asked. That was the $64,000 question, as they say, and I knew I probably would have to pony up much more than that in order for Reuben Sifuentes to prevent me from going to prison.

"It's not going to be easy, Ms. Bouvier. I'm not going to mince words with you or make any false promises. I've heard through the grapevine that Zion Bram plans to take you down with him. But I'm going to fight like hell to make sure that doesn't happen."

I couldn't believe what I was hearing. Why? Why would Zion do that? How could he be so cruel and dispose of me in this way? None of this made any sense. All I had done was show him support in our business dealings and love in our personal relationship. So why was he so determined to destroy me? Maybe because he thought the government would go easier on him if he helped convict all those who had been a part of his scheme. So fingering me would be a tactical maneuver for him.

It was so fucking unfair. I felt like crying. But I was damned if I was going to let Zion Bram have this effect on me, even if he wasn't around to see it. Zion had put himself so deep inside my head that I was afraid he might have some kind of psychic insight into what I was feeling and thinking. A ridiculous superstition, I know, but one that I couldn't totally dismiss. You see what love can do to you when it's not meant to be?

I looked up, realizing my reverie had made me miss Sifuentes's last few sentences. "It's going to be an uphill battle," he said, "but I'm confident that in the end we'll prevail."

I could tell he was getting ready to wind things up. As he rose from his desk, he said, "One more thing, Ms. Bouvier. I advise you in the strongest terms possible to stay away from Zion Bram. Do not see him. Do not speak to him. Not even if he tries to contact you. We can't risk the two of you seeming like coconspirators."

And with that, Reuben Sifuentes ushered me out of his office and said he would be in touch with me shortly.

The following day I returned to work—not to ZB Financial Services; that office was closed and sealed off with yellow police tape—but to my own firm, Bouvier Public Relations. There I was greeted by Megan, who treated me as though she were completely unaware of any of the press and newspaper articles written about me. It almost made me want to tear up; that kind of loyalty can't be bought. And I didn't realize until that moment what a good employee and friend Megan really was. I reminded myself to give her a raise, if I could ever afford to again.

I entered my office, sat down at my desk, and called for Megan, asking for a status report on all non–ZB Financial business.

Megan took a seat opposite, me and cleared her throat but otherwise remained silent. I waited for her to begin, but when no report was forthcoming, I said, "Megan, do you have something to tell me."

She looked down, unable to meet my eyes. "There is no status report," she said.

I loved Megan, but I was beginning to lose my temper. "How can that be? You've had plenty of time to prepare it. What have you been doing during my absence?"

She rose to her own defense. "It's not that I didn't prepare a status report. It's just that there's no status to report."

"What do you mean?"

"I mean, I'm sorry to tell you this, but we have no business," Megan apologetically pronounced.

"No business!" I exclaimed.

Before I could finish my thought, Megan interjected. "All our clients have deserted us. They don't want to be associated with you because you're associated with Zion, and they think that association will hurt their business."

"So all our clients are gone?" I said.

"Yes."

"Every one of them?"

Megan nodded.

I was asking redundant questions because I couldn't wrap my head around what she'd said. My business was defunct, kaput, gone with the wind.

"Well, what about all that new business we were hoping to acquire?"

"They're gone as well. They didn't even want anyone to know they were taking meetings with us."

"I'm that much of a leper in the PR community?"

"'Fraid so."

I sat back and tried to take this in, but it was too enormous of a thing to get my arms around. Thanks to my relationship with Zion Bram, I was now without clients, without a bank account, and facing a possible prison sentence for something I hadn't done. The only thing I was guilty of was using poor judgment by falling in love with the wrong man.

I felt utterly defeated. For the first time in my life, all I wanted to do was be a quitter, go home, get into bed, and pull the covers over my head until his whole thing blew over.

I sighed and said, "Well, then, I guess there's no reason for either of us to be here."

And with that, I walked out of the office, leaving Megan behind to turn off the lights and lock the door. Zion had put one more nail in my coffin by driving a stake through my business. He was a vampire of sorts, sucking the lifeblood out of anyone he came in contact with.

What followed was six months of absolute hell, probably the worst half year of my life. Since I was innocent of all charges, Sifuentes encouraged me to cooperate with the government. He was with me during the interrogations. Every week I spent five or six hours being deposed by different government agencies. There was a man from the SEC, a man from the FBI, and even one from the CIA to question me. I met them in various government offices that were all basically the same space—a bare room with a table in the middle and chairs on either side. In the center of the table was a tape recorder that the interrogator would turn on and off, depending on whether my testimony was on or off the record. The room itself, no matter in which government office building it was located, always looked familiar to me, and one day I realized why. It looked like one of those squad interrogation rooms you see on nearly every TV cop show. All that was missing was the two-way mirror the detectives use to look inside from the next room without the person under suspicion being aware.

It was always the same interrogators, and in those six months, I got to know them very well.

My SEC interrogator, Mr. Jay, was a colorless sort of man who always wore dark worsted suits and glasses with clear rims. Pale, with thinning sandy hair, he possessed a voice that was equally lacking in color. He spoke to me in a monotone and asked questions without any rising or falling inflections in his voice. He was so boring during our time together that it was all I could do to keep my eyes from drifting closed in that airless, windowless room where our meetings took place. I could tell he was a man thoroughly lacking in imagination—a bottom-line, balance-sheet kind of guy—and he created in me a prankish urge to throw him a curve ball by answering one of his questions with the most outlandish response I could think of.

Interrogator number two, Mr. Sewell, was from the FBI and looked like he bought his suits off a plain pipe rack. They were ill fitting and made him look like a schlump. But what he lacked in fashion sense, he made up for with bulldog persistence when it came to questioning me. Actually, at times, a comparison to a pit bull might have been closer to the mark. Unlike the SEC interrogator, who retained a neutral stance throughout, the FBI guy was always in my face, asking me the same question over and over, always hoping to shake me up and catch me in a lie, which he never did. During these sessions I was in no danger of drifting off to sleep. In fact the FBI interrogator kept me on my toes and on my guard. At the end of these sessions, I usually was exhausted and badly in need of sleep.

A CIA agent, Mr. Miller, was my third interrogator and the oddest of the bunch. Like a phantom he had the weirdest way of ghosting into a room to begin our sessions and ghosting out at the end, as though he didn't want to be observed entering or leaving our shared space. Sometimes he dressed in a bespoke suit that made me think of Yale's Skull & Bones or Princeton's eating clubs. At other times his clothing was more casual, as though he'd just wandered in after a sail or safari or stepped off the links. Sometimes he was friendly and spoke to me in a conspiratorial way, as though it were the two of us against the world. Other times, however, he was cold and removed, as though he were a body snatcher. Sometimes he would seem distracted, as if he had other things on his mind. And sometimes he would be laser sharp and bore in on me with a piercing stare. When he walked into the room, I never knew which version of him was going to greet me. I suspected he kept switching looks and attitudes in an attempt to keep me off balance and drive me to incriminate myself. But because I was innocent and always kept to the same basic story, that never would happen.

Together all three of them questioned me about my relationship with Zion and attempted to create a timeline based on my testimony. They wanted to know what I knew about his company and his confederates. They asked me the same questions repeatedly in as many different ways as they could. They tried to trick me and fake me out. They played good cop and bad cop and every type of cop in between. But the answers they got out of me were always the same, because basically I knew nothing about how Zion's business operated. My job had been to bring people inside the tent. But what went on inside the tent was something I had no real knowledge about, so I was innocent. That was my story, and I stuck to it like the proverbial glue.

Of course, during this period, I wasn't in contact with Zion, nor had I heard from him. Wherever he was—and I didn't wish to know where that was; I reminded myself daily that I really, truly didn't want to know—he was keeping a low profile until the trial.

The most difficult part about those six months before the trial got underway was the fact that I went through it almost totally on my own. Oh, don't get me wrong. I had friends, and they wanted to help me in any way they could. But I was too embarrassed to see them, so I made up excuses and told them I couldn't be with them for one reason or another. The same went for my family. I was too embarrassed to see them either, and I also didn't want them to suffer any embarrassment on my behalf. So I stayed away from them too.

It was a lonely existence.

At the end of those six months, after what I knew would be my last deposition, I went home and turned off my phone. I didn't want anyone to get in touch with me. The trial was scheduled to begin the following month, and I needed to sort things out in my head and in my heart and put closure on my relationship with Zion.

I ended up doing everything you're supposed to do after a bad breakup. I napped often and showered infrequently (it didn't matter since I had no desire to go outside). I ate too much Häagen-Dazs (a cliché, I know) and drank too much red wine. I watched too many soap opera and old movies. I turned on the stereo and played a lot of music I knew would make me cry. Luther Vandross and Phyllis Hyman consoled me in ways no one else could. In other words I was as depressed as hell. And I had no interest in getting myself out of this pathetic condition.

Then, after a couple of weeks of this self-indulgence, my doorbell rang. *Who could it be?* I wondered. At first I wasn't going to answer it; my depression held more sway than my curiosity. Then it rang again. I pulled the covers over my head and burrowed into the little cave I'd created for myself. The doorbell rang a third time, this time muffled by the covers over my ears. Now I was starting to get annoyed. Didn't whoever was calling know how depressed I was? Didn't they know how much I wanted to stay in my cocoon-like state without ever transforming into a beautiful butterfly? By the fourth ring, my annoyance turned into full-out rage. How dare someone have the nerve to interrupt my depression? I threw the covers aside, leapt out of bed, and stormed into the living room, where I headed for the door.

"Who is it?" I said, doing nothing to mask the anger in my voice.

"It's me...Jonny," said the voice from the other side.

"Jonny?" I said, incredulous. Of all my friends, he was the only one I hadn't heard from during my six months of deposition hell.

"Yes, it's Jonny. I've been out of town on business, and now I'm back."

So that's why I hadn't heard from him.

"I'm sorry, Jonny, but I'm not feeling well. Can you come back another time?"

There was a pause, and for a few moments, I thought he had gone away. Then he said, "Omega, I know what's going on with you. I'm sorry I didn't reach out to you before. But now I'm back, and I want to help you."

That was nice to hear, but instead of being appreciative, I said, "There's nothing you can do to help me."

"Well, I'm not a lawyer—that's true. But I am your friend, and I'd like to see you and take you out to dinner...if you'll let me."

I started to tear up at the thought of how thoughtful and gallant Jonny was being. I felt horrible for giving him a hard time.

"You want to take me out to dinner?"

"Yes."

"But I look terrible, and my condo is a mess."

"I'm sure a shower and some makeup will remedy that. And I couldn't care less about what your place looks like."

I sighed. The guy had an answer for everything.

"Okay," I said. "I'm going to let you in. But close your eyes and don't look at me. Because I look like crap. You promise?"

"Yes, Omega, I promise," he said in a voice that let me know he was humoring me.

I unlocked the door and opened it. True to his word, Jonny's eyes were shut, and his hands were covering his eyes. I took him by the arm and led him to the living-room sofa.

"Stay here," I said. "I'll be as quick as I can."

I ran into the bathroom, threw off my robe and pajamas, and turned on the shower. "Go into the kitchen and make yourself a drink," I called out to him.

"Thanks. I will."

I heard Jonny go into the kitchen and open the refrigerator. I stepped into the shower and let the water wash away all the depressed feelings that had been oozing out of my pores for the past several weeks. It felt good to feel clean again. And with the grit and grime gone, I felt my feelings lift. By the time I got out of the shower, I was actively looking forward to going outside and being with Jonny.

Wrapped in a towel, I padded into the bedroom, where I looked in my closet and picked out something fresh to wear. I wasn't totally feeling it yet, but I was optimistic that the combination of my outfit and Jonny's outlook would soon turn my mood around.

Wearing capris, a cute blouse, and flat sandals, I allowed Jonny to take me out to dinner at a place that wasn't his. We ate at a loud restaurant on Ocean Drive that was a fifty-fifty split of tourists and locals. Afterward, as I knew he would, Jonny suggested that we go dancing at a club a few doors down from the restaurant. I protested that I wasn't in the mood, but he wasn't hearing any of it.

"This is Dr. Jonny talking," he said, "and the doctor knows what's best for you."

Bowing to the inevitable, I followed him into the club. There was a line to get in, but Jonny, of course, knew the doorman, who whisked us immediately inside. Almost as quickly we hit the dance floor, and I found myself dancing salsa for the first time since being with Zion. At first it felt odd, feeling a man's touch other than Zion's. But in no time at all, I was over it and completely gave myself to being Jonny's dancing partner.

We danced for hours. We danced until we were exhausted and our feet hurt. And as we danced, for the first time in six months, I forgot about Zion, forgot about all those months of depositions and being treated like a criminal, forgot about my self-imposed exile from my friends and family. That night, on the dance floor, there was only Jonny, and I was grateful for his company and friendship.

But like all good things, this night had to come to an end. And end it did, with Jonny walking me to my door. I was glad he understood that we were only friends, so there was no awkwardness about whether I'd let him inside for anything more. He kissed me on the cheek; we hugged; and then he said good night, vowing, now that he would be back in Miami for a while, to keep tabs on me and make sure I was okay.

Back inside my condo, I collapsed on the sofa. My leg muscles hurt from all that dancing. I knew I'd eventually find my way to my bed. But in the meantime, it was pleasant just to sit here and think about what a fun time I'd had and what a wonderful friend Jonny was. I felt reenergized, as though my spirit had been somewhat restored. Thanks to Jonny, I felt like myself again. I was Omega Bouvier—hear me roar. And I knew that whatever was in store for me, I would face it and deal with it and rise above it, because Jonny had reminded me that I was a survivor.

With those thoughts I went into my CD collection and found Gloria Gaynor's song "I Will Survive." I played it over and over. I danced and twirled around my condo, singing the lyrics that profoundly became my personal anthem.

I slept well that night—the first time in a long time. I got up the following morning and took a long jog on the beach. It had been a while since I'd heard the crunch of sand under my feet and breathed the fresh ocean air. It was revitalizing, and my spirit felt renewed. I returned home, cleaned and organized my apartment, and mentally prepared myself for the trial the following week.

So many thoughts were cruising through my head, but when I finally calmed my mind, I recalled a Scripture my mother had taught me when I was young. I don't know where it's found, and I vaguely remember the words. It says, "Do not be anxious about anything, but in every situation, by prayer and petition, with thanksgiving, present your requests to God. And the peace of God, which transcends all understanding, will guard your heart and mind."

Dear Father, Jehovah, forgive me of my sins. Please be with me. Give me the strength to get through this. In the name of your Son, Jesus Christ, with faith I pray. Amen.

Fifteen

During the ZB Financial trial, I frequently found myself in windowless rooms.

Besides Reuben Sifuentes's law office and my condo, I was shuffling in and out of the Dade County District Court on the appointed days that Sifuentes told me to attend. The courtrooms often were empty, save for the presiding judge and a few onlookers. All the furniture was wooden and grandiose. We looked like children in an adult-sized room, playing pretend. If there were windows, they were narrow and located high up, close to the ceiling. There was no way to know whether I would spend hours in the courtroom or just a few minutes. The trial hadn't even begun, with the jury selection going on and the prosecution building cases on the federal and state level. The rooms were empty and dreary for now, but once things really started, the place would be full of reporters, former clients, coworkers, and curious onlookers.

Reuben Sifuentes was thorough in making sure my case and hearings weren't intertwined with Zion's. He discounted any evidence that came up in other hearings and used the instincts of a theatrical dramaturge to craft a story for my defense.

I was a young, driven, professional woman, blinded by love and ambition. I followed my contract, and I followed Zion, with no knowledge of corruption or dishonesty. There was nothing in my character to make me a liar or a con. My only mistake was remaining loyal to my employer and my lover. With no knowledge of the numbers or the deals involved, how could I be held accountable?

This was the story Sifuentes relayed repeatedly at each hearing. The prosecution grew tired of it, citing that if I were so intelligent and competent, how did I not know anything about Zion's deals? It went back and forth like this, with the judge stopping to stick to formalities.

I dressed the part, staying refined and reserved in gray blazers and low heels. I would show a hint of color in my skirt or earrings, staying true to my youth and innocence, which had gotten me into this mess. I couldn't wear anything Zion had bought me, especially since the prosecution had a list of everything Zion ever had gifted me off the company account. Although the government seized most of Zion's gifts, they missed a few items that were purchased in cash.

I would sit somberly but proudly. I was innocent. While I had lost my love and felt betrayed, I had no reason to feel remorse or regret. Sifuentes would describe me as a modern woman in the arena of a man's world, trying to do right and remaining aware of the corruption around me. I had decided this sorry episode in my life wasn't going to hold me back or beat me down.

Sifuentes told me Zion's trial would be held first. Mine would be postponed until Zion's judgment. "The good news is that if Zion isn't sentenced, then you won't be either. Even if he is, afterward the judge may find there isn't enough evidence to charge you and have your case acquitted," he relayed to me, after the final hearing.

"Okay, well, then what's the bad news?" I asked.

"Evidence and testimony from Zion's case could be used against you in yours. The jury already will have predispositions based on the first case."

"But what if nothing's said about me in the first case?" I proposed, thinking there was little in the financial evidence to do with me. Maybe my name wouldn't come up at all.

"If the rumors are true about Zion wanting to incriminate you too, then your name will come up in his testimony and in his lawyer's case. The more people he takes down with him by cooperating, the less severe his sentence."

I blinked again, still not believing Zion would try to take me down with him. If he did, he would have to lie about my involvement, but I guess I shouldn't have been surprised, as he'd been lying all along to me and to his clients; we were all his marks. Still it hurt me to think that he would try.

"Omega, I think you're going to have to testify against him," Sifuentes finished.

It wasn't something I'd considered doing yet. Testifying in my own case...yes, of course I would speak up on my own behalf. Sifuentes agreed that my protestation of innocence would be believable on the stand, and my case could benefit from my defending myself. However, the idea of testifying in Zion's case—seeing the man I had loved, only to seal his fate as a criminal—was an extremely heavy burden to bear.

"Okay," I said softly, looking down at my hands and nodding.

The idea, though, never really settled right with me, and I felt the burden of my testimony hanging over me as Zion's trial started. It was covered by the newspapers and TV, which meant I was learning more and more about the truth behind Zion's scams. The dark parts of the business were occluding my memory of our time together, like the moon blocking the sun during an eclipse. I spent my days worrying over how to get through my own trial, how I would get back on my feet, how I would restart my career and my life.

Megan would visit me at the condo, bringing me zero news about new clients but being supportive nonetheless. Jonny remained a close confidant, feeling staunchly that I should throw Zion under the bus in any way I could. He believed without question that I wasn't involved in Zion's scams, and I appreciated his unquestioned, unshakeable belief in me.

Coupled with the idea that I would have to face Zion in the courtroom, there was also the problem of my failed career. It was starting to look unlikely that I would be able to continue in public relations. Even if I relocated to another city, I had a feeling the reputation of Bouvier Public Relations in connection to ZB Financial would follow me wherever I went. So I took some of my newly found free time to consider my career options and figure out if changing it altogether would be necessary.

It was. However, I had only recently learned how to survive and fight in the PR world, and I worried that I was too far up the ladder to start all over again at an internship level in another field.

Some days I woke up nauseous, frightened by the thought of what might happen to me.

I also couldn't stop thinking about Zion. He was ingrained in me, as I still really loved him. I couldn't connect the two different sides of him. The side that had whisked me away to the Caribbean, showing me the locals he cared about deeply. The part of him that was tender and passionate in bed, doing everything in his power to take care of me. This just didn't seem like the man who would lie and steal people's life savings and ultimately turn on me and send me to jail.

Sifuentes walked me through my testimony, extrapolating on what I shouldn't bring up and where I should claim ignorance. Fortunately there was a lot of honesty in my ignorance, because every time Sifuentes rehearsed a possible question the prosecution might pose, I was shocked.

Yes, I knew Zion had traveled to Switzerland that week. No, I didn't have any idea why. No, we weren't in a relationship at that point. No, I never saw any files on potential clients and their holdings. I didn't even know Reesey was a part owner and investor in almost every facet of ZB Financial.

There was a moment in the testimony rehearsal when I thought Zion had taken pains to leave me out of a lot of the incriminating activities. He had taken me to dinners with big clients, but I couldn't recognize any of their names. He never told me when he was traveling; I'd just hear about it through everyone else in the office. Even the example of how he communicated with the PR team around me was evidence of my innocence, as apparently Frederick knew more about the operations than he let on. Sifuentes felt strongly that without any curve balls, I could come out of the trial clean and with my reputation intact. He also felt strongly that Zion wouldn't escape punishment. The evidence was stacked high against him, and while his lawyers might be able to shorten his sentence, he was doomed to be found guilty. And that fact made me feel very sad.

I chose not to attend the first few sessions of Zion's trial. I figured that the less I knew about it, the better off I'd be. Instead I sat at home, waiting on an update from Sifuentes or Megan or any of my few remaining friends or acquaintances who still gave me the time of day. I kept the television off to avoid any information about the proceedings. I focused on my future and what I needed to rebuild my life. I researched where I could consider moving and how I would go about selling my condo, if necessary. I rented a stack of VHS movies and played them over and over in the background. It was a solitary existence I had retreated to.

One video I burned through again and again was *Mahogany*. It was one of my favorite movies, and despite its sad nature, watching the spirit of Diana Ross reverberate through my living room made me feel a little bit stronger. Beautiful, talented, driven, and challenged, her movie personality was a personification of the dramatic character that Sifuentes was weaving in the courtroom to represent me. Learning that you've loved the wrong man, all the while being blind to it, then wondering if you somehow secretly, unconsciously had known all along. Having the hope that maybe someday he won't be the wrong man after all. I cried the first few times I played the tape, and after sitting with it in my condo, rewinding it, and watching it over and over, the movie gave me a renewed sense of hope. Even if things were falling apart for me, I had the inner strength and the hope to get through it.

I was set to testify the following morning. I didn't want to spend any more time worrying over the events that had passed or the events to come, so I slipped *Mahogany* yet again into the VCR and started on an old family recipe for banana bread in the kitchen. I remembered my mother making it when I was little, when it was deep winter and all the kids were pent up and wanting to go outside. The bread would fill me with warm memories.

The buzzer to my front door went off. I looked down the hallway and scanned through the list in my head of who might be coming by. I thought it could be a neighbor complaining about my late-night TV-viewing habits. Maybe the doorman with a package from earlier in the day. I couldn't think of anyone else who would be paying a visit at this hour. With a long silk kimono wrapped around me, I walked down the hallway to greet the surprise. When I peeked through the peephole, my stomach dropped like an elevator with its cables suddenly cut.

He was somber in manner but still so very good-looking. His suit fit perfectly, with his tie removed, as if he were coming home from another long day at the office. He glanced up at the peephole as if he knew I would be staring out at him, shocked. He buzzed again, and I jumped.

I slowly undid the dead bolt and opened the door to face him. "What are you doing here? You shouldn't be here!" I said sternly, crossing my arms. My heart was caught in my throat, and my body was reacting to the sight of him. I was shaking inside like a blender set on its highest setting. I didn't want to be drawn in by his presence, but I couldn't help it. Worry and apology were stirring in his face, but I didn't want to believe it was real.

"Omega, please let me come in," Zion said softly. The sound of his voice made me tremble. I wanted him to come in so badly, but I also wanted him to leave and forget I'd ever been in his life.

"You should go," I said adamantly. "It'll look very bad for me if you're here. You've ruined enough for me already." I said this with a bite to my tone. It was one of the phrases I'd been practicing in my head in case I ever did see him again, but I honestly didn't think I'd have to use it.

He looked down shamefully and whispered, "I know. But I had to try and see you."

A war was waging inside me as I tried to figure out if this was the Zion who wasn't going to incriminate me in court. Was this the Zion who truly loved me and wanted to please me? Was this the Zion who was making some kind of sacrifice by coming to my door, some kind of grand gesture?

Or was this the same Zion he had been all along? The lying, scheming manipulator who had stolen millions of dollars of other people's money—and my future. They both shared the same face, so I couldn't find a way to decide which was which.

"Please let me in." He looked straight through me as he asked, and I couldn't help but open the door. As he walked past me, he placed his hand briefly on my side. Through my silk kimono, I felt the familiarity of his fingers. A voice inside was screaming for me to back away and kick him out of my life for good this time. Instead he walked to the living room, where he sat on the couch and placed his head in his hands as if this day were no different from any other.

I walked to the TV and turned off Diana Ross and Billy Dee Williams in midscene. I wasn't sure why Zion had shown up, but I could guess it was to tell me something about what had happened or why. I had told myself weeks ago that there was nothing he could say that would change the way I felt about the trial and the terrible time he was putting me through. I had set aside my feelings in order to blame him and not allow him back into my life. Then, when I saw him at my door and had him so close again, all my resolve was beginning to fade. A sick sensation settled in the pit of my stomach, and I knew I was lost.

I sat in the chair next to the couch, maintaining my distance so I wouldn't be within striking distance of him, then sat back and tried to appear calm. I didn't want him to think I'd been shaken by his arrival.

"What do you need, Mr. Bram?" I asked, my tone deliberately cold.

He looked up pleadingly, "You, Omega. I need you. Things have been so out of control lately. I know I owe you an explanation, an apology." He paused, studying the stern set of my face. "But somehow I feel that wouldn't matter, would it?"

I said nothing in response, as I didn't know what to say and was afraid to allow myself to speak. Zion had read me again, as he did so well. He knew there was nothing he could say to say to fix it—nothing except ask for forgiveness based on what we'd had outside of work. All indictments and trials aside, when I looked at him, I knew he still loved me. It hurt me to mistrust him and to feel betrayed. It also hurt to see the man I loved hurting too.

"Everything has fallen apart. I don't know how to possibly go back. I hate that you've been brought into this." He placed his hands over his face again.

I still couldn't respond. I didn't trust myself to answer.

"Despite that, I miss you. I wish you were by my side," he finished, then sighed deeply. He leaned forward, locking eyes with me. Then he reached out and placed a hand on my knee through the fabric of my kimono, squeezing to reassure me of his feelings.

It was too much. I pushed his hand away. "You can't just come back here and think I'll forget about everything that's happened! You lied to me! You lied to everyone!" I stood up and paced the living room.

"It's hard to explain. There's a lot you don't know about, Omega. I wanted to keep you out of it. You know me. You have to know I'm not as awful as they're making me out to be." He stood up to follow me, holding out his arms to bring me in. I walked away, refusing him. I wasn't going to accept his explanation, not when there was so much at stake for me. I couldn't stand by his side.

"What about my case, Zion? I'm being prosecuted too! You know I had nothing to do with your scams, yet I'm on a list of names of people who were involved. How did that happen?" I asked, feeling the anger and aggression build up, remembering that it was supposed to have been Zion who told the prosecution about my involvement, even when I'd had none. I turned my back to him, balling up my fists, thinking what he was saying couldn't be true but how desperately I wanted it to be.

"They're lying! They're just trying to rattle you! They want you to give up more information about me, maybe even make it up so they can stick me with more charges. I never wanted to get you in trouble. I never wanted to hurt you." He stood behind me, close enough for me to hear his breathing. "After tomorrow I don't know if I'll ever see you again. Please, Omega."

Zion wrapped his arms around my waist, pulling me to him, with my back against his broad chest. I wanted to walk away and fight the urge to lean into him. But I couldn't—damn him, I couldn't. He was pleading and desperate, and while logic told me not to believe him, I still did.

I knew I was a strong person. I was rebuilding myself to fight for my reputation and my life. I knew I was a good person, and I wouldn't be sentenced, because that would be too unjust. I had prayed every night to be released from the chaos around me, and I knew someday peace would come. Yet despite all the trouble Zion had brought my way, I still loved him. I couldn't help myself. I loved him more than I had loved any man, and a part of me felt as if I were sacrificing myself to him to prove my love. A part of me never would be able to let go of what we had.

"Please, Omega. Look at me." He spoke softly into my ear again, and the tension I held inside me was released as I focused on Zion's whole body against mine. I looked up to the ceiling, closed my eyes, and then turned to face him. I missed staring into his eyes, and I got lost in them for a moment as we held our gazes. He pulled me closer, and I felt his longing.

He kissed my forehead then my cheek. He growled, deep down and low, and began to kiss my neck. "I love you, Omega," he said, lifting his head and looking into my eyes. A thrill went through me as his words penetrated my ears and his look seared my soul. The intensity of his declaration made me shiver right through to the very core of my being.

"I love you too, Zion," I said, almost whimpering to him, feeling in a safe enough space to say it. I took a deep breath and exhaled slowly, savoring the thought of our shared confession.

His hands moved inside my kimono, touching only the center of my chest. He pulled the kimono open, letting the fabric brush across my fully hard nipples. I shook at the feeling. No man had touched me in all the time that Zion and I had been apart. In truth no man ever had touched me the way he did.

Zion breathed heavily into the crease of my neck, sending a shiver down my spine. I knew he was looking down at me, my robe open and exposing me, his hands holding it open without touching my skin. My breasts were rising and falling with each breath. I wore nothing beneath the silk kimono, and now Zion was watching every part of me. He already knew every inch so well. I was so ready. He always had the ability to arouse me so quickly.

I reached up to run my fingers across the back of his neck, arching my back so he could take in more of my body. He groaned again in response and pushed his erection against me, pulling back on my hips, making my arch further.

"Is this what you want?" I whispered, gulping down the longing I felt for him.

"Yes," he said gently. He kept his hands wrapped up in my kimono, pulling my hips against his hardness but holding back from touching me more.

We were on the verge of diving in. He didn't want to push me and was waiting for my signal. I felt how tense and stiff he was. I heard his breath, thick and ragged, against my skin. I knew if I said no, he would walk away. If he had left me then and there, I would have fallen on my living-room floor, curled up, and just died. I missed him already. I knew he would have to leave eventually. I decided to take the plunge with him. My heart was pulling so much harder at me than my mind.

"Take it," I said.

He moaned loudly and pulled my kimono completely off, letting it drop to the floor around my feet. I felt like a flower whose petals had unfurled. In an instant his hands were caressing my back, squeezing my buttocks, then my hips, then my buttocks again. He kissed and sucked along my shoulder, nipping me and making me yelp. He was so hungry. It had been so long since we'd been together. I surrendered my body to him for the feast.

He picked me up, my legs wrapped around him as he carried me across the living room. With my head on his shoulder and my nose at his neck…oh, how I missed his scent. He lowered me onto the sofa and pinned me so that my buttocks hit the back of the couch. I braced myself in reaction to his force, placing my hands on the edge of the cushion.

Slowly Zion ran his fingers over my breasts and belly, following his touch with his mouth, sucking hard and long on each nipple, until he was on his knees before me. He separated my legs and gently traced the outline of my lower lips with his tongue, glossing wetly over them. He used his tongue to open me and began to eat me out. His tongue was like a bee buzzing around a flower's unveiled pistil, finally finding that exquisitely tender bit of nerve that had recently only known the touch of my fingers. Soft, hard, soft, hard—he knew how I loved to have my clitoris stimulated. I looked down at him and saw him looking up at me as he continued to lap at my vagina. He always did enjoy watching me, and now his look only added to the sensual concussions that were rocking my body. Wave after wave of sensations crashed over me as his tongue led me to an orgasm that left me shattered.

I leaned back against the top of the sofa cushions, but Zion wasn't finished with me. Of course he wasn't. This hadn't been enough for him in the past, and it definitely wasn't enough for him now. He knew me and knew what my body was capable of. And in that short space of time, I knew he wanted to take me someplace new, someplace we'd never reached before in our lovemaking— some new sensual experience that I would remember for the rest of my life and against which all other future lovers would be judged. And heaven help me, I let him. I let him.

I was barely finished orgasming when he slid two fingers into me, where I was still wet and craving for him. Again he watched my face as he slid them in and out of my vagina quickly, grazing my G-spot and making me crazy yet again. His rhythm matched the desperate pace that we wanted from each other. With his two fingers, he brought me to a second orgasm, and I was so ready for it. My arms shook as I came, barely holding my body up against the couch. My mouth let out moans, followed by his name.

But still Zion wasn't finished with me. I knew he loved to watch what he did to me. He had told me so. With his hands on my hips, he turned me around, so now my front was to the back of the sofa. There he was on his knees behind me, playing with me and making me shout out his name. "Zion, Zion, *Zion!*" It was as if every cell of my body were a miniature version of myself calling out to him. He tasted me from behind, right there on bended knees, making me give into him, once again probing the inside of my vagina with his hot tongue while squeezing my vaginal lips with his fingers as if they were ripe orange segments, allowing my juice to drip onto his face. He was on his knees, making me his again, after begging me to let him. As I orgasmed yet again, I collapsed forward onto the couch.

I felt him rise to his feet, and I heard him unzip his pants, but I was too tired to turn around. He scooped me up with one arm, underneath my breasts, holding my weak body against his, and I felt the smoothness of his shirt against my damp skin. He penetrated me quickly and pounded his body hard against me again and again, and then he held still.

I was suddenly filled with him, and it was bittersweet. I felt so complete with him inside me, even as rough as it may have been. Zion was everything I wanted in that moment. I was overwhelmed with emotion and couldn't contain my tears. Yes, I was crying, but it was only me wanting more of him. Zion felt the need in me as he thrust himself deeper and deeper inside me. No man had ever been this physically deep inside me before. With his other hand, he grasped the side of my face and kissed my neck, whispering, "Yes, I love you, Omega, yes." Even his voice sounded as desperate and wanting as I felt.

With that he thrust against me again. He made the couch move and my back arch each time he drove himself into me. He held on to me tightly so that our faces were side by side as he gained speed. His urges never had been so animalistic and powerful. I gave in to his need and let my body take on everything that was building up between us. We climaxed at the same time, screaming loudly, as we rode the intensity of our orgasms.

Finally we both slumped over the couch, catching our breath. Slowly Zion backed away. This time he actually came out of me.

"I'm sorry, Omega," he said, lifting me up and carrying me to the bed.

"I know," I said back, fighting back the realization that this was the end.

I slept in Zion's arms that night, under the infamous painting that hung above my bed, curled up against him, as I had many nights in the past. However, I knew these were the last moments we'd share.

Before the sun rose, I felt him crawl away from me, slip into the living room, and open the front door. I pretended to be asleep. I didn't need to say good-bye because I knew I would see him again soon. In court.

That morning was the day I would have to testify against him.

Sixteen

When I woke up, Zion was gone. If it hadn't been for the slight lingering hint of his scent and the light impression he'd left on his pillow, I might have imagined I'd dreamed the events of the entire night before. It had been both wonderful and horrible, and I ran into the shower to rinse myself of his sweat and semen. What did I allow to happen? As the water streamed down my body, I couldn't stop the tears that flowed with it. As I thought about what transpired the previous night and what was going to happen later that day, my stomach was in knots, and I shook uncontrollably. I had to give myself a pep talk and pull myself together—quickly.

I dressed in the most conservative way possible: a suit, white blouse, neutral stockings, heels, and the simplest of jewelry— nothing ostentatious, nothing that might send the wrong message to the jury. I had been coached on this by Reuben Sifuentes, who knew how important my appearance would be to the jury's opinion of me. I put on as little makeup as I could get away with and pulled my hair in a ponytail. I looked at myself in the mirror and saw that I was channeling my spinster schoolteacher look. There—I was ready for my day in court.

Actually it was Zion's day in court. I would only be a witness for the prosecution. I knew now why Zion had come to my door last night. It was his last-ditch attempt to affect my testimony by making me believe that he still loved me and that he was innocent of all charges against him. And I had wanted to believe this because, if it were true, if Zion were innocent, then it meant his love for me was real, and I hadn't made the mistake of my life by allowing myself to fall in love with him.

I left my condo and drove to the courthouse, my hands still shaking as I gripped the steering wheel. I'd never been a witness before, and I didn't know what to expect. My only real knowledge of the inner workings of a courtroom had come mainly from watching *Law and Order* and other legal TV shows. But I was sure the reality would be much different. I was also sweating lightly as I thought about the impending testimony I would give that day. Sifuentes had rehearsed me over and over, coaching me on what to say, what not to say, and how to say it. He also had warned me not to lie under any circumstances. I knew I had nothing to worry about in regard to that because I was innocent, and as long as I kept that thought foremost in my mind, I would be fine. Or so I kept telling myself.

I arrived at the Dade County District Court, parked my car, and waited for my lawyer on the steps that led into the building. Sifuentes was right on time. He was followed by a small herd of reporters who knew he was always good for a printable quote or two. He was wearing an expensively tailored suit over a blue shirt with a white collar along with a neon-yellow bow tie that would have burned the retinas if it had been a part of a TV test pattern.

Over this he wore an opened alpaca-hair overcoat, even though the weather was far too warm for this sort of outfit. I could see the light sheen of sweat on his face and appreciated that sometimes you have to suffer in order to look good. This is a rule women learn at an early age, and it was interesting to see it put into practice by a man.

As he came up to greet me, the reporters gathered around us and pushed microphones into his face.

"Is your client going to testify today?" one asked.

"Is she going to incriminate Zion Bram?" another wanted to know.

"What's she going to tell the jury?" a third reporter chimed in.

Reuben Sifuentes held up his hands as though to ward them off. I knew all about these maneuvers from my years of practicing the art of public relations and was happy to see that he knew how to handle the press and have them eat out of the palm of his hand without giving anything away. He smiled at them and said, "Now you know I can't tell you that. That information is privileged. But if you're lucky enough to get a seat inside the courtroom, you'll have your answer soon enough. Now if you'll excuse me…"

With that he took me by the elbow and led me up the steps and into the courthouse. He escorted me up to the courtroom where Zion's trial was being held. There was a bench right outside the door, and he motioned for me to sit. This was where we would wait until my name was called.

As I sat there, staring at the far wall of the courthouse corridor, I couldn't help allowing my mind to wander. And for some reason, as it riffled through my recent memories, it settled on one from the beginning of my relationship with Zion—my professional relationship, that is.

It was the first time I'd actually watched him at work. We were in a hotel ballroom that was filled with about three hundred people—men, women; young, old; middle class, working class; rich, poor; black, white, Hispanic, Asian. They ran the gamut of diversity. But there was one thing I noticed that they all had in common—a look on their faces of hope commingled with fear. Hope of fulfilling their financial dreams, fear of falling short of their goals and being looked upon as a failure, not just in others' eyes but in their own as well.

Of course I was the one responsible for filling this room. My PR team and I had gotten the word out and brought them here. This was the payoff of what we had been working so hard to achieve, so it was especially gratifying for me to look out and see that every seat had been filled.

Standing in the wings, I looked to my right and saw that Reesey, Zion's éminence grise, was right next to me. How had he gotten so close without making a sound? I guess my attention had been focused so much on the crowd waiting for Zion that I had blocked out everything else. On the other hand, maybe stealthily walking up to someone was among his bag of tricks. It wouldn't have surprised me in the least if it had been. We nodded politely to each other. Then Reesey crossed his arms in front of his chest and waited for the big show to get underway.

We stood in the wings and watched as a man took to the stage. He introduced himself then told the audience how lucky he was to have listened to Zion. He stated how much money he had made in the past and how much more he planned to make in the future by sticking with Zion and his plan. He said he was a man of humble means who was now able to lead a much richer (in all senses of the word) life thanks to Zion's unique wealth-management strategies. Because of Zion's influence, he had been able to buy a house for his family (they previously had lived in a cramped apartment down in Del Ray Beach) and put his two children through college, and he had enough left over to buy property (ironically back at Del Ray Beach) for himself and his wife to retire to when the time came. It was the American dream comes true.

The man, who was white, finished up to great applause. Everyone in the audience could see themselves being this man and achieving the same level of success he had. As he came offstage, he was replaced by a second man, this one black. He stood onstage in front of the audience and delivered a similar spiel. The details were different, but the message was the same: "No matter your background, no matter where you come from or how much money you have (or don't have), listen to Zion, follow his plan, and you'll end up where I am, standing on a stage and talking about how much better my life is now because of Zion Bram."

I shook my head, in awe of how savvy Zion had been to start his company with these two examples of bootstrap capitalism at its finest and most inspiring.

To an equal degree of applause, the second man walked offstage and into the wings before disappearing into the darkness of the backstage area.

And from this same darkness, a new person appeared. It was Zion. He looked from Reesey to me and smiled at us. I smiled back but said nothing. I could tell Zion was putting on his game face in preparation for taking the stage, and the last thing I wanted to do was distract him at this important moment. He was wearing an immaculate dark-blue Hugo Boss suit with Bruno Magli loafers burnished to a high shine and a blindingly super-crisp white shirt. Pass me my shades—this man was practically glowing. The creases on his pants were so sharp, I could have used them to shave my legs. And of course and as always, he wasn't wearing a tie, his one concession to his true laid-back nature.

Reesey picked up a microphone that connected to the speakers in the ballroom. "And now," he said, into it, "please, give it up for...*Zion Bram!*"

Zion waited for the applause then walked onstage. Actually "walk" isn't the best way to describe it. He moved with a combination of bounce and glide to give the impression that he actually was levitating as he crossed the stage to the podium.

He stood at the podium and waited for the applause to die down. It took a while, thanks to the help of several ringers in the audience whose job it was to cue the rest of the audience as to how they should react. It seemed to be working too, because, just as the applause seemed to die down, it would start up again in wave after wave. I watched Zion stand there and eat it up, bask in it. Like an actor, he seemed to feed off the applause and allow it to power his performance.

And then he began to speak. For me it was a revelation. I'd never seen this side of Zion before. Oh, I'd seen him socially, on the dance floor, his moves so cunningly smooth and seductive. And I'd seen him professionally, in the office, knowing how to be disarming in order to get his way, especially with those who didn't share his ideas. And I'd seen him, in a combination of social and professional arenas, at his dinners, holding court and being effortlessly charming.

But this was a new Zion, one who surpassed all those other interpersonal skills. This was Zion pouring on the charm to a level that reached high into the stratosphere of charisma. This was Zion combining words and body language to put forth his financial philosophy in a way that galvanized the crowd into action. This was Zion as a spellbinder, telling a story that held his audience in the way all great storytellers have done, going back to the early griots of West Africa who told their histories to captive village audiences. This was Zion to whom attention must be paid.

I peeked out around the wings and beheld his audience. It was as though they were all in a trance. Zion was their Svengali, their personal financial guru, and they hung on to his every word. He was mesmerizing in the degree of his intensity. He held the crowd spellbound.

And a small confession here: he held me too.

Because, as I stood there and listened to him speak, I felt a strong emotional tide running through me. It was the same emotion I'd felt the first time we danced together. But now it was on a much grander scale, as though equal to the amount of energy he was pumping into the room. I felt that emotion pool in my stomach and make it constrict along with my lungs, making breathing difficult. I felt as if I were in desperate need of oxygen, and Zion was its only source.

As I stood there, I felt something else grow—my desire. Listening to him address the crowd with Old Testament vigor, I fantasized about Zion. I imagined what it would be like to kiss him and taste his essence and thought it would be amazing.

I then imagined us back at my condo, making love on the silk sheets I'd purchased just for the occasion. I heard him whisper to me in that voice that held the slightest trace of an Afro-Caribbean accent. I felt his naked body hard against me, overpowering me in my reverie, the way his voice was overpowering me now. I saw him raise my arms over my head, holding me immobile, knowing this slight taste of bondage would send me over the edge when I finally achieved orgasm. I stood there and wondered—if Zion and I eventually did come together—would it be this way, as I imagined it, or possibly even something much greater than my mind could conceive.

Then something happened to snap me out of the moment. I felt someone stare at me. Shaking my head reluctantly to erase my erotic reverie, I looked up and was surprised to find Reesey staring at me. He held my gaze for a minute, forcing me to look away. But in that brief glance, I caught a look of complicity on his face. It was as though he were a mind reader and knew what I'd been thinking about. No, that was impossible. Reesey might have been many things, most of them mysterious and downright intimidating, but being a mentalist wasn't one of them—of that I felt sure. So why did I feel so spooked? Maybe it was the knowledge that I'd just made myself so vulnerable to Zion, without his knowing it, and here was his right-hand man, a very short distance away, who seemed to intuit my daydreams. I felt my cheeks begin to warm and knew I was blushing.

And that brought me out of my courthouse reverie. I was surprised to find myself back on the bench in the corridor, sitting next to my attorney and waiting to be called to testify. I wondered what was happening inside the courtroom and how Zion was faring with his testimony. Most important, I wondered whether he still planned to implicate me as a partner in his Ponzi scheme. I looked over at Reuben Sifuentes, who didn't seem to be paying any attention to me, unlike the way Reesey had. I had no idea how much time had passed, but a growling in my stomach told me it was likely time for lunch.

A short time later, a lunch recess was called. Sifuentes escorted me outside to a small park that bordered the courthouse building. While I waited on a bench, he went over to a lunch truck and came back with two Cuban sandwiches and two steaming cups of Cuban coffee. It was a pleasant, sunny day, and we sat among secretaries and clerical workers from the courthouse. The sandwich and coffee were delicious and just the sort of pick-me-up I needed. Sifuentes and I made small talk as we sat on the park bench, and if I hadn't known better, I could have sworn this was just another ordinary day instead of one that could significantly alter my future.

Between bites I said to my attorney, "So how do you think it's going in there?"

He paused before answering, either to swallow a bite of his sandwich or contemplate my question. After a moment he said,

"It's hard to know. It's obvious that Zion has a silver tongue and a knack for talking his way out of trouble. He also has the best defense attorney in the state of Florida, whose gift for oratory is only surpassed by mine."

He looked at me and smiled. I looked at him and dutifully smiled back.

He continued, "But this time, with the evidence stacked up against him, words will only get Zion so far. His only real hope is to cut a deal with the feds and the state and implicate as many coconspirators as he can to make sure he does as little hard time as possible."

I knew this already, but it was good to hear it one last time so I could figure out what I was in for.

With our lunch finished, Sifuentes collected our trash and placed it in the nearest receptacle. He then led me back inside the courthouse, where we once again took up our positions on the bench reserved for witnesses waiting to testify. I settled down for another long wait, this time pledging not to let my mind wander into my recent past with Zion.

This time we didn't have long to wait. Or at least my attorney didn't. The courtroom door opened, and the bailiff came out and spoke to him. He then returned to the courtroom. Before I had the chance to wonder what that was about, Sifuentes turned to me and said, "The judge has declared a short recess and wants to see me in chambers along with the prosecuting attorney and Zion's attorney."

"What about me?" I asked.

"You stay here," he said. "And keep your fingers crossed, if you believe in that sort of thing."

With that as his last word, he stood up, buttoned his suit jacket, and disappeared down the corridor in the direction of the judge's private chambers, leaving me to sit there and stew in my own juices as my fate was being decided less than a hundred feet away. As I contemplated what was being said in the judge's chambers and enumerated all the possible outcomes and how they might alter my fate, I began to get very nervous. It was probably the most nerve-wracking half hour of my life until I saw Sifuentes heading back in my direction with an unreadable look on his face. Damn him, couldn't he act like any other human being and give me a smile or a frown, a thumbs-up or thumbs-down, just indicate in some way what my future was to be—freedom or being incarcerated in some federal correctional facility?

He sat down next to me, and I turned to face him. I guess he could see by the expectant look on my face that I was hoping, despite his legendary gift for verbose oration, he would instead be concise and put me out of my misery with as few words as possible.

"Omega," he began.

"Yes," I answered. It was just one word, but was it enough for him to detect the slight quivering in my voice?

"I've just come from the judge's chambers, and he gave me a rundown of Zion's testimony in court."

"Yes," I said again, hoping he would understand that my one-word answers were a plea for him to cut to the chase and tell me the real deal.

He took a deep breath before continuing. I felt like killing him if he didn't get on with it, but he finally said, "At the end of his testimony, Zion asked for special permission to address the court. He said you had nothing to do with his scheme. He said he had misled you, and you were completely innocent. Based on Zion's testimony, your depositions, and the overwhelming evidence acquired by the federal agents, the judge is going to have all charges against you dismissed, and you won't have to take the stand to testify against Zion. It's all over for you, kiddo. We're all done here."

It took a moment for me to take it all in. More than a moment in fact. It was many moments. I felt my mouth drop open in surprise and simultaneously felt a lightening of my body, as though a great weight literally had been lifted from my shoulders; I felt so light that I thought I might just drift away.

On impulse I reached over and grabbed at Sifuentes, holding him in a death grip and squeezing the life out of him, keeping myself tethered to the ground—and reality.

"Thank you, thank you, thank you," I said.

"You don't have to thank me. I didn't do anything. Thank the judge…and Zion too, I suppose."

And I realized he was right. Zion had held my fate in his hands and, in the end, had decided to do the right thing by me. It must have cost him; I'm sure it must have. *Why did he do it?* I asked myself. Maybe he had done it out of love. But love of me or love of his perversely virtuous opinion of himself? I would never know for sure, but it didn't matter, because, for whatever the reason, Zion finally had done right by me.

I let go of Sifuentes, and he smoothed down his jacket where I'd gotten it wrinkled out of shape.

"What do I do now?" I asked him.

He paused for a moment before saying, "Anything you want."

I nodded at him. "Thank you," I said one last time. Then, as if in a trance, I got up from the bench and walked down the corridor. The judge had adjourned the court session for the day. And as fate would have it, as I passed by the courtroom, someone opened the door, and I caught a slight glimpse of Zion standing and speaking with his attorney. As if in slow motion, our eyes met for a few fleeting moments, and we exchanged faint smiles. I sighed. With a conflicted heart, I refocused my attention forward and continued walking down the corridor and out through the courthouse door. That was the last I saw of Zion Bram.

It was early afternoon. The sun was shining down on the park. The light never had seemed brighter. I looked up into the clear, cloudless sky, and it never had appeared more spectacular. I heard birds singing and children laughing and playing nearby, and these were the sweetest sounds I'd ever heard.

On trembling legs I walked down the courthouse steps and let the breeze ripple across my face. My prayers had been answered. Thank God, I had my life back.

There was only one question now: what would I do with the rest of it?

Seventeen

The gallery was located in SoHo, and its red brick walls had been restored to their nineteenth-century glory. They were hung with photographs whose substance mirrored the walls. The photos depicted close-ups of buildings, concentrating on individual architectural details: a lintel here and a pediment there. There were many close-up shots of plain bricks and mortar. And in fact that's what the exhibit was called: *Bricks and Mortar*.

Earlier in the evening, standing around sipping cranberry juice and eating fancy hors d'oeuvres, I was introduced to the photographer Jane Willets. She was an attractive black woman with beautiful steel-gray natural hair and a warm disposition. We stood there talking, and she told me all about her philosophy of bricks and mortar and how what holds buildings together mirrors the fabric of society that holds mankind together. Each human's design and facade are distinctive, and what lies within us is equally as distinct. Each person has a unique story, history, purpose, life-span, and reason for being, too often perceived and judged by exterior characteristics. In her photographs, Jane showed the viewer aspects of architecture that one passed every day on the street without noticing, but in the context of her pictures, they became something revelatory.

As I wandered around the gallery, I kept catching sight of Jane talking with other guests. When this happened and our eyes met, we'd nod knowingly at each other, as though we were lifelong friends. I liked Jane immediately upon meeting her, and I could see myself befriending her. She was just the kind of thoughtful, well-adjusted person I needed to have at this point in my life.

I was here with a friend, Samantha, my old Dartmouth roommate, who had relocated to Manhattan after graduation and now considered herself a dyed-in-the-wool New Yorker. For the first time, she allowed me to refer to her as Sam, saying that kind of moniker was very on point in New York City, where she knew any number of chic women who were known by a man's first name.

Samantha—sorry, Sam—had invited me to come up to New York and stay with her after I'd been exonerated of all charges in Zion's criminal case. It seemed like a good idea to get out of Miami for a while, so I readily accepted her invitation. I decided to drive there alone. There's nothing like a good road trip to think and clear my mind. I took my time traveling up US Interstate I-95, stopping through Georgia, North Carolina, and then Maryland for a brief visit with my family. It was so good to see everyone, and my parents were especially happy to have me home. And now that my long legal ordeal was over, I felt I could see them and look them in the eyes again. It was a short but sweet visit and the first time I'd been home since college. I only hoped my mother didn't sense anything else different about me.

And now here I was in New York, staying with Sam at her Upper East Side apartment and attending chichi events, such as this photography-exhibit opening. I loved the city. It was so different from Miami and so different, for that matter, from any place else I'd lived. It was a city of affluence and power, of art and culture, where people were all different but somehow seemed to get along, living together on one slender island bracketed by two mighty rivers. It was a city where many people walked or rode public transportation to get to their destinations. So I left my car in a garage space in Sam's building and got around like a native New Yorker. I learned the city in no time by remembering notable buildings and landmarks within the geography of the city.

"How are you doing?" Sam had walked up to me at the photography exhibit, breaking my train of thought.

"Fine," I answered in the same noncommittal tone that I'd recently perfected and that had become my default setting for those kinds of questions.

"Good."

That was Sam, always checking up on me, always making sure I was okay, as though she were talking to someone who had survived a plane crash or war atrocity, someone suffering from PTSD, which, in a way, maybe I was—or in my case, PZSD, post-Zion stress disorder.

Sam had been invited to the exhibit opening by a friend, an artist type (as opposed to an actual artist) who lived in a loft not far from the gallery. I could tell she wanted to spend time with him, and I knew she'd eventually be exiting the gallery with him, leaving it up to me to make my way back to her apartment on my own. I didn't mind. It gave me more time to enjoy the exhibit and hopefully more time to spend with the fascinating Jane Willets.

It had been two months since that day in the Dade County District Court, when Reuben Sifuentes had given me the good news. A lot had happened in that time, most of it to Zion. He had been found guilty and sentenced to a 15 year prison term. He also was forced to make restitution to the tune of $750 million. But even with that, there were still many bilked clients who never would get a cent back of their initial investment with him through ZB Financial Services, whose offices had been permanently closed.

As for me, I had gotten my life back, more or less. Most of my friends had called or written in the wake of the judge's decision, and I had met them all individually for lunch or dinner and had a good old time reminiscing about our shared pasts. But there was a distance now that never could be bridged, as though—even though I'd been declared innocent—there was something about me that would forever seem tainted in their eyes. It bothered me how they could be such fair-weather friends. But I suppose you eventually find out who your real friends are.

Of course my business was a shambles. No one wanted to hire me as a result of Zion having tarnished my reputation. Even though I was innocent, perhaps it didn't speak well that I had been duped by him. For this reason I was considered untouchable in the Miami PR community. Megan and I put our heads together and tried to figure out a strategy to resume business, perhaps in another state, where the name "Bouvier Public Relations" wasn't the punch line to a cruel joke.

And there was something else, something I'd been dancing around for the past two weeks. Feelings were coursing through my body that I'd never experienced before. Nausea at odd times of the day. A feeling of being bloated. Hot flashes at unexpected times. I thought I knew the cause of these sensations, but I put off finding out for sure because the thought of it was too much for me to face. But in the end, I faced my fears, went to my local pharmacy, and made a dreaded purchase.

Looking at one of Jane's *Bricks and Mortar* photographs, I suddenly felt lightheaded and looked around for a place to sit. But there wasn't a chair to be found. Fortunately, at that moment, Jane had been looking in my direction. She rushed over and said, "Come with me," then led me to a room in back of the gallery that was filled with empty picture frames and ordered me to sit in a chair. She found a bottle of sparkling water, poured some of it into a glass filled with ice, and handed it to me.

"Drink this," she said. And I did. I sipped it down slowly. "It's not good for you to get dehydrated, especially in your condition."

"My condition?" I asked, playing dumb.

"Yes. You're pregnant, aren't you?"

It was the first time I'd heard anyone outside of myself acknowledge this fact.

"Yes," I confirmed.

"How far along are you?"

"About two months."

"Drink some more water," she said. "You're looking kind of pale."

I did. Then, after a beat, I said, "How did you know?"

Jane shrugged. "I have an eye for that. It's a gift, like the ability to divine water."

"Too bad you can't figure out a way to make a living at that."

She laughed, and I joined her. It had been a long time since I had made anyone laugh or felt the urge to laugh myself.

Jane looked me up and down and said, "How are you feeling now?"

"A little better." I said. "Thanks for the water."

"You and your husband must be excited to be expecting."

"No. I'm not married. And to be honest, I'm not thrilled to be in this predicament."

"Does the father know you're pregnant?"

"No."

"Where is he?"

I paused, trying to figure out how to best answer that. Then suddenly a flood of memories of Zion, the whole ordeal, and the reality of my pregnancy came crashing down on me like a ton of bricks. My eyes filled with tears, and I couldn't contain the tsunami of feelings that overwhelmed me, causing me to break down. I sobbed and sobbed. Jane hugged and consoled me. In the arms of a complete stranger, I was helpless. It was all too much for me to bear.

"There, there, my dear," she whispered while patting my back.

When I finally settled down, Jane handed me some tissues and told me to take a few more sips of water. As I collected myself, I felt a real sense of relief. Something about Jane made me trust her, and I was grateful to be able to express myself without judgment or shame.

Finally I just decided to tell her the truth. "We're not together anymore. He's serving time in prison."

"Oh."

It was an old story, I know, for a certain type of woman. But I'd never considered myself one of those women. I was too smart to be in this situation. This wasn't supposed to be my story. But who knows? Maybe I was one of those women after all.

"I'm sorry," Jane said. I shouldn't have asked you so many questions. It's really none of my business."

"It's okay," I said. "Thanks for caring anyhow."

"Does your friend know?" She was referring to Sam, who was still wandering around the gallery in the company of her artist-type friend.

"No, and I don't plan to tell her."

"Why not?"

"I'm afraid she'll overreact and go into hyperactive mother-hen mode. And I have no room in my life for that type of scrutiny right now."

"I can see how you wouldn't care for that."

"No."

"You seem like the independent type."

"I like to think I am."

"Well, you know, there's such a thing as being too independent. That can get you into trouble, especially when you're expecting a child. You never should be afraid or too proud to ask for help."

"You sound like you're speaking from experience," I said.

"I am," Jane said simply.

As I looked at her, I saw how strong and wise a woman she was, as though the bricks and mortar she photographed were also the stuff of which she was made.

Jane looked at me then said, "You look like you could use some fresh air. Let's go out for a walk."

"But what about your opening?" I asked.

"Oh, these things bore me," she said with a shrug, "especially my own."

"Let me just tell my friend we're leaving."

I returned to the gallery and located Sam, who was leaning into her date and hanging on to his every word. It took me several moments to get her attention. I told her I was leaving and would see her back at her apartment. Fortunately Sam had given me her spare key. From the intense looks she and her date kept giving each other, I was pretty sure Sam wouldn't make it back to the apartment that night.

After returning to the back room, I accompanied Jane out the emergency exit and into a cobblestone alley. We followed the alley out and found ourselves on one of the cobblestone streets of SoHo, teeming on this beautiful spring night. We passed the gallery and glanced casually inside, where patrons were busy visiting with Jane's photographs. Given the number of people in attendance, it clearly was a successful event. I imagined it would feel very special to be the artistic creator and at the center of all that energy and attention. But Jane apparently didn't feel that way. She loved, it seemed, taking the photographs and having them on display but had a difficult time dealing with the adulation and social responsibilities that went along with that.

We walked for a while, and Jane was right—the fresh air was like a restorative to me. But after a while, I started to feel tired, a fact that sharp-sighted Jane also picked up on before I could say anything.

"Feel like stopping?" she asked.

"Yes," I said, "these heels are killing me"

"Takes some getting used to, this city. Walking on these concrete sidewalks can be murder—even if you're not wearing heels."

We found a Greek diner nearby and decided to stop there for something to eat. SoHo, I understood, was in the middle of a gentrifying process that was transforming a once-forgotten neighborhood of lofts and warehouses into a haven for new galleries, restaurants, and shops. This diner seemed to be one of the last few holdouts of SoHo's previous life.

Inside we found a booth and had an attentive waiter standing before us. Within minutes our food was placed in front of us, which was a good thing since I was ravenous lately—when I wasn't nauseous, that is. Jane ordered a large salad, and I had a cheeseburger and fries. I mean, what else do you order in a Greek restaurant?

As we ate, we resumed the conversation we'd started in the back room of the gallery.

"If you don't mind my asking, what are you going to do?"

I took a bite of my cheeseburger before answering. "Honestly," I said, "I have no idea."

"Well, you have to make up your mind soon," Jane said.

"I know."

"If you need the name of a doctor, I can give you a referral."

"Thank you," I said, honestly touched that this person, a woman I'd only known for a little more than an hour, would show such kindness toward me, a virtual stranger. I couldn't help smile.

Jane caught it and asked, "What?"

I shook my head. "I feel silly."

"Don't. What were you thinking?"

"I feel like I'm Cinderella and you're my fairy godmother."

Jane smiled back at me. "Well, I don't see any pumpkins, but I can ask if they have pumpkin pie on the menu."

That made me laugh. And my laughter started Jane laughing. In no time at all, the table was convulsed with laughter far beyond Jane's lame attempt at humor. But maybe that's what made it so funny.

And as I laughed, a profound sense of peace came over me. Maybe meeting Jane hadn't been accidental. Maybe viewing her photographs likewise wasn't an accident. Maybe there was a master plan, and maybe they were part of my place in it. Maybe there was a solution to my problems. And maybe life didn't have to be so overwhelming as long as there were people like Jane, my family, Sam, Jonny and Megan back in Miami to provide support.

It's amazing how history repeats itself. I thought back to my mother and that tale from so long ago. Once, she had been in the same position as me (both with me then and as me now), dealing with a possibly unwanted pregnancy. She had made her decision, and then had it reversed by an act of fate that she had interpreted as coming from the hand of God. If it hadn't been for that decision, I wouldn't be here now, in a diner in SoHo, far from the small town I'd come from and called home, with a virtual stranger who now seemed like an agelong friend, trying to make up my mind about a similar situation.

And as I sat there, I realized in that moment that I did have choices. I could have the child, and everything would be all right. I could have the child and give it up for adoption, and everything would be all right. Or I could…Whatever decision I made; it was my decision to make. In the end I have to be able to stand before God with a clear conscience and look myself in the mirror. It had to be a decision I could live with, whatever that may be.

I felt lighter and freer than I had in a long time. My ordeal with Zion was behind me, even if I was now carrying his seed, something I'd never reveal to him. I might be finished in Miami. I might be finished in PR. But perhaps this was an opportunity of sorts, and Manhattan was beckoning me.

I said all this to Jane, being vague about the story of the events surrounding my own birth. She nodded sagaciously and said, "You know what New York is the capital of?"

"No," I said, shaking my head.

"Some people think power or money. Others say media or fashion. But New York is really the capital of reinvention. You come here, and you can be anything you want."

I took another bite of my cheeseburger and nodded at Jane's words of wisdom.

"I mean, take a look at me," she said. "I'm a sharecropper's daughter from Tuscaloosa, Alabama. But I came here and reinvented myself, first as a fashion photographer, then a fine arts photographer, and now a documentary photographer. If I can reinvent myself, so can you."

I nodded again, knowing she was right.

We finished our food and left the diner. Outside, the beautiful spring night held the promise of renewal. I said good night to Jane, thanked her for all her thoughtfulness, and promised we'd get together real soon.

Jane hailed a cab and left, leaving behind an evening of good memories. Even though it was far, I decided to walk a ways uptown, at least until I got tired, and then get a cab for myself for the ride back to Sam's apartment. I needed time process Jane's words. She had given me much food for thought.

The streets were crowded with New Yorkers, all going about their business at a fast pace. A diverse collective, no two people alike, from every corner of the earth. Rich, poor, old, young— from every tribe, nation, religion, and ethnicity—each one having his or her own story, sharing this space in time. There was such perfection within the imperfection. And I marveled in that thought.

As I headed uptown, I was mesmerized by the tall buildings, bright lights, and architectural landscape of this incredible metropolis. Thanks to Jane and her exhibit, I looked at mere bricks and mortar with greater insight. I had an epiphany that instantly put a smile on my face.

"You know what?" I said to myself, with a slow-dawning lifting of my spirits. "I think I'm gonna like it here."

Eighteen

The ocean waves stopped crashing in my ears as I came back to myself. I freshened up in the ladies' room and applied fresh lipstick before heading back to my table in the restaurant. As I passed the bar, I checked the time on my diamond-and-gold Omega watch and briefly turned my attention back to the TV. Bernard Madoff was no longer on the screen, and the TV anchors were now on to a new story. But the Bernie Madoff story would have staying power in the weeks and months to come, and people would become obsessed with him and the brazenness of his con artistry.

Zion and his confederates had stolen hundreds of millions of dollars. But he looked like a piker compared to Bernie Madoff, who had swindled billions from his trusting clients. That made me laugh. If there was one thing Zion couldn't stand, it was being treated as a small-timer. He had been taught to dream big by a book given to him by a great-uncle who was probably a con artist himself. Maybe that's where Zion had gotten it from. Whatever the case, he was a small fish in a large pond compared to the ocean of deceit Bernie Madoff had practiced.

Over the years my attitude toward Zion had softened. Maybe he did love me in his own way. Maybe he never meant for me to become ensnared in the web of lies he had created. In the end I had decided to learn from him and move on.

And as you can see, in the intervening years I hadn't done too badly for myself. Jane Willets had been right; New York is the capital of reinvention. And I had reinvented myself as a real-estate entrepreneur who owned her own Fortune 500 company. I was a woman thriving in a male-dominated industry. I could afford to live the life I had imagined and eat in restaurants such as this and pick up the tab for a tableful of associates and not even blink twice at the bill.

I'd had meaningful relationships with men since Zion, although none had ever come close to the degree of passion he had unleashed in me. Or maybe it was just my youth and inexperience that led me to feel that way so many years after the fact. Or maybe it was just memory that had heightened that long-ago experience for me. Maybe no one in the years since had swept me up and won me over the way Zion had, but I remained hopeful that there was still a man out there in the future who would once again ignite that kind of passion in me. There was no one in my life like that now, but I was confident that he was out there and that our paths would cross when the time was right. In the meantime my life was full. I was thriving, happy, and loving life.

And then there were my friends. The number of them had grown since I had moved to New York, worked in real estate, and then started my own company. But at the core, there was still Sam, Jane, and Megan. Megan had remained in Miami, where she opened her own PR shop and became as successful as I had dreamed of being down there. We spoke all the time and saw each other several times a year. She eventually had dropped her habit of choosing men who were bad for her and was now married to a successful Miami sports doctor who made a fortune attending to all the local professional athletes. Sam also was married, and her children referred to me as "Auntie Mega." As for Jane, she remained steadfastly single, living a solitary bohemian lifestyle in Costa Rica, where she served the interests of impoverished women and children. She had found her calling, and I was thrilled for her.

I noticed I was the only woman at the bar and resolved to return to my table before one of these drunken businessmen made a clumsy attempt to pick me up. I threaded my way through the all-male throng, saying, "Excuse me, excuse me" and smiling at them, moving quickly so as not to give them an opportunity to rub up against me.

Finally I was through the crowd and stopped to catch my breath. I felt a pair of eyes staring at me; centering their attention on me and making me feel flushed. Had it suddenly gotten hot in here? Was something wrong with the air conditioning? I turned around and noticed a tall, distinguished-looking man standing in the corner of the bar, someone I hadn't noticed before in the thickness of the crowd. To my shock it was a familiar face. Someone from long ago. But it couldn't be. Could it? And as he stood there staring at me, it was as if time stood still. I was taken aback and felt a little weak in the knees. I whispered to myself, "Oh…my…God! What's he doing here? Okay, Omega put your game face on. It's time to take care of some old business!"

CPSIA information can be obtained at www.ICGtesting.com
Printed in the USA
LVOW10s2139100116

470045LV00003B/91/P